ALSO BY LAURA DALEO

Immortal Kiss

Bound by Blood

The Vampire Within

The Soul Collector

The Doll

Once We Were Witches

My Name is Death

The Vow

Laura Daleo

AUTHOR LAURA DALEO

The Vow is a work of fiction. Names, characters, places, and incidents either are the product of the author's imagination or are used fictitiously. Any resemblance to actual persons living or dead, events, or locales is entirely coincidental.

Published in the United States by Author Laura Daleo, San Diego, California

Print ISBN: 9780997846102

ebook ISBN: 9780997846119

The Vow is a dark paranormal fantasy novel written by Laura Daleo. Claire Mathews was puzzled at not seeing her dad waiting for her at the airport. He was always very careful to be on time for any family activity. She grew even more confused and a bit alarmed when her attempts to call her parents or her brother, JJ, met with no success. Finally, she loaded her bags into a waiting taxi and made her own way home. Her driver took a second look at her when he arrived at her destination, as if to make sure she had it right. Claire was stunned to see the police tape festooning the front of her parents' home. The police cars and the Medical Examiner's van she saw turned her surprise into dread. Detective Reynolds was sent over to see her, and she met his questions with barely disguised impatience. Yes, she was a student, and home for the summer holidays -- but where were her parents and brother?

Laura Daleo's dark paranormal fantasy novel, The Vow, is set in a world where vampires and humans live peacefully under the conditions set forth by The Vow. I'll confess to being a bit jaded by urban fantasies featuring vampires, but found Daleo's offering to be a most agreeable change from the standard fare. Her plot is precisely drawn and apt to please anyone who enjoys not only fantasy, but also well-written police procedural mysteries, and her characters are engaging and credible. Who killed Claire's parents and what happened to JJ? Claire's reactions to her sudden loss are the stuff that makes psychological thrillers tick, and her quest for answers and justice kept me hooked into this decidedly different vampire fantasy. Daleo's insights into the vampire psyche are profound, and those characters in her book of the vampiric persuasion are especially worth spending some time with. The Vow is most highly recommended.

—Reviewed by Jack Magnus for Readers' Favorite

A vow of peace set forth on this day, March 31, 1885, joins mankind and vampires in one world, ending all bloodshed between species. The union of harmony must remain faithful despite the passing of time. Defiance of the vow by either race will render such truce null and void. If such a time comes, God help us all.

CHAPTER 1

Seriously, where were my parents? With a sigh of frustration, I gathered my overnight bags for the third time and slung them over my shoulder. My phone calls ended up in voicemail, and my text messages went unanswered. Even my brother, JJ, hadn't responded. My parents were paradigms of punctuality, so overlooking their own daughter's arrival at the airport seemed unlikely. An explanation existed, but what could it be? I looked around again, skimming over the many faces, but not one of them belonged to my parents. "Oh, screw it. I'll take a cab," I mumbled under a strained breath as I trekked through the airport doors and headed toward the taxi zone. I raised my hand, signaling a cab.

A taxi sped over to me, bumping up against the curb and idling as it broke formation from the multitude of yellow cars. The driver lowered the window and asked, "Where to, Flower Child?"

As I glanced down at my lace crop top, floral kimono, and cutoff shorts, I wondered how the cab driver had known my dad's nickname for me. In all honesty, my closet was filled with vintage pieces adorned with lace, embroidery, or fringe, but I didn't identify as a '60's hippie. I constantly reminded my dad that the proper term for the style was Boho Chic, but in his eyes, I was his Woodstock Flower Child—the one he'd forgotten to pick up from the airport. I replied, "2863 Derrick Place," as I opened the back door and tossed my bags onto the seat. I sat with my arms crossed, an image of a pouting child flashing through my mind, but I had no intention of letting my parents forget this one. *One guilt trip coming right up.*

Twenty minutes later, the driver turned onto my parents' street and slowed down. The moment we reached my house, he glanced in the rearview mirror and raised his eyebrows. "Here?" he asked.

I barely managed a nod, fixated on the police cars, yellow crime tape, and crisp white van decorating the front of my parents' house like some bizarre Halloween scene. I blinked and then stared blankly after reading the words *Medical Examiner* emblazoned across the van. Was this some sick joke?

"That'll be twenty-five dollars," the cab driver rattled off.

After flipping open my wallet and paying him, I slowly stepped out onto the street. I dropped my bags on the pavement as I stood before my childhood home. A sickeningly cold feeling swept over me as a swarm of neighbors hovered nearby. Their eyes were on me, their faces painted with gloom. I shivered at the sudden prickling of my flesh, like hundreds of ants crawling up my spine. Somehow, I made it onto the sidewalk.

An officer in dark blue rushed toward me, blocking my path. "That's far enough, miss. No one is permitted inside."

"That's my parents' house." I didn't wait for a reply but instead pushed past him. "I don't need permission."

He grabbed my arm, preventing me from moving forward. "Miss, I can't allow that. We are dealing with an active crime scene." He released my arm. "Please stay back."

Was my parents' house a crime scene? I glanced once more at the words strewn across the white van. *Oh God. Mom? Dad? JJ?* Slithering into my pores and gnawing at my bones, the chill mushroomed. Sunlight drenched my body, but I was unable to escape the vicious winter storm building underneath my skin. Something was horribly wrong. The feeling of desperation crept up my throat as I stared back at him. "What happened?"

The corners of his mouth tightened, forming a thin line. "At this time, I cannot discuss that with you."

"Then who can?"

"Right now, no one."

What the hell happened at our house? Was there a murder? Behind my eyes, "murder" flashed on and off like a failing neon vacancy sign. I needed to get inside, and this fool was in my way. "You're telling me there isn't a single person who can explain to me why I can't enter my own home?"

He glanced at my bags and then met my eyes. "You live with your parents?"

As I struggled to keep my voice from quivering, I nodded my head. "I'm home for the summer."

"College?"

"Yes. Finals are over." I mentally chided myself. Why would he care about finals? I peered over his shoulder. "Can you tell me where my family is?" My gaze fell on him. "You need to let me in."

"Evidence is being collected. I'm afraid you'll have to wait here."

Like hell, I will. A flurry of questions flew out of my mouth. "Why is the medical examiner here? Has someone died? Are my parents and brother all right?" I clutched my stomach in fear, and my voice grew frantic. "What happened?"

Rather than answering me, he called out to the army of police scouring through trees and bushes, "Jenkins, find Detective Reynolds. Tell him I need him."

They ignored his request and continued their search.

A pinched expression appeared on his face as he shook his head. Focusing on me, he calmly asked, "What's your name?"

"Claire, Claire Matthews."

"Wait here, Miss Matthews." With that, he walked away and disappeared into the mystery beyond the front door some thirty feet away.

Watching the front porch turn into a revolving door for police officers wearing rubber gloves and blue booties over their shoes, I stood alone facing the house full of memories. Some officers carried evidence bags, a few took notes, and others gathered around the doorway exchanging dialogue. A flood of tears blurred my vision, but I gathered my resolve and swept them away with my fingers. There was no reason to cry. Not yet. Perhaps robbers broke in while no one was home, and they turned on each other. A neighbor may have heard the scuffle and called the police. The repetitive drum of my heartbeat softened as my imagined theories slowed the panic racing through my veins. Deep down, however, I couldn't shake the feeling that something awful was lurking behind the front door.

In the doorway, the officer reappeared, accompanied by an older man with much blonder hair than mine, dressed in a gray suit. He plastered a solemn TV cop expression on his face—the same one actors adopted when they delivered the dreadful news. He proceeded down the walkway, narrowing the gap between us. My pulse accelerated into frantic thumping. Maybe all of this would disappear if I closed my eyes, tapped my heels three times, and said *there's no place like home.* Sadly, I already *was* home.

"Miss Matthews, I'm Detective Reynolds," the man said, extending his hand. His large palm swallowed mine up, the heat of his flesh warming my icy fingers. "May I ask you a few questions?"

"Not until I see my family."

"I understand this is difficult, and the last thing you want to do is speak to a detective right now, but information helps me do my job." His inquisitive eyes swept over me. "How old are you?"

"I'm twenty...but can't you just tell me what's going on?" I begged rather than asked.

He shoved his hands into his pockets and focused on my bags. "In college?" Giving a nod toward the house, he then asked, "Do you live here?"

"I go to school in San Francisco," I answered, my voice on edge. "I'm home for summer break."

"Were your parents expecting you?"

What kind of question was that? "Yes, of course."

"When did you last speak to them?"

A wild impulse to blast past him and run straight into the house seized me, but I remained perfectly still. "Please just let me go inside."

His tone of authority matched his attitude as he went on to say, "Miss Matthews, I need your cooperation to help your family. Please answer my question."

If I wanted to get inside the house, I had to play his game of twenty questions. "A couple of days ago."

"How did they sound? Did you notice anything peculiar about the conversation?"

Why the third degree, and what did he care about our topic of discussion? "They sounded fine." I paused, staring him down. They were *my* parents. If they had behaved strangely, or if I thought something had been off about them, I would've done something—called somebody or come home early. Again, and with emphasis, I stated, "They were fine."

He rubbed his chin, as if in thought. "What about background noise? Did you hear anything unusual?"

Each question irritated me, and I had reached my limit. "I'm not answering another question until I know what's going on." I took a deep breath. "Are my parents...dead?"

He put his hand on my shoulder, the somber-cop face returning. "I'm sorry, Miss Matthews. The man and the woman inside the house are dead."

His words crashed down on me, threatening my ability to stand. My breath caught in my throat, and I stumbled backward. How could I survive without my parents? I looked away from him and focused on the street. Tears spilled from my eyes, splashing against the hot asphalt and hissing out of existence. I finally managed a couple of breaths, then a couple more, before finding my voice and looking up at him. "Wh-What happened?"

"I know this kind of news is never easy," he said, his eyes soft with compassion.

A glimmer of hope lifted the gloom. He said a man and woman. He didn't name names. They could be anyone. "Who are they? What are their names? Maybe they're not even my parents."

He nodded but appeared doubtful. "We still have to identify the victims, and for that, I need your help."

I stiffened and rooted my feet to the ground. "Please, don't ask that of me. There must be someone else who can identify them?"

"Is there anyone else? What if they are your parents?"

I looked away from him toward the growing horde of neighbors. The hungry scavengers crept closer and closer, eager for a juicy morsel of gossip or perhaps a glimpse of a dead body. Maybe they should be the ones to identify the bodies.

"Miss Matthews?"

I looked back at the detective, biting my lower lip as I struggled to formulate a response. If the man and woman inside turned out to be my parents, I should be the one to confirm their identities, yet I couldn't bring myself to answer him.

"Will you help me?" he asked, his voice optimistic.

I opened my mouth, but nothing came out. I just didn't see how I could bring myself to fulfill his request.

Stepping closer to me, he lowered his head to level his gaze on mine. "I want to catch their killer, but first, I need to know who they are."

My hands trembled as I finally spoke. "I don't think you realize how difficult what you're asking me to do is."

A sigh escaped his lips. "Unfortunately, I do."

My gaze briefly turned to the house, then to him. In spite of how difficult it was, I had to find out if the people inside were my parents. "I need a minute."

"Take your time."

My mind struggled to make sense of the jumbled details as I stood motionless, taking deep breaths.

The detective did not relent, continuing to ask further questions. "Are there any grandparents, aunts, or uncles I should contact?"

I shook my head. "It's just me and my brother, JJ."

"When was the last time you spoke with your brother?"

The warmth from my body seeped out of my pores, and I rubbed at the chill left behind. "He's seventeen. He lives here. Are you saying he's not here?"

A kind expression smoothed out the lines etched into his forehead. "The fact is that we don't know where he is at the moment. We searched his room and his computer. Despite our efforts, we couldn't locate a cell phone. He left his wallet on the dresser in his room. "Do you know where he might have gone?"

With each new detail the detective revealed, the nightmare grew more horrifying. I shivered as my arms fell to my sides. "He could be with Nate and Parker, but his cell phone must be with him. He treats that thing as an extra limb."

"Have you tried calling him?"

"Yes, of course. It just goes to voicemail." I looked around as if he might suddenly appear. "Where are you?" I uttered half-aloud.

"We need to find him," Detective Reynolds said, a slight edge to his voice. "He may have answers. Who are Nate and Parker?"

I couldn't respond. A horrible feeling swept over me, pressing against my chest. My parents might be dead. JJ was missing. I sank to the curb, shaking my head.

He sat next to me, not speaking for a minute or two, and then said softly, "I've been doing this job for more years than I can count, and I've never been able to find the right words to provide any comfort. All I can say is that I'm sorry."

The set of wrinkles in the center of his forehead, coupled with his thick brows, reminded me of my father. A giant sob swelled to life in my throat. I forced it down and shifted to face him. "How did they die?"

He pressed his lips together. "I have to warn you; it won't be easy to see. The victims appear exsanguinated."

"What does that mean?"

"Drained of their blood," he explained. "The bodies are somewhat mummified."

I gasped. "Are you saying vampires did this?"

"We believe so."

Vampires? I touched the base of my throat as if warding off a bite. "What about The Vow? They gave their word. They haven't killed since."

"That was a hundred-plus years ago," he said with a frown. "We could have a rogue vampire on our hands. One who no longer holds any respect for The Vow."

"How is that possible? They have The Vampire Centers now. There's no need to feed off humans."

"I don't disagree with you, but receiving transfusions from a Vampire Center is human intervention. A vampire with a preference for traditional methods could potentially bear responsibility. The thrill of the hunt and all that."

"Hunting? No, we coexist. They don't kill anymore."

"Well, looks like they do now."

A spark of rage flickered inside me. If my parents had lost their lives to a vampire, why? My dad owned an insurance company, and my mom was an artist. They were decent, ordinary people; nobody important or unique. Why pick them to drain and murder? The hairs rose on my arms. Could either Nate or Parker be the killer? But they were JJ's best friends. They wouldn't do that to him, or would they? I was desperately searching for a solution. I turned to Detective Reynolds. "My brother—"

His eyes narrowed as he regarded me. "Your brother, what?"

I didn't want to throw them under the bus, but they were vampires, and JJ was missing. "My brother's friends, Nate and Parker, they're vampires."

He titled his head to the side and gazed at me intently. "Would either defy The Vow? Are they capable of murder?"

"I—I don't know. They're JJ's friends, not mine."

He pushed to his feet and towered over me. Rubbing his chin, he glanced at the house, then stared back down at me. "Where do they live?"

As I stood, memories of the first time I'd met Nate and Parker played inside my head. *It had been spring break, and my first year away at college. I'd been painfully homesick. Everyone had dashed off to Palm Springs, South Beach, or Vegas—except me. I'd run home and into vampires, Nate and Parker. They'd been with JJ, standing by the curb in front of our house.*

JJ had rushed over, throwing his arms around me and squeezing hard. After releasing me, he'd said, "God, I missed you." He had plastered that goofy smile across his face.

"I missed you too," I'd told him, my focus on the vampires.

JJ had waved them over. "Claire, this is Nate." He'd pointed to the taller of the two wearing a beanie, which rested slightly above his brilliant green eyes. Turning, JJ gestured to the shorter one, a boy with long, dark-brown hair, bushy eyebrows, and nearly black eyes. "And this is Parker."

Both had been observing me intently, their mouths agape.

"Bro, your sister's hot," Nate had said, giving me a flirty smile.

JJ had shot back a glassy stare and punched Nate's arm. "Don't even go there. She's off-limits to both of you."

Detective Reynolds placed his hand on my shoulder, pulling me back to the present. "Miss Matthews, did you hear me? Where do they live?"

"In East Village, the Vampire District," I answered, their images fading from my mind.

Detective Reynolds looked over his shoulder and called out to one of the officers. "Stevens."

Two police officers snapping pictures and placing yellow markers down glanced in our direction. Detective Reynolds waved to the one with broader shoulders and a bit more belly.

He lumbered down the walkway toward us. "Got something?"

"Maybe. Take a ride over to East Village and see if you can find..." He paused and turned to me. "Do you know their surnames?"

I shrugged and shook my head.

He turned back to the officer, seemingly unaffected by my response. "See if you can find two vampires, first names Nate and Parker, and bring them in for questioning. Take Jenkins with you."

"Will do," Stevens said, jotting in a notepad before calling out to the other man. "Jenkins, we're taking a ride out to East Village."

I watched them climb into one of the cars. "What if they find JJ? I should be there."

"Stevens will contact me with any information they discover."

My mind raced in a different direction. I had to know what happened inside my parents' home. "What led you to believe the killer is a vampire?"

"I'm trying to spare you the details."

"I *need* the details." I pressed my fingertips against my temples. "My brain is freaking out, conjuring up the unimaginable. I think it's better if you just tell me."

In a blunt directive, he rattled off his findings. "Their bodies bore multiple bite marks, and not a single drop of blood remained within them. We've got one smart killer. They wiped everything clean. Not a shred of evidence left behind." He raised his palms. "Without evidence to go on, I don't know where to begin."

I stared him down. What kind of detective was he? "So you're giving up?"

The corners of his mouth curled upward, and he almost smiled. "I never give up."

An unsettling thought leapt inside my head. What if JJ wasn't with Nate and Parker? What if he were indeed missing, or worse? "What are you doing to find my brother besides seeking out the two vampires?"

"We're searching the area, questioning neighbors, and tracking down leads. Hopefully, someone has seen your brother, or other clues will provide us with some useful information. We'll find him."

His words didn't reassure me; they sounded more like an attempt to appease me. Months from now, I hoped I wouldn't see JJ's face plastered on milk cartons and bumper stickers. And if those were my parents lying dead inside their house, I needed closure—a trial and conviction. Was justice even possible? The vampires' powers of enchantment manipulated human minds, so even if the police caught the killer, he or she could quickly eliminate themselves as a suspect with the power of suggestion. The killer may never see the inside of a jail cell. If vampires had indeed taken my parents' lives, I resolved to exact my own justice, even if it meant hunting them down myself. A sense of resolve flooded through my body as I faced the detective again. Abandoning my bags on the street, I took a step toward the house and said, "I'm ready now."

A stern look settled over his face, wiping out any traces of his previous compassion. "Remember, this *is* still a crime scene. You can't touch anything."

"I understand."

My neighbors' beady eyes followed us all the way to the front door. The famous theme from Alfred Hitchcock's *The Birds* played inside my head, growing louder and louder: *Ristletee, rostletee. Hey, Donnie-dostle-tee. Knickety-knackety. Rustical quality. Now, now, now.*

"Miss Matthews, please put these over your shoes," Detective Reynolds said, his voice terminating the haunting song.

I took the pair of blue booties and slipped them over my ankle boots. The police officer blocking the doorway stepped aside. The mahogany frame stood wide open, void of the door's solid barrier. The frosted inlays were smashed and scattered across the entryway, twinkling like diamonds in the sunlight. Stepping over the tiny pieces, I entered my childhood home. The house seemed undisturbed. The brown furniture, colorful throw pillows, many houseplants, and table lamps claimed their customary spaces. Even the pictures on the walls hung perfectly centered and free of dust. My home's appearance didn't suggest any evidence of foul play.

"They're in the master bedroom," Detective Reynolds said, guiding me up the stairs.

Could I do it? Could I look into two pairs of lifeless eyes and determine if they belonged to my parents? An icy chill crept into my bones, making me shudder, but I had to know. Following the detective up the staircase, I soldiered on like a character from one of JJ's video games.

When I reached the second-floor landing, I could see JJ's closed bedroom door. Hundreds of arrows seemed to impale my heart, causing my body to remain motionless and my mind to spiral out of control. Where was he? Was he hurt? Did he need help? My brain screamed, *"Search his room,"* at me.

Detective Reynolds veered to the right toward my parents' bedroom, but I listened to my instincts and turned left toward JJ's bedroom. I made it all the way to his door, my fingers wrapped around the doorknob, ready to give it a turn, when the detective's stern voice pervaded my ears. "Miss Matthews!"

I whirled to face him.

He waved me over. "Stay with me at all times while we're in the house."

I remained frozen by JJ's door. "I need to see my brother's room. Maybe there's something you missed."

"Rest assured, we were very thorough."

I knew my brother. He had hiding places scattered throughout his room. The police may have thought they'd discovered everything, but I needed to search all his nooks and crannies with my own eyes.

In three strides, Detective Reynolds stood at my side, shooing me away from the door. "The only room you can gain access to at the moment is the one belonging to your parents. Is that clear?"

My heart crumbled in disappointment. I expelled a defiant, "Yes."

As he led me in the direction of my parents' room, I glanced over my shoulder at JJ's door. One way or another, I would get inside his room, with or without the detective.

When we reached my parents' door, Detective Reynolds blocked the doorway with a thick arm, giving me a grave look. "Remember, their appearance is rather...gruesome. The ME estimated they've been dead for three days."

I swallowed hard and cleared my throat. "I got it."

He removed his arm and allowed me to enter.

A thick, foul stench polluted the air, hovering all around me—the unmistakable aroma of death. It slithered up my nostrils and down my throat, robbing me of my breath. I gagged on the rancid odor and pulled my shirt up and over my nose. *God, give me strength.* Taking in shallow breaths, I approached the bed.

They lay side by side, their dove-colored flesh resembling a withered plum depleted of its juices. Several bite marks disfigured their skin, giving them a pincushion-like appearance. Goosebumps prickled my skin as I stared at their frozen, yet peaceful, expressions. I let out a hysterical shriek when I met their eyes. *Mom...Dad!* With my hand clamped over my mouth, I smothered the scream.

The detective stood next to me, settling his hand on my shoulder. "Are they your parents?"

I couldn't speak but gave a slow nod. The walls began to inch forward, closing in on me. My parents had been everything to me—my strength, my happiness, my security. I needed air, but my damned feet refused to move.

"Are you all right?"

What a stupid question. Of course I wasn't. The open doorway fell into my line of sight. *Run!* I bolted from the room and into the hallway. Racing down the stairs, I ran straight out the front door. I didn't stop until I hit the pavement of the roadway. After ripping the blue booties from my boots, I grabbed my bags from the street's gray surface.

"Miss Matthews, please, wait!"

I wanted to rid myself of Detective Reynolds and all his bothersome questions, but he seemed determined to get what he wanted out of me. I turned and faced him, throwing my bags over my shoulder.

As he caught up to me, he said, "I have a few more questions."

"My parents are dead. Find their killer. Find my brother. That's all you need to know."

"That's what I'm trying to do." He held up his hands in a placating gesture. "Just give me a couple more minutes."

I agreed. After all, we *did* both seek the same goal—to catch the killer.

"Do you know of any other vampire acquaintances besides Nate and Parker?" he inquired with a raise of his brows.

"No."

"You're sure?"

"Pretty sure."

"What about your neighbors? Do any of them associate with vampires?"

"You'd have to ask them."

He took an evidence bag out of his coat pocket, which contained a keyring bearing two keys. "We found these keys locked in a box inside your parents' closet. Do you know what they're for?"

Narrowing my eyes, I studied the keys. A red rubber tip coated the small one, and the other looked like a regular house key. Neither looked familiar. "I've never seen them before."

"One more question. Do you know of any vampire who had reason to do this to your family?"

He seemed to enjoy asking the same question multiple ways. His approach didn't change my answer. "Like I said, other than Nate and Parker, I don't know any vampires."

"Thank you, Miss Matthews. If you think of anything, please call me. Here's my card."

I took the small rectangle and stuffed it into my pocket.

"I'll need your contact information as well." He pulled out another card and a pen. "Please write down your cell number."

I scribbled my number on his card and handed it back to him. "Please, find my brother. He's all I have left." As tears moistened my eyes, I blinked them away.

He gave my shoulder a firm squeeze. Kindness brightened his eyes. "You have my word." He glanced back at the house and then at me again. "Do you have a place to stay?"

I answered him with a lie. "I can stay with a girlfriend."

"Can I have one of the officers give you a lift?"

Pointing up the street, I said, "She's just up the block. Thanks, though."

He stared at me for a moment and then gave me a slight smile. Shoving his hands in his pockets, he turned and headed back to my once happy home. As I watched him retreat, I almost called out to him. I had nowhere to go.

CHAPTER 2

In a public restroom stall, I sank to the floor. My chest heaved with sobs I couldn't control, leaving me gasping for each breath. After what seemed like hours, I pushed to my feet, washed off my face, and ventured out into the mall. I stood motionless, staring blankly at the world around me. I wanted to grieve, hide from the cruel world, and crawl into a hole and die. But none of those things would bring my parents back. I needed to gather my strength, get my head together, and come up with a plan to fix this.

I wandered into a Starbucks and tucked myself away at a corner table. I took a sip of hot coffee and tried to make sense of it all. The Vow controlled the vampires. Their thirst for the hunt had ceased to exist for as long as anyone could remember. The Vampire Centers fed them, and one stood in every city, so why had some random vampire chosen my parents to feed upon and murder? Were Mom and Dad hunted strictly for sport, or had the vampire wanted something more? Was there a tangible object that the vampire was willing to kill for? Maybe my parents had resisted or fought back, yet other than the broken glass, signs of a struggle had appeared nonexistent. Could Detective Reynolds be right? Had a rogue vampire been responsible?

As a child, the creatures' doll-like features had fascinated me, the way the moonlight shimmered across their porcelain skin, sparkled in their bejeweled eyes, and illuminated their silken hair. I'd always thought of them as beautiful creatures rather than monsters, but the slaughter I'd witnessed in my parents' bedroom had to be the work of a monster. Everyone knew their history; heard the stories of vampires killing humans and vice versa, but all of that had happened long before The Vow. I surmised something significant must have set this vampire off for him or her to break the pact that kept both vampires and humans safe...I wasn't one to simply wait for answers.

Could Nate and Parker be the killers? Seriously considering this possibility for the first time, I bolted upright, choking on my coffee.

What did I know about them? Could they be capable of killing? *Don't go there. Remain optimistic and maintain your faith.* I sank back into the chair and shook away the horrid images but then began to wonder why JJ had never called me back.

Was it possible he didn't have his cell? He always had that damn thing with him, but my calls headed straight to voicemail. Maybe it *was* still in his room. He had a habit of hiding the phone from our parents under his mattress. Maybe the police had overlooked it. *There is only one way to discover the truth. Go back to the house and search his room.* The fact that the room was part of a crime scene presented a slight dilemma, but I rationalized that it was still my home. Besides, I needed some cash, not to mention a car. I would sneak into his room, steal some cash and the car, and quickly escape. With my plan settled, I nursed my coffee and waited for nightfall.

After the sun dropped below the horizon and the night sky emerged, I ditched Starbucks and hailed a cab. A feeling of déjà vu overtook me as I sat in the back seat of the yellow car. Here we go again; only this time, I possessed full knowledge of the tragic reason behind my parents' absence at the airport. Chills scurried down my arms, causing me to shudder, but I couldn't change the past. My focus shifted to the future and JJ.

The cab rounded the corner onto my street and stopped four houses up from my parents' at the address I gave him. I watched him drive away before glancing up and down the street—no police, no neighbors, just me. Certain I was in the clear, I turned toward my house. An eerie darkness shrouded it, as if it were a graveyard, absent of life and warmth. Shadows prowled around the porch as fragile beams of moonlight played across the front door. The porch light flickered as if beckoning me to come closer. Crime tape still blocked the entrance.

I took one step forward and then came to a standstill. What if the vampire returned? The thought sent my heartbeat into rapid-fire, echoing against my eardrums. I hummed a soothing melody in an attempt to calm myself, one my mother had sung to me as a child. It held me there, offering me the strength to stand my ground. I then headed up the walkway to the porch and ducked beneath the tape. When I unlocked the door and entered, dead silence greeted me.

The grandfather clock's sudden chime pierced me like a powerful blade of terror. I dropped my bags onto the floor and clapped a hand over my mouth, suffocating a scream, but this was *my* home; why should I be scared? Taking in a few reassuring breaths, I flipped the light switch by the staircase. The second floor materialized in the light, and my gaze darted toward JJ's bedroom door.

I took the stairs two at a time, exerting no effort in my pursuit of his phone. As I turned the knob and pushed the door open, my pulse accelerated once more. The subtle orange glow of his desk lamp lit the room. Clothes exploded from the hamper, spilling out onto the carpet. CDs lay everywhere, on the floor, the bed, the desk, and his nightstand. His bed lay unmade, the comforter piled in a heap at its center.

Kicking CDs out of my way, I cleared a path to his bed. I reached down and pulled up the right corner of his mattress. Nothing. I lifted the left corner. Again, nothing. I bent down and looked under the bed. There was only a carpet and a few balls of dust under the bed. I released a sigh of frustration and kicked the bed, and a small thud sounded from beneath. Dropping to my knees, I checked again. There it was! I let out a squeal of delight and grabbed it up. I tapped the screen, but darkness stared back. Dead battery? I slipped his phone into my pocket and headed back down the hall.

The gruesome images of my parents' corpses flashed before my eyes as I stood in front of their bedroom. The foul odor of decay lingered just inside their doorway, turning my stomach. How could I enter their room knowing their bodies were there? At the same time, a heartwarming memory of me crawling into bed with them and watching a scary movie while eating popcorn filled my head. I closed my eyes, resting my head against the smooth wooden frame, holding onto that thought. If I wanted the cash and the car keys—I *needed* them, not wanted them— avoiding the room wasn't an option. *I can do this. I have to do this.* I inched forward and flipped on the light. An empty bed came into view.

I gasped with relief, though the putrid stench contaminated the furniture, walls, and carpet, soiling my mother's picture-perfect room.

When I'd turned thirteen and JJ had been ten, our father had sat us down and rambled on about the importance of keeping an emergency fund. He'd kept his own in a sock, and right now, my survival depended on finding that sock. I ransacked their dresser, pulling drawers open and throwing clothes onto the floor, searching for my dad's stash. My fingers brushed over a bulkiness unlike the others in the drawer. I gave it a squeeze, and the crackle of paper met my ears. The money sock sat in the palm of my hand. As though I'd been penniless for years, I sank to the floor and pressed it against my heart. For a brief moment, I allowed joy to lift my spirits before dumping the contents onto the floor. Several hundreds, a few twenties, and a credit card tumbled out. I scooped up my pot of gold, gave the credit card a kiss, and shoved everything into the pocket of my jeans. When I rose to my feet, my mother's jewelry box atop the dresser came into view. Lifting the lid, I found the silver cross necklace I loved so much tucked into the corner. A swell of grief tugged at my heart as I slipped the chain around my neck. "I'll never take it off, Mom," I whispered, my eyes skimming over the family pictures standing on their dresser: my parents' wedding, me as a baby, baby JJ, and JJ receiving his first science award. I took a second look. My high school graduation photo was missing.

"Don't move. Put your hands in the air." The male voice exploded into the room.

As I turned toward the sound, the tiny hairs on the back of my neck pricked. An overweight police officer stood in the doorway, his gun aimed at my chest. My pulse drummed along the surface of my skin as I backed away, colliding with the dresser.

Jerking his gun to the left, he ordered, "Get away from the dresser."

It took every ounce of strength to push myself free and raise my hands.

"Empty your pockets."

I tried to reason with him. "I'm not stealing. This is my parents' house."

He ignored me, keeping his gun raised. "Pockets."

"I'm Claire Matthews. This *is* my parents' house. *My* house."

He tightened his grip on his gun and raised his voice. "For the last time, empty your pockets!"

My hands quivered as I threw the money, credit card, and cell phone onto the bed.

He picked up the credit card. "Obviously, you're not Paul Matthews."

"He's...he was...my dad."

After holstering his gun, he settled his hands on his hips. "Do you have any ID?"

"In my bags downstairs."

Gathering up the items on the bed in one hand and taking hold of my arm with the other, he said, "You and I are going to go slowly down the stairs and retrieve your bags."

Step by step, we descended the stairs like an elderly couple. When we reached the entryway, he made me stand against the wall while he knelt by my bags. His chubby hands rummaged through my clothes, my underwear—all my personal things. It made my skin crawl, besides being a complete violation of my privacy.

He located my wallet and flipped it open, his eyes darting back and forth as he examined my driver's license. When he lifted his head, his eyes met mine. "Well, you are who you say you are."

I swiped my hand across my forehead in relief. "Thank God. I thought you were going to arrest me."

"I *am* taking you downtown. You broke into a crime scene and stole evidence. I've got no choice but to take you in."

I barked out a laugh. "You can't be serious! I have a key, and I can't steal what's mine."

He stated with finality, "You'll have to work that out with Reynolds."

A dull, nagging pain speared my temples. This day just kept getting worse. I gave him my most charming smile. "Can't you just call him and work something out?"

He mimicked my laughter. "Do I look like Monty Hall? Whatever deal you make will be worked out downtown. Now, let's go." He took my arm and escorted me out of the house and into the back seat of his squad car. Settling behind the wheel, he then pulled out a plastic bag and dropped JJ's cell phone, the credit card, and the cash into it.

I slid down in the seat and put my head in my hands as he pulled onto the street and headed for the ominous station downtown.

"Tough day?" he asked, glancing in the rearview mirror.

"You have no idea." *And thanks to you, Mr. Policeman, I don't have any cash, a car, or my brother's cell.*

"Be straight with Reynolds, and he'll go easy on you."

I didn't share his optimism. Detective Reynolds would undoubtedly deliver a lecture—or worse, possible consequences—to me.

The downtown precinct loomed before me when he pulled his squad car into the lot and turned off the engine. After kicking his door wide open, he scooted off the seat and came around to collect me. He marched me through the station's front doors, firmly grasping me by my arm. Police officers, detectives, and a few civilians crowded the narrow lobby. The multitude of voices blended, bouncing off the crisp ivory walls. It made my headache pound all the harder.

"This way," he said, pushing through the crowd.

He led me to a long row of connected chairs and deposited me into one of them. He dropped my bags at my feet and said, "Wait here." After two steps in the opposite direction, he spun to face me again. "After reconsidering, please place your hands behind your back."

I bolted upright. "You're not seriously going to cuff me to the chair, are you? I'm not planning on running away if that's what you're thinking."

"I've heard that one before."

"You can trust me. I promise."

He pressed his lips tightly together and shook his head. "I've heard that before too."

"Maybe from a guilty person. I'm not going to run."

"It'll just be for a few minutes until Reynolds comes to get you." He gestured toward the chair. "Now sit back down, please, and put your hands behind your back."

I let out a groan, plopping back down and flinging my arms behind me. "This is so unnecessary."

Someone to my right snickered. My gaze fell upon a vampire with crystal-clear emerald eyes four chairs down. Was this cop crazy? Vampires had just killed my parents. I didn't even want to be in the same room as them, let alone sit so close to them. I whipped my head back toward the police officer. "Don't leave me alone right next to this vampire."

"You're not next to him. You're four chairs away. Besides, his cuffs are silver-plated, so he's not going anywhere. Sit tight while I find Reynolds." The cop snapped my cuffs into place and headed down the hallway.

"What is that supposed to mean?" I shouted after him.

"Silver weakens my powers," the vampire answered for him.

His velvety-soft voice ignited my curiosity. The overwhelming urge to take another peek at him burned inside me, but I refused to give in. I kept my eyes on the polished tile of the floor.

"What are you in for, Blondie?"

I pretended not to hear him.

"You should've batted those big baby blues at him. Those'll keep you out of jail."

His voice sounded enchanting, like music from a flute or harp. One peek couldn't hurt. I began to turn my head. *He's playing me. He wants me to look.* I locked my gaze back on the floor. "Leave me alone."

"I can't. You look just like a Barbie doll. Would you believe me if I said my name is Ken?"

I rolled my eyes but didn't face him. "So not funny."

"I'm not trying to be funny. I'm trying to get your attention. Apparently, my charm isn't working very well."

"You got that right."

"Come on. Just one little glance my way."

"Look, I'm not interested."

He laughed. "Well, well, well. It appears that I have a challenging task ahead of me. I could offer you a taste of my blood. Girls tell me it tastes like candy."

His pesky, persistent chatter made his voice less appealing and more annoying. "Stop talking. I need quiet. My head is pounding."

"I can fix that."

"I don't want your help."

"But I can take away the pain."

For the love of God, I wanted to scream. He just refused to give up. I twisted in my seat to face him, finally, donning my most annoyed scowl. "If I had to choose between your blood and pain, I'm sticking with pain."

He tilted his head full of caramel-colored curls and blew me a kiss. "Aw, come on. I'm just trying to help. Plus, I'm bored. Since we're both in this situation, why don't we make the most of it?"

Why couldn't he just shut up? Closing my eyes, I pressed the base of my skull against the ridge of the chair and rolled it back and forth.

"If you merely gaze into my eyes, I can cure you."

I couldn't hold in the groan any longer and let it slide past my lips. I threw a dirty look his way. "Will you shut up?"

He smiled and winked at me. "What can I say? I'm a vampire. We're persistent."

"You want to talk? Okay, fine. Tell me why some vampires kill."

A bewildered look spread across his face. "We don't."

"Well, some vampire or vampires killed my parents." I stared him down. "Was it you?"

He offered me an expression of disgust. "Where the hell did that come from? How could I have known your parents?"

I narrowed my gaze and pressed him. "I didn't ask if you knew them. I asked if you killed them."

Both his feet bounced upon the floor. Had I triggered a reaction? "Look," he said, his tone rising an octave or two higher, "just because I'm a vampire doesn't mean you can blame me for what happened to your parents."

"Why are you avoiding my question?" I glanced down at his feet, then back at his eyes. "You're nervous."

His eyes darted about the room as he cleared his throat. "I'm not nervous."

"Like hell you're not." I jerked at the cuffs, lunging toward him. "Did you kill a man and a woman a few days ago?"

He rooted his feet onto the floor and pressed his back against the chair. "I'm not saying another word."

A jolt of realization ran through me. He knew something.

Approaching footsteps interrupted my little interrogation. A tall, thin police officer stepped between us, unlocking the vampire's metal cuffs. "Your story checks out, Marty. You're free to go."

"No, no, no!" I blurted out. "He can't leave. He knows something about my parents' murder. Get Detective Reynolds, please!"

The police officer glanced at me, then the vampire, and raised his palms. "Marty, what's she going on about?"

The vampire shrugged. "Beats me."

"Don't let him go, please," I begged.

"I'm sorry, miss. I have no reason to hold him." The police officer turned his back on me and walked away.

The vampire he'd called Marty gave me a wink and then vanished before my eyes. My heart sank, and to exacerbate the situation, Detective Reynolds appeared around the corner, a scowl etched on his face. "Care to explain what you were doing there?"

I concisely expressed my thoughts to him. "I'm trying to find my brother."

He huffed loudly. "And I'm not?"

Detectives did find people. That was their job, but that didn't mean I couldn't do some investigating of my own. I glanced up at him and batted my big baby blues as Marty had suggested. "I can't just sit around and wait. I went looking for his cell, and you can thank me for finding it, but the battery was dead. What about you? Any news on Nate and Parker?"

He sat down next to me, unlocking my handcuffs. "Their place was cleared out, and no one has seen them for a while."

I rubbed my wrists while pointing out the obvious. "Maybe they ran?"

"It does raise suspicion, but it could also be a dead end. You're going to have to trust me to do my job."

He did seem sincere, but giving up control to someone who wasn't family didn't seem right. My emotional connection prevented me from giving up, at least not just yet. "Now that you have JJ's cell, can I see what's on it? Maybe there are some text messages or voicemails that can lead us to some real clues."

He shook his head. "Lead *me*, not *us*, Miss Matthews. Furthermore, we have classified your brother's cell phone as evidence."

"Please, call me Claire. And remember, if it weren't for me, you wouldn't have his cell. I think you should share any information you find. I might be able to offer insight you wouldn't have knowledge of."

He stared at me for a moment, then laced his fingers. "You're right, Claire. You did find it, but if you'd told me where to look, the police would've found it first. This is a formal murder investigation. I trust you understand that, correct?"

He was determined not to budge, just as I was. "I know, but that's my brother who's missing. And my parents were murdered in the home where I grew up. This experience is also personal."

He gave me a stern look. "And that's why I can't have you involved. You're too invested, and I'm the detective, remember?"

He may have been, but where were the results? Yes, he'd just gotten started, but I lacked patience. He needed to find clues, interview witnesses, and track down evidence. That took time, and maybe JJ didn't have time to spare. He could be hurt, or worse. I wouldn't relinquish my rights as a sister. No matter what Reynolds said, I was committed long-term. The cuffed vampire's actions resurfaced in my brain. "I think I might have something." I glanced at the empty chair where he had been sitting. "A vampire named Marty was sitting right there. I think he may know something about my parents' murder. He got all dodgy and defensive when I mentioned their death at the hands of a vampire."

He pursed his lips and exhaled deeply. "See, this is what I mean. Marty's going to go back to the vampire community and spread the word that the police are looking for a vampire and possibly stall my investigation."

A warm flush flooded my cheeks. "Oh, I didn't think about that. Sorry, I just reacted when he got all squirmy."

He pulled out a notepad and scribbled something on the page. "I know you meant well. I'll check him out."

"Now that I think of it, there *is* something else."

He raised his brows and stared in my direction.

"I noticed a picture missing from my parents' dresser. My high school graduation photo."

His thick brows furrowed together when he cocked his head. "Maybe your parents just put it away?"

"Maybe, but it seemed odd since it's claimed that very spot for two years. So, I thought you should know."

Again, he put his pen to the pad. "I'll check the evidence. Maybe it got bagged for prints."

"So, am I free to go? You're not going to charge me with anything, are you? I was just trying to find some answers."

"You can go." He glanced down at my bags. "I take it your girlfriend wasn't home."

I fended off his statement with another lie. "I must have missed her. I'm sure she's home by now."

He placed his hand on my shoulder, his eyes filled with compassion. "You don't have a place to stay, do you?"

The truth in his words resonated deeply, intensifying the headache at my temples. That was my home, so where else could I possibly stay? I did my best to stay optimistic. "Not really. Maybe I can just stay at a hotel or something." My optimism deflated. I couldn't manage to pay for a room without a single cent to my name.

As if he read my mind, Reynolds handed me the cash I'd taken from my parents' house. "This should help."

I gave him a grateful smile. "Thank you. It will."

He also placed the keys to my parents' Jeep in the palm of my hand. "CSU bagged these, but they're not evidence, and you could use the car too."

In the midst of all the gloom, the two small victories filled my eyes with tears. I tried to blink them away, but I couldn't escape my emotions.

Yes, I wanted—no, I needed—the Jeep. Wiping away the surge of tears, I whispered, "You don't know how much this means to me. Thank you. Thank you so much."

He offered up a warm smile and said, "If there's anything else I can do for you, just let me know."

"Can I get a couple of aspirin? I've got a horrible headache."

"I'm not surprised after the day you've had. Two aspirin, coming right up."

CHAPTER 3

Ispent the next few weeks living out of a suitcase at Motel 6, waiting for an offer to be made on my parents' house. I could no longer call it home, what with the gruesome memory of identifying the corpses of my mother and father etched into my brain and the lack of my brother's presence inside its eerily silent walls. When all was said and done, I just wanted to be free of it. In all honesty, the relief of not having to return to the house outweighed any traces of guilt about selling it. The logical decision was to let someone else call it home, and I'd practically given the place away when an offer finally came in, but with a recent murder hanging over its roof, potential buyers weren't exactly lining up around the block. Despite my conscience weighing heavily, I accepted the offer.

I stood on my parents' front porch, my muscles, nerves, and bones aching with grief. However, to finalize matters with the new owners meant packing up mine and JJ's things. All of our things would to be delivered to my new condo—purchased with the benefit of our parents' life insurance policies. Everything else inside their house sat waiting for Saint Paul's Donations to retrieve. In forty-eight hours, I could leave both the motel and the house behind, but first, the task at hand was packing.

Outside their house, I stared down at my braided sandals, and raw, burning breath rose in my throat. As I looked up, I saw the same nosy neighbors from the day the police had discovered my parents' bodies, venturing out and gathering at the edge of their driveways like packs of coyotes. I expected to see drool seeping from their flapping mouths. The itch to shout out at them tickled my tongue. Didn't they have anything better to do? Did the word privacy mean nothing anymore? I rolled my eyes, turned my back on them, inserted the key into the lock, and hurried inside.

Climbing the stairs, memories from the funeral monopolized my thoughts. A man in a crisp, navy-blue suit had joined me, standing with his hands folded and his head lowered, listening along with me to the kind words spoken by the minister. I clung to every word, trying to fill the void in my heart.

When the funeral had ended, the man in the suit had identified himself as my parents' attorney. He had voiced a quick, "I'm sorry for your loss," handed me an envelope, and then left me alone at the gravesite. I'd stared at the envelope, the sun blazing down on me and warming my skin. How long I'd held it in my hands before opening it, I don't recall. After I'd finally torn open the seal, I'd stared at a check for five hundred and fifty thousand dollars. In all my time growing up, we had lived in a vacuum. There had been no outsiders, no other family members. It was just us, but the isolation had ended for JJ when he had met vampires Nate and Parker after I'd gone off to college. So, I hadn't wanted money. I'd wanted my parents and my brother.

Shaking off thoughts of the past, I pulled my focus back to the present and continued to my room. As I pushed open the door, my familiar surroundings came into view: whitewashed furniture covered in bright floral-print cushions, built-ins crammed with a myriad of knickknacks and books I'd collected over the years. My picture-framed clock I'd made during my freshman year at college sat on my desk, and the funky tree-shaped sculpture of my design stood on my dresser. A poster autographed by my favorite band, The Wanted, hung above the bed across from the closet, slightly ajar with its overstuffing of my zillions of pieces of clothing. I climbed onto my bed, hugging a pillow and heaving a melancholy sigh. My lips began to quiver, and one by one the tears fell. It became painfully clear that packing simply wasn't in the cards today. I would do it first thing tomorrow, after a good night's sleep in my old bedroom.

A few hours later, a gruesome nightmare ripped through my brain and jarred me awake. In it, dead bodies had hovered above my bed. A scream swelled inside my throat but failed to escape. *You're not real. Get out of my head.* I bolted upright and sprang to my feet, flicking on the light and pressing my back against the wall. The spine-tingling vision began to grow faint as the personal treasures scattered about my bedroom came into focus. Loneliness washed over me. God, I missed my family so much.

Fleeing the solitude of my room, I hurried down the hallway, rushing into JJ's room. I stepped over the clutter on the floor and sat on the edge of his bed. The subtle scent of Calvin Klein hit me when I picked up one of his sweatshirts from beneath my feet. I could smell him. My chest caved inward with grief. The room spun around me, throwing me into the past when JJ had been thirteen and I, sixteen.

As he jumped up and down inside my memory, pulling at his blonde curls, JJ gushed with pride. "Mr. Clark picked my science project for the school fair."

I'd given him a high-five. "I'll work the booth with you if you like."

JJ had grinned and given my shoulder a nudge. "That's because you have a major crush on Mr. Clark."

Heat had spread across my cheeks as I'd replied with an exaggerated shake of my head. "Not. True."

"Then why does your notebook have his name written all over the inside?"

My mouth had fallen open before I'd quickly snapped it shut, my hands flying to my hips. "Have you been snooping around in my bedroom again?"

In response, he had wrapped his arms around his torso, puckering his lips and blowing kisses. "Oh, Mr. Clark, I love you."

I'd charged after him. "You little brat! You're going to get it."

JJ had raced out of his room and down the stairs, with me only seconds behind.

At the bottom of the staircase, Dad had wound his arm around JJ, halting his escape. "Are you tormenting Claire again?"

The memory faded away, and I cried into JJ's sweatshirt. Wiping away tears, I whispered, "JJ, please, don't be dead." I took one more sniff of his sweatshirt, laid it on his bed, and quickly left his room.

CHAPTER 4

The next morning, Saint Paul's Donations gathered the remaining furnishings and mementos of our entire lives—minus my own and JJ's things. I sat on the curb in front of the house, my eyes fixed on the pavement, my chin resting on my knees, indulging in a moment of self-pity. Heavy footsteps approached from behind, and a male voice said, "Excuse me, Miss Matthews. One of my men found this journal buried under some clothes in your parents' closet. I know you said you would rather not keep anything, but this looks rather old and personal. It might be of some importance to you, and you might not want a stranger's eyes reading it."

I turned to find a short, stocky man covered in sweat. He bent and handed me a worn, brown leather journal bound with a leather tie.

Fingering the worn leather, I nodded at him. "Thank you."

"You're quite welcome. My men and I are about finished. As instructed, we left the two upstairs bedrooms alone. I'll have some paperwork for you to sign shortly."

"Thank you."

He nodded and hurried off back inside the house.

I unfastened the leather binding, flipping the journal open. The upper right-hand corner bore the scribble "Property of William J. Matthews." I re-read the last name. Matthews? Had he been a relative? I scanned the first line written beneath the name.

December 1, 1883—As I hunted the vampire, grave danger once again overshadowed my life.

Vampire hunted? I gripped the edges of the journal while my pulse bounced with excitement. Who was William J. Matthews, and why did my parents have his diary? I sat completely still as I turned the page. Only fragments of the entry were still readable, insufficient to fully comprehend its significance. I skimmed through several pages, discovering more of the same. Not until I skipped to the middle of the journal did a full page of legible words meet my vision.

June 29, 1884—With each passing year, the vampires evolve. They grow stronger, more rebellious, making my task exceedingly difficult, yet not impossible. However, their razor-sharp sight, keen sense of smell, and sensitivity to sound exceed my human capabilities. I am always one step behind in my pursuit.

July 1, 1884—I must engage with the vampire. It is imperative that I study him, learn his habits, and comprehend the reasons behind his behavior. If I am ever to destroy him, I feel I must first befriend him.

July 31, 1884—I have assembled a vampire kill kit consisting of five essential items: a wooden stake, a knotted rope, a vial of holy water, a cross forged of pure silver, and last, but not least, some cloves of garlic. These are vital weapons, but none of them compare with that of the sun. This daytime star is their most deadly adversary, their ultimate demise.

I looked up from the journal and shuddered. William J. Matthews had been a vampire slayer. But that didn't explain how his diary had ended up in my parents' closet, hidden no less. I inhaled deeply as I flipped to the subsequent page.

October 15, 1884—Deceived by the vampire, I became trapped in his lair. However, I am rather smart. Drawing a line of garlic toward the door, I held my silver cross in one hand and the vial of holy water in the other. I inched toward the crypt's exit and kicked the door wide open. The first light of the day slowly made its way inside. As my gaze locked with the vampire's, I grinned, raised my hat, and made my escape. Lady Luck had blessed me once again.

January 15, 1885—My mind is awhirl. The vampire race has proposed a vow of peace, which would end the bloodshed and bring our worlds together. Can we trust such a vow? Could we ever coexist? I will voice my concerns at the town meeting, but I fervently hope for a possible truce.

The remaining pages contained no other entries, though I knew what the outcome of the vote concerning The Vow had been. Had William lived to see it come to fruition?

"Excuse me, Miss Matthews. We're all done. I've got paperwork ready for your signature," the stocky man said, handing me a pen and clipboard.

I snapped the journal shut and rose to my feet. "Where do I sign?"

"Here and here."

He gave me a copy before he and his men left me standing in the driveway alone. Just like that, their truck disappeared down the street, taking with it all my parents' possessions. I smothered the swell of emotion inside me. Those had only been material things; they didn't matter. Finding the vampire responsible for their deaths, and even more importantly, finding JJ, did. Learning more about the identity of William J. Matthews and how he might be connected to our family seemed a good place to start.

The starkness of the rooms, once cluttered with the objects of everyday life, surprised me as I entered the house. The happy, uncomplicated, secure world I once knew had vanished, replaced by grief, turmoil, and uncertainty. As the overwhelming desire to destroy the murdering vampire intensified with every heartbeat, I dug my nails into my palms. "I'm going to find you, bloodsucker, and when I do, you're going to pay." I marched up the stairs to my bedroom and scooped up my laptop. Climbing onto my bed and sitting back against a mountain of pillows, I logged onto the internet. I did a Google search for Ancestry. com and clicked the link to the page. The instructions seemed fairly simple: start with yourself, add what you know about your family, and then the site would complete a search and construct your family tree.

But for me, the task was anything but simple. I pushed the laptop aside and fought the urge to abandon the search. I couldn't stand the sight of one more mysterious hint regarding my family tree leading to nowhere. I just wanted one answer—William J. Matthews' connection to my family. Was that too much information to ask for? I stretched my arms overhead and rolled my head from side to side, determined to pick up where I'd left off.

My "small" task evolved into hours of scrutinizing census, birth, death, marriage, and military records until a single strand of resolve emerged from my family tree. William J. Matthews had been my great-great-grandfather on my father's side. For the longest time, I stared at the screen, re-reading the words as if they might evaporate before I could grasp their meaning. Maybe his journal had come into my parents' possession through a distant relative I'd never met. Had they read it, and in fear of The Vow, they had hidden it from JJ and me?

Perhaps even more slayers made up a part of our family? A phrase from William's journal rushed back, filling my thoughts. *I must engage with the vampire. It is imperative that I study him, learn his habits, and comprehend the reasons behind his behavior. If I am ever to destroy him, I feel I must first befriend him.* William's words thrust forth an idea. I knew how to find my parent's killer, and that was by becoming a volunteer at The Vampire Center.

CHAPTER 5

The following day, the movers delivered mine and JJ's things to the new condo. The moment they left, I jumped over the maze of boxes to ransack my pile of clothes. I had no interest in unpacking or settling in. All I could think of was putting my plan in motion. I chose a paisley shift dress and ankle boots to wear. I nodded my approval of my appearance in the mirror, grabbed my car keys, and drove straight to The Vampire Center. The arched brick structure with blacked-out windows monopolized the entire block of East Broadway. I swung the Jeep into the massive parking lot, killed the engine, and stepped out onto the asphalt. As I sized up the building, my heartbeat thumped in my dry throat. I trembled, but not from the temperature, but from nerves. The brilliance of my plan lost its appeal. I knew nothing about The Vampire Center, not to mention the requirements of becoming a volunteer. And what if they didn't need any volunteers? What then? How could I ever gain a vampire's trust or learn anything about their behavior? *Get it together. How hard could it be?* I squelched my defeatist nature as my resolve came back with great strength. I took in a couple of deep breaths and marched forward with all the confidence in the world.

The tinted glass door slid open automatically, welcoming me inside. My boots squeaked against the polished floor in the hushed silence of the empty lobby. After rounding the right corner, I entered a waiting area filled with oversized chairs, magazine racks, and a few coffee tables. A circular reception desk occupied the room's center, where a gray-haired woman stood behind it, flipping through charts. Looking up, she asked, "May I help you?"

Hoping to sound like one of those humanitarian—well, vampitarian—types, I cheerfully responded, "I would like to inquire about volunteering for The Vampire Center."

A warm, inviting smile spread across her face, deepening the wrinkles beside her eyes. She held out her hand. "My name is Nancy Carter, the head nurse, and who are you?"

I couldn't have her knowing my real name, what with the murders and all. "Claire Jones." *Geez, was that the best I could come up with?*

"Well, Claire, this is your lucky day. It just so happens we've lost several volunteers and are in desperate need of more. Are you looking for day or night shifts?"

She'd stumped me. "Whatever you have available would be fine."

She came from behind the desk and pointed to the waiting room chairs. "Have a seat, and let's chat."

The massive chair engulfed me completely. I slid forward so I could rest my feet on the floor.

"Day shift volunteers tend to our human donors, which is from whom the center's blood comes."

"I assumed the blood came from hospitals."

"In the beginning, yes, but now we have so many donors, we don't need to take the blood supply from the hospitals."

"That's amazing." Again, I attempted to sound enthusiastic.

Nancy beamed. "Yes, it is. We've come a long way, and we're very proud of our center. Do you have any volunteer experience?"

Should I lie and tell her I had? What if she asked for details? It seemed honesty was my best chance there, but playing the naïve newcomer might be a better sell. "No, I haven't, but I've always wanted to be a part of a bigger cause, and The Vampire Center seems ideal for me."

"Wonderful. Both volunteer roles are essential to us. Day shift donor volunteers check the human donors in, enter their blood type into the computer, and prepare labels and blood bags. Then, the transfusion volunteers prepare the bags before greeting the vampires and escorting them into the room to sit with them during their transfusion. This job entails either reading, conversing, or telling a story to help them pass the time."

I certainly wasn't there to waste my time with human donors who couldn't help my cause. "I'm sure you probably need both, but being a transfusion volunteer sounds fascinating."

"Normally, I would ask for at least one reference, but since I'm in a bind and need to fill slots tonight, I'll get to that later."

Thank God for that, as I didn't have a clue whose name I would give her—certainly not Detective Reynolds.

"I think you're a perfect fit for the transfusion team with your cheerful personality," she said, glancing at her watch. "It's coming up on four o'clock. I would be extremely grateful if you could start tonight."

"That would be great." The sooner I could start gathering information about who may have been responsible for my parents' deaths, the better.

She smiled, rose to her feet, and waved me forward. "From four to six thirty, transfusion volunteers prepare for the night shift. I'll show you around and introduce you to the other nurses and volunteers."

I followed her as she led me down a corridor lit by fluorescents, leading into a massive slate-colored room. At least fifty dentist-style chairs lined the north, south, and east walls. Beside each stood a smaller reading chair, designated for volunteers, I assumed. A library jam-packed with books covered the entire west wall. The bold plaid privacy curtains, the spines of the numerous books, and the vibrant green of the potted plants were the only sources of color in the room.

"This room is where the magic happens," Nancy said, spreading her arms. "Come seven o'clock, it will be bustling with vampires."

"Does it hurt them?" I asked. "The transfusion, I mean."

"On the contrary, they're quite relaxed but often become a bit bored. That's where our volunteers come in." Pointing to the rows of books, she added, "The publication date range is vast, as some vampires prefer books from their eras."

Maybe following the example of William Matthews wasn't such a good idea. Being an inexperienced and defenseless twenty-year-old girl, attempting the interrogation of vampires might prove to be a major challenge. Perhaps this type of mission *was* better suited for Detective Reynolds and the police.

Nancy touched my shoulder, an expression of concern creasing her forehead. "Are you all right, Claire? This whole process can be rather overwhelming for first-timers."

I pushed aside my insecurity and gave her a confident nod. "I'm just excited. I can't wait to get started."

A satisfied smile replaced her frown. "Then let me introduce you to the girls."

"Sounds great."

We traveled down the incandescently lit corridor once more. About twenty feet in, she stopped at a closed door to our right. Muffled chatter filtered through the frame before Nancy swung the door open wide. "This is the storage area, or as we like to call it, the blood room."

The potent stench of human blood lingered thickly in the air. I wanted to gag—certainly not the reaction one would expect from a veteran transfusion volunteer. None of the other ten or so women standing about the long rectangular room seemed to mind. I decided if they could deal with the smell, then so could I. I raised my chin, striving to stand a little taller as I walked into the room. Half the women retrieved blood bags from the refrigerators and stacked them along a workstation that stretched the length of the wall, while the other half sorted the bags and placed them into machines of some kind.

Nancy smiled proudly. "We have ten refrigerators and twelve blood warmers. These volunteers are getting ready for the night shift. As I explained earlier, preparation is the responsibility of the transfusion volunteers."

I regarded the machines, taking in what Nancy said. So the strange contraptions warmed the blood, but didn't vampires run cold?

She placed her hand on my shoulder, pulling my attention away from the warmers so she could lead me toward the women. "Claire, this is Melissa, Sara, Martha, and Jeannie. Girls, Claire is joining The Center as a transfusion volunteer."

I offered my hand and said, "Nice to meet you." Not one of them reached out and accepted. Judging by their pinched expressions, an addition to the team wasn't welcome news.

A large woman with a pierced lip rolled her eyes at Nancy. "Really? Another blue-eyed blonde? The vampires are going to go nuts." Her gaze darted toward a blonde woman standing on her right who looked close in age to my mother. "No offense, Jeannie."

Jeannie shrugged her shoulders. "None taken."

A goth girl dressed in black, with hair of the same shade, plastered a nasty scowl on her face and crossed her arms. "You just stay away from Connor. He's mine."

"You don't stand a chance with Connor, Sara," a woman covered in costume jewelry fired her words at the goth girl. "He's just too sweet to tell you."

"Melissa, you're just jealous because he always sits with me," she shot back.

Great, a catfight. What the hell was I getting myself into?

Nancy whistled loudly and clapped her hands. "Now, now, ladies, calm down. We're adults, not children, remember?" She turned toward the large woman. "Martha, you know as well as I do how short-staffed we are and how backed up things get around here. We *need* volunteers."

Martha tugged on the silver stud embedded in her lip and nodded reluctantly. "I still say the vampires are going to go crazy over her."

Nancy glanced at me before facing the group. "At first sight, yes, but they'll relax afterward, so quit fretting." She turned to the goth girl. "Sara, Connor's personal affairs are just that—personal. You can't claim him as if he were a possession."

The girl's pale cheeks advanced to shades of red as she answered, "Yes, Nancy."

Nancy then turned her attention to the costume-jewelry queen. "Melissa—"

"I know, I know," she said, interrupting Nancy. "I have to play nice."

The rest of the women remained silent, focusing on the task at hand, preparing the blood. A sense of relief settled inside my stomach.

For a moment, I thought I might have joined a dating service rather than a Vampire Center.

Nancy shooed them away. "Okay, now, everyone get back to work." She turned to me. "Come, and I'll show you how I work the front desk." After she had closed the door behind us, she told me, "Don't pay any attention to them. Their feathers get a little ruffled when a new volunteer starts."

Territorial was more like it. "Why is that?" I asked.

"Some of the volunteers have been with us a long time and have built relationships with the vampires. Regrettably, this has led to feelings of jealousy within the group. They understand that The Center does not tolerate such behavior."

"I hope they don't think I'm here to steal anyone's vampire."

She smirked as she spoke. "Of course they do."

I certainly wasn't a threat to their love lives or crushes. I planned to use The Vampire Center to hunt down my parents' killer. If those women were privy to my real intentions, what would they think of me then? "I'm only here to volunteer. Hopefully, the girls will realize that."

She shook a finger at me. "Don't be concerned with the chips on their shoulders. They'll get over it; they always do." Nancy placed a few clipboards on the counter, then grabbed several sheets of paper from a drawer. "These are the sign-in sheets. Vampires fill in their name and blood type. We enter their information into the computer, which prints out in the blood room. We then select the warmed blood for them. As chairs become available, the vampires' names are called, and they're brought to the transfusion room and paired with a registered nurse and volunteer. Any questions?"

"Why do you warm the blood?"

"Now, that's a good one. When the centers first opened, we pumped cold blood into them. The vampires caused a big stink, saying it felt unnatural and like an insult to them after they'd been accustomed to drinking from humans." She tapped her temple. "If you think about it, it makes sense. Before The Vow, they drank from a warm host. We now warm the blood in an effort to accommodate the vampires' preference for the traditional method."

She had a point, and I gave The Center props. Without their ability to cater to their vampire clientele, humanity's fate would be in grave peril.

She chuckled. "I'll let you in on a little secret. The warmed blood gives them a slight buzz."

I cracked a smile. I'd never laid eyes on a wasted vampire before.

"Any other questions?"

"Just one. Why did the women say the vampires would go crazy over me? Should I be concerned?"

"Don't worry, you're in no danger. It's quite the opposite. They'll make a fuss over you, that is all. They have a weakness for blue-eyed blondes."

A stampede of footsteps came rushing toward us from behind. I turned to look, and my mouth fell open. A large herd of vampires had swarmed into the reception area, their glassy eyes shifting in my direction. Pervasive gazes locked onto me, glowing with such radiance they were almost blinding. I took a step backward, moving away from the group.

"Here we go," Nancy muttered. "Claire, come behind the desk with me while I check them in."

I didn't hesitate. As I hurried behind the desk to stand next to her, an army of vampires charged straight toward us, causing my eyes to widen and my pulse to pound in my throat. It almost made me forget my reason for coming. Was one or more of these vampires behind my parents' murder? Would I gain any useful information from them? Just how did one go about interrogating a vampire? Could they read my thoughts and anticipate my next move? Could they expose my small-scale investigation, leading to my expulsion from The Vampire Center? What would I do then? I blew out the tension in one breath and cleared my head, focusing all my effort on keeping it blank and empty. I needed to unwind, maintain a positive outlook, and let events unfold naturally.

After checking in the first wave of vampires, Nancy took me back into the transfusion room and sat me down in one of the reading chairs. "Jessica will bring in your first vampire. Are you ready?"

Was I? There's only one way to find out. "I'm ready."

She patted my hands. "Sit tight."

A redheaded woman carrying a bag of ruby-colored blood escorted a vampire, who appeared to be stuck back in the seventies, into the room and straight toward me. His attire—a sweater vest and plaid pants—made me giggle, but fireworks brought on by excitement also exploded inside my stomach. I sat stone-still and locked a smile onto my face.

She reached out her hand. "Hi, Claire, I'm Jessica. I'll be the transfusion nurse working with you tonight." She turned to the vampire. "And this is Max."

"Nice to meet you both," I said.

Jessica winked at me. "Max, you hit the jackpot tonight, getting a pretty young blonde to sit with you."

As he lowered himself into the transfusion chair, his dark-green eyes wandered over my face, his expression starry-eyed and lovestruck. "I'm in heaven right now," he told me, his eyes fixed on my own.

Oh, good lord. It's going to be a long night! "Why, thank you, Max," I said, widening my smile.

Jessica hung the bag above his chair and then inserted the needle into his vein, after which she released the clamp. A steady flow of crimson colored the line and disappeared into his pasty arm. He closed his eyes and rested his head on the back of the chair, releasing a long, low sigh. I watched a warm glow spread across his pale cheeks.

"I'll be checking in with you off and on during the night," Jessica said, then added, "but if you need me or have a question, just yell. I won't be far."

"Okay. Thanks."

"I'll leave the two of you alone." She smiled. "Have fun."

Fun? That was the last thing on my mind. I needed information. I had no idea how to go about collecting information, but I needed to start somewhere. I shrugged my shoulders and said, "So…"

Max glanced first at me and then at the floor. "This must be strange for you, sitting there watching me feed my body with human blood?"

"I don't think it's weird at all. It's what your body needs."

He shifted in his chair, crossing and uncrossing his legs before locking his eyes on mine again. "You're both beautiful and kind."

"I'm a volunteer; this is what we do. Just relax. Why don't I read to you?"

A radiant shimmer lit up his dark green eyes. "Can we talk instead?"

My heartbeat spiked, eagerness spilling into my veins. *Yes, tell me everything. Tell me why some vampires kill.* "Of course we can."

He leaned toward me. "Tell me all about you."

I dismissed his request with a wave of my hand. "My life is boring. Besides, I'm sure you have far more intriguing stories. I would much rather hear about you."

"Really?"

"Yes."

He cocked his head and gazed up at the ceiling before looking back at me. "Well, for starters, I love tequila. All vampires do. It's our drink of choice."

I took a mental note: *Vampires love tequila.* My mother used to tell me, "You can catch more flies with honey than vinegar." I took her advice and put on a show of interest. "No, you don't say! It's my favorite too." Truthfully, I hated the stuff.

He grinned. "We should have a drink sometime."

I kept baiting him, probing for more. "Maybe we will. Tell me something else about you."

"I turned after The Vow came about, and for that I'm grateful." He paused, offering me a heartfelt expression before continuing. "I could never hurt a human being."

The Vampire Center was all he knew. Most likely, he didn't know the first thing about feeding on humans, but did he know others who had? "What about vampires who turned before The Vow? How do they feel?"

A frown of troubled lines creased the center of his pale forehead. "What do you mean?"

"They used to feed off humans. Maybe they miss doing so?"

He gave a decisive shake of his head. "Not true. We are all delighted those days are over."

He couldn't possibly know every single vampire, and I knew of at least one who missed old times. I just needed to find a vampire willing to give said killer up. I returned my focus to the sincere and gentle Max. "I can't imagine what things must have been like before The Vow came about."

"Being forced to kill to survive..." A shudder ran through him, cutting his words short. He changed the subject expediently. "Kicking back in a graveyard and drinking tequila among the tombstones with my buddies, now, those are fun times. We never get too drunk, though. Alcohol makes us forget about the sun coming up."

This is another tip worth remembering: *Check graveyards for drunken vampires.* "Have you ever seen that happen—vampires caught by the sun?"

His gaze broke focus, revealing gloom behind his blank stare—a painful memory perhaps? "I have," he answered, his voice just above a whisper. "I watched while they burned alive."

I sat back and pressed my hand to my chest. "What a horrible way to die."

He nodded in agreement. "Indeed. We have to respect our golden reaper."

"And stay away from it," I added.

He barked out a laugh. "Yes." That starry-eyed look returned as he held me once again in his gaze. "I could stare at you forever."

"Why?" I probed. What was it about blue-eyed blondes that fascinated them so?

"Humans think we have a weakness for girls like you, but they're wrong. It's not just any blue-eyed blonde." He winked at me. "You're special."

Genuinely intrigued, I scooted to the edge of my chair. "How so?"

His green eyes seemed to glow as they moved over my face. He tapped at his chin as he said, "Your beauty is pure, nearly flawless, like a vampire's, but you are undoubtedly human. Such preternatural beauty fascinates us. A vampire can't help but be drawn to you."

I pressed my fingertips to my warming cheeks. "What a lovely thing to say."

"This can't be the first time someone has told you you're beautiful."

"Never in such an enchanting way."

He looked up at the blood bag, just a few drops away from emptying. "Our time is almost up. I enjoyed sitting with you."

I hated to see Max go. I rather liked him.

Approaching footsteps cut off my planned response. Jessica came between us, placing her hand on my shoulder. "I'll finish up with Max. You can go check in with Nancy."

I reached my hand out to the vampire. "I enjoyed our time together too," I said, giving his hand a gentle squeeze before leaving him with Jessica.

The crowded waiting room filled with vampires evoked childhood memories of flawless porcelain dolls. The steady pitter-patter of my heart hammered against my eardrums as a pair of jade-colored eyes sparkling like fireflies stopped me dead in my tracks. The person bearing those eyes bore a striking resemblance to a modern-day James Dean. An untucked white T-shirt appeared beneath his black leather jacket and hung over a pair of black jeans. Combat boots with the laces hanging loose and untied completed his look. He swept his brownish-blonde bangs back from his brow and gave me a single nod. Hooking his thumbs into his belt loops, he sauntered my way, extending his hand once he stood before me. "Hi there, I'm Connor, and you are?"

Was this Sara's Connor? Was this the Connor Sara had warned me to avoid? I wasn't taking any chances, especially on my first night volunteering. I gave him a fleeting smile, then turned to address Nancy. "Jessica sent me to check in with you. Who's next?"

"That would be me," Connor replied, slapping the counter as if he were playing bongo drums.

Nancy arched a single brow. "Connor, three others are ahead of you. Return to your seat and wait your turn."

He winked at her. "Then move me up the list. I won't tell anyone." He gave my shoulder a playful nudge. "And you still haven't told me your name."

Nancy barked out her order like a drill sergeant. "Connor, *sit down*."

He heaved a loud sigh and meandered back to his seat, where he flopped down while keeping his eyes glued to me.

I leaned toward Nancy and whispered, "Is that Sara's Connor?"

A tsk-tsk sound echoed in her throat. "Really, Claire, you sound just as silly as Sara did before. Yes, that's Connor, but he certainly does *not* belong to her."

Connor leapt to his feet and strutted toward us again. "I heard my name." A smile dripping with charm spread across his face. "I managed to catch yours as well." He effortlessly pronounced my name without hesitation. "Claire. I like it. Sit with me tonight, will you?"

As I stood next to him, my heartbeat climbed sharply, urging me to sit with him and stare into his dreamy eyes, but neither inciting a war with Sara nor hooking up at The Vampire Center was first on my agenda. Finding my parents' killer demanded all my attention, and I planned to keep it that way. "If you're not next on the list, then I'll be unable to sit with you," I retorted in my most blasé voice.

Connor rubbed his hands together and said, "If I sing to you, would that change your mind?"

"Sing?"

He spread his arms wide and belted out, "*At long last love has arrived, and I thank God I'm alive. You're just too good to be true. Can't take my eyes off of you.*"

The vampires in the waiting room rose from their chairs, cheering and whistling, egging him on.

Connor turned toward his fans and took a bow before facing me. "So?"

How did he think singing would change anything? He had definitely inherited the arrogant-vampire gene. "Even if I knew that song, it doesn't change your place in the line."

His mouth fell open in a dramatic manner. "You're kidding, right? Everyone knows Frankie Valli."

"Frankie who?"

Boisterous laughter spilled from his lips as his eyes drifted over my face. "Okay, not your era...I get that. Who's your favorite band then?"

"I don't have time for this. I have to get back to work."

Nancy waved him away. "Connor, I'm not going to tell you again."

With a determined flare glimmering in his eyes, he held up a finger. "One more minute." He turned to me again. "Tell me the name of your favorite band."

He wasn't about to give up until he got what he wanted. I blurted out, "The Wanted."

The fireflies in his eyes fluttered and brightened. He exuded a radiant smile, as though he had just unearthed a delightful secret. He didn't sing, but in a smooth, buttery voice, he recited, "I can't say that I'll be chasing the sun with you, but now that I've laid eyes on you, my universe will never be the same."

He reclaimed my attention, and I couldn't keep my lips from forming a flirty smile. "You're rather clever, aren't you?"

"I like to think so."

Hurried footsteps came rushing up behind me. A squeal filled with excitement pierced my eardrums. As I turned, Sara bumped against my arm, running past me to greet Connor.

Her face beamed as she gazed up at him. Grabbing his hands, she exclaimed, "I'm so happy to see you." She smiled sweetly as she flipped her hair back, tucking it behind an ear. When she glanced over at me, however, her face twisted into a nasty scowl.

The glowing fireflies dimmed in Connor's eyes as he said with less flair, "Hello, Sara." He glanced at me over her shoulder. "Sara, I was hoping to—"

"Continue reading *To Kill a Mockingbird*?" Sara asked, cutting him short. "I've already pulled the book for us."

I'm definitely not getting in the middle of that. I turned my back on them and looked at Nancy. "Who's next?"

"Randall," Nancy called out.

A vampire with bushy blonde hair, clad simply in jeans and a T-shirt, popped up from his chair. He slipped his arm under mine, locking eyes with me. "Hello, Claire."

I politely removed his arm and greeted him in return. "Hello, Randall."

Connor narrowed his eyes at Randall and grumbled something under his breath, shaking his head.

"What did you say, Connor?" Sara inquired, seemingly oblivious to the events unfolding before her.

Still staring at me, Connor mumbled, "Nothing."

His brilliant jade-colored eyes caressed every inch of my face. My heart fluttered as I lingered within his gaze. Something undeniable had sparked between us. But then, the smitten Sara had made it clear he was off-limits. Her grimace intensified, hardening her features as she narrowed her eyes at me. As much as I hated to turn away from Connor and walk with Randall to the transfusion room, I did just that, and without a single glance back.

CHAPTER 6

fter midnight, I climbed into my Jeep and laid my head against the seat. My first night as a volunteer had proven to be far less than enlightening. In fact, every vampire I'd sat with had shown me nothing but respect and kindness. There wasn't a single wicked, evil, or ruthless vampire in the bunch—but it didn't change the fact that my parents were dead and my brother was missing. As long as the killer was out there, I had no choice but to keep volunteering at The Vampire Center.

I noticed a neon sign flashing *Cops-R-Us: Open 24 Hours* as I drove down the street. An image of Marty in silver-plated handcuffs flashed through my head. I slammed on the brakes, made a sharp right, and snagged a parking spot. According to William's journal, gathering information was only one aspect of vampire hunting. The other part involved building a vampire kill kit. With my eyebrows drawn together, I wondered, could I destroy one? The thought made me shudder. I would never be capable of doing such a thing. My goal was justice, answers, and truth, not more death. What if these vampires refused to cooperate? If I never found out who murdered my parents, what would be my fate? Was there only one way to gather data: to force a vampire to speak?

My purse in hand, I rushed into Cops-R-Us in search of silver-plated handcuffs. Guns, knives, tactical gear, and restraints of every type imaginable covered the walls of the store's compact interior. An overwhelming feeling fluttered inside my stomach as my gaze wandered over the items. Rows and rows of handcuffs stared back at me like pupil-less eyes: swivel, hinge, tri-fold, double-hand, standard, thumb, leg, tactical, stainless, Peerless, Smith & Wesson. Where the hell were the vampire cuffs?

"May I help you find something?" The male voice sounded from behind me.

Relief overtook me. With all these gadgets, I most certainly needed some help. "Yes, thank you," I answered as I turned.

A man with wavy black hair and a full beard stood smiling at me. "What can I help you find?"

Would it sound weird if I asked for vampire cuffs? Probably not the smartest approach, what with the peace created by The Vow and all. But I needed silver-plated ones; there was no getting around the fact. There was only one way to approach the situation. "I'm looking for handcuffs—silver-plated handcuffs, to be exact."

"We sell 'em." As he scanned the wall, his smile faded. "Damn. Looks like we're out of stock."

Just my luck.

His expression brightened, accompanied by a snap of his fingers. "Do you care if they're used?"

As long as they worked, I could care less. "Used is fine."

"Sometimes cops like to trade in their old cuffs for new ones. Let me check the back. I'll even throw in a pair of silver-plated leg irons."

"What are those?"

He looked me over and said, "If you intend to restrain something as powerful as a vampire, you're going to need them. They go around the ankles."

"I never said anything about a vampire."

He barked out a laugh. "The silver-plated cuffs gave you away. As long as I make a sale, I don't care what you use them for." He waved me forward. "Wait up front while I check in the back." He hurried off and left me standing at the counter.

I flipped open my wallet. One hundred and twenty-three dollars sat inside the fold, but paying with a credit card would link me to the purchase. Not a smart move. I just hoped my cash would cover the cost.

"Whatcha buying?" I knew that voice—Connor. He stood beside me, eyeing my open wallet.

I snapped it shut. "None of your business."

The clerk came back and placed the pair of handcuffs and leg irons on the counter.

Connor grinned and gave me a playful nudge. "I hope you're planning on doing something kinky with those."

The clerk smirked and nodded. "Now I get it. These are for him."

"They're not for…" I thought better of finishing that statement. Connor gave me a legitimate excuse for buying them. "Let's just get on with it."

The clerk chuckled and offered Connor a nod of approval.

"How much?" I queried, ignoring both of them.

"Five hundred for both—and that's a steal!"

My mouth fell open. Was he crazy?

Connor grabbed the cuffs and held them up, giving them a thorough once-over. He tossed them back at the clerk. "These are bent and scratched. Do they even work?"

The clerk quickly nodded his head. "Yes, of course. I'll show you." He snapped the cuffs and irons closed, slipped in the key, and popped both sets open. "See?"

"So they work, but the price is still too high," Connor argued, crossing his arms over his chest.

"It's a fair price," the clerk insisted.

Connor leaned over the counter, his face inches from the clerk's, and his eyes growing intensely bright. "You'll sell them to the girl for fifty dollars and not a penny more."

The clerk stood motionless, his gaze unfocused and cloudy. "That will be fifty dollars."

"You can't just make him sell them to me for less," I whispered.

"He's playing you. Fifty dollars is the real price. I promise you."

I gazed intently at Connor, scrutinizing his face for any indication of deceit. His steadfast gaze mimicked my own. "Fine," I huffed, reaching into my wallet and handing the cash over.

The clerk placed the restraints in a bag and slammed his hand down on the glass counter. "Sold."

"Thank you," I said, scooping up the bag and heading quickly for the front door.

Connor jogged ahead of me and was leaning against my Jeep as I walked outside. "Still want to know what you're planning to use those for."

I opened the driver's door and tossed the bag inside as it hit me. How had Connor found me here? Had he been waiting outside The Center for me? Was he following me? Before I could confront him, he beat me to the punch.

"All correct," he confessed with a wicked grin.

I crossed my arms and mustered up a scowl. "During my entire night of volunteering, not one vampire read my mind, but *you* just had to take a peek, didn't you? Didn't your maker tell you it's rude to invade other people's thoughts?"

"Ha! My maker taught me the trick."

"Well, don't do it again."

He touched his right temple. "Your request has been duly noted."

I let out an exaggerated sigh and waved him away.

"I like you too," he said in response.

"I never said I liked you."

"You didn't have to. It's written all over your beautiful, blushing face."

"You're mistaken. That would be annoyance."

Again, he flashed his charming smile. "Well, whatever your expression, you're still gorgeous." He reached out and lightly ran his fingertips over my arm. "That peek I took at your mind exposed your real intention regarding the loss of your parents and your missing brother. Let me help."

I pushed his hand away and climbed into my Jeep. "Those are my personal thoughts. If I wanted you to know them, I would've said them out loud."

"I only wanted to help."

My pent-up emotions rushed to the surface, and I closed my eyes so he wouldn't see my tears.

He put his hand on my shoulder and said tenderly, "I can help you."

I brushed off my face and peered up at him. Maybe he *could* help. The question at hand was whether I should allow him to help. "Why did you follow me here?"

He tilted his head. "I—I can't explain it. I sense a connection with you, as if our souls share a common bond."

"Or maybe it's just the blue-eyed-blonde thing."

He swept his hand through his bangs and shook his head. "It's definitely not that."

He did make a good point. Something about him weakened my resolve, but I couldn't give in to it. I had to stay focused on finding the killer and JJ.

"Give me a chance. You can trust me." He appeared and sounded so sincere.

I decided to test his sincerity and rattled off, "So, you know a vampire killed my parents and possibly abducted my brother. Got any ideas about who that might be?"

His eyes widened, then quickly narrowed as he cocked his head. "None, but are you searching for this rogue vampire on your own?"

"Well, there's a detective assigned to the case."

"So you're working together?"

I looked away. "Sort of."

"Playing it close to the vest, are you? I get it, but do you want my help finding this vampire and your brother?"

A tiny voice inside my head whispered, *Let him in.* I sighed and met his eyes. "Why do you want to help me? You don't know me. You have no stake in this. This is my fight, so why?"

A wrinkle of impatience pinched at his brow. "Does it matter why? Besides, you can't take on this vampire assailant by yourself."

I held up the restraints. "I can with a little help."

He bent down so we were eye level and, in a stern voice, said, "William had cause to carry a kill kit; you don't."

I chucked the restraints into the back seat and grabbed onto his arm, searching his eyes. "William J. Matthews?"

He winked at me. "The one and only."

My hand fell from his arm to hang limp in my lap. My mouth slackened until I finally managed to find my voice. "You knew him? He was my great-great-grandfather."

A Cheshire-cat-like smile played across his face. "See, I knew there was a deeper connection between us. Every vampire in the late 1800s had knowledge of him. He was quite the clever slayer."

He knew my great-great-grandfather. It didn't seem possible. What were the chances? "Did he hunt you?"

"He did. I trapped him once, but being the cunning devil he was, he escaped."

I gasped. "I think I read about you in his journal, something about garlic and holy water?"

He slapped his thigh and let out a loud laugh. "Yes, I remember. He threw cloves of garlic on the floor and shielded himself with a cross and holy water before filling my lair with daylight. I watched him tip his hat and stroll right out my front door."

Hope swirled around inside my stomach. Maybe Connor *could* help me. "Tell me everything. How did he hunt you exactly? How did he protect himself at night? I can use his methods to find my parents' killer!"

"You don't need to know any of that. William lived during a time when vampires killed to eat. Those days are over."

I raised my voice and clenched my hands into fists. "No, they're not. The Vow means nothing to the vampire who committed the murder of my parents. He or she can't get away with that."

He tucked a strand of my hair behind my ear and murmured, "And they won't, but you can't hunt them alone. Let me help you."

I needed to trust someone, and Connor knew William. I took that to be an omen. Moreover, having a vampire on my side could either be a valuable advantage or the deadliest error I could ever commit. I firmed up my resolve and nodded slowly. "Okay...I want your help."

CHAPTER 7

ight two at The Vampire Center was winding down with only one more vampire waiting to sit in my chair. Jessica, accompanied by Marty, the dubious vampire I'd encountered at the police station, advanced toward me, causing me to nearly lose my balance. An internal war waged inside my brain; should I hurl accusations at him and accuse him as an accessory to murder, dash off and call Reynolds, grill the bastard myself, or keep my mouth shut? Sitting perfectly still, the unshakeable feeling that he knew something about the murders sank into my bones. Realizing my opportunity, I decided on grilling the jerk. I owed it to my family to make him talk.

He slapped his thigh and laughed out loud. "Blondie! What *are* the chances? I never expected to see you again, and of all places—The Center. Small world, right?" He leaned in a little closer. "I'll admit, I've thought of you often."

"I've been thinking about you too," I said, feeling blood pump in a heated rush through my veins.

"Wow, a girl like you thinking about a vampire like me. That's completely wonderful!"

I was tempted to choke him, yet maintaining composure facilitated my strategy to extract the truth from him. "You ran out on me at the police station. Why?"

"Yeah, sorry. Cops make me nervous. Hey, why don't I make it up to you by buying you a drink?"

A drink? How could he possibly believe a drink would fix his transgression of withholding information about my parents? I opened my mouth to blurt out a smartass remark when I recalled Max's little tidbit: *Vampires love tequila.* I could use that drink to my advantage by getting him drunk and convincing him to talk. I set out to make it happen.

"Ah, come on. We'll have fun, I promise."

I knew it would raise suspicion if I just gave in, especially with his squirrelly reaction at the station. Playing a little hard to get seemed to be my best strategy. "We'll see."

He focused directly on my eyes and lowered his voice. "If you have a drink with me, I'll tell you what I know about your parents' murder."

Images of their dead bodies exploded into sight behind my eyes like a bomb. I shuddered and squeezed my eyes shut, forcing the vision to fade before glaring at him. "I knew you were hiding something!"

"Have a drink with me, and I'll tell you everything," he pressed, his tone begging.

My whole body trembled as I clenched my teeth and grinded out my words. "No. Tell me now!"

He pressed a finger to his lips. "Shh, don't make a scene." He slid back in the chair and wrapped an arm around the back. "The way I see it, if you want to know, you'll come along. I'm not going to hurt you. Anyway, what's one drink?"

Damn him; he held all the power. What choice did I have? Fine, I would play by his rules. "One drink, but you better have information for me."

Rubbing his hands together like some disgusting fly, he answered, "Great." He glanced around the room before whispering, "I would rather not start any rumors inside this place, so meet me out front when you've finished your shift."

With a violent shake of my head, I whispered fiercely, "No way. I'm not letting you out of my sight. We leave together. I won't take a chance on your running away again."

"I'll meet you out front, I promise."

I narrowed my eyes, studying him. "I don't trust you."

Flashing his pearly fangs, he promised, "I'll be there." He jerked his head to the right. "Shh, Jessica's coming."

Jessica came up and glanced at the empty blood bag. "You're all set, Marty," she said, removing the IV from his arm. She turned to me. "You're all done, Claire. See you tomorrow."

I stood up, feeling a tingling sensation throughout my body. "See you then."

Marty shot me a secret wink. I cringed for a brief moment before stopping at the front desk to get my purse. Sara and Connor had finished up about a half hour or so ago. Most likely, Connor was lurking about somewhere, waiting to sneak up on me. I couldn't have him tagging along. Marty would never speak with Connor by my side. As I walked out the front door, I kept my eyes fixed straight ahead. Upon seeing no sign of Connor, I exhaled a breath of relief, only to collide with him the next moment.

He steadied me with his recently warmed hands, offering me one of his dazzling smiles, and asked, "Where are *you* off to?"

I slipped past him and mumbled, "Nowhere."

His form whooshed by me, brushing my arm as he passed. He stood in front of me, blocking my path. Suspicion filled his features as his eyes darted back and forth, searching mine. He raised his brows and crossed his arms in a disapproving manner over his chest. "Why the hell are you meeting with Marty?"

I heaved out an annoyed sigh. "I told you to stay out of my head."

"I wouldn't have to get inside your head if you were just honest with me."

Marty was a means of discovering the truth, and I didn't feel I owed Connor an explanation. I pushed past him, walking toward the street. "I haven't lied to you. It's my truth, and it doesn't belong to you."

The pitch of his voice changed, growing more impatient. "Marty is a liar. He has undoubtedly told you lies."

Did he know Marty so well? Gaining information about my family trumped my partnership with Connor. "I'll take my chances."

He caught up with me and spun me around with strong hands. Gazing into my eyes, he said, "I would rather not see you get hurt."

"I'm a big girl. I can take care of myself."

He swept his hand through his bangs and peered at me while narrowing his eyes. "Did I do something wrong? Are you upset with me?"

I gave him a half-smile and touched his arm. "You didn't do any-thing wrong, and I'm not angry. This matter is about my family, nothing more."

"Did he tell you he knew something?" He asked, his voice persis-tent. "You can't trust him, Claire. I know Marty all too well. I've been bailing him out over the course of his entire immortal life. Trust me, he's nothing but trouble."

The rumbling growl of a motorcycle engine silenced my response. I turned around to find Marty pulling up on a bike. He winked at me, patted the back seat, and shouted over the thunderous roar, "Get on."

Connor grabbed my arm, holding me back. "Don't go, Claire."

Marty had offered me something Connor didn't have to give. It was that simple. "I have to," I said, choosing to leave him standing there alone.

"Did I interrupt you and Connor?" Marty inquired, his voice devoid of any hint of sincerity.

I narrowed my eyes, pinching my brows together. "That's none of your business."

He grabbed a second helmet from a compartment on the back of his bike and shoved it at me. "Here, put this on."

I pushed the helmet away. "I'm wearing a dress. I'll drive my Jeep and meet you."

"That's even sexier." He winked at me. "And I promise not to bite."

I rolled my eyes. "Not funny."

He indicated the direction with the tilt of his head. "Balboa Park is just a couple of blocks that way. We can share a bottle of tequila."

"You want to drink in a *park*?"

He looked up into the night before glancing back at me. Flashing a smile, he said, "We have a gorgeous warm night, twinkling stars, and each other. What more could we possibly ask for?"

Don't make me gag. "This isn't a date. I'm accompanying you to gain information, nothing more."

"But I'm such a catch. You may want to take advantage of me."

"Not gonna happen."

"Well, you're mine for tonight, so get on the bike."

"Like I said, I'll follow you in my Jeep."

"I'll drive really slow. You'll be safe."

"We can go back and forth about the subject all night long, but I'm not getting on that bike."

"I like strong women, but you're making me nervous. Red flags are popping up all over. I must take a peek into that beautiful head of yours." Marty's mind plunged deep inside my own, like a probing worm, twisting and turning, fishing for information. Two could play this game. I called forth memories of my mother, her face, her laughter, her voice—and the image of her gruesome death into my head. He didn't dig any further. He gave me a thumbs up. "False alarm."

"And you're a jerk."

"Sometimes, I am. Go get your Jeep, and let's get rolling."

I spun around, biting on my lower lip. I loathed everything about him, and the thought of sharing a drink with him...words couldn't adequately express the depth of my repulsion, but my desperate need for answers outweighed my exasperation. If going to the park was the cost I had to bear, then I was willing to accept it.

****

In the main lot, we parked side by side. There was not a single person in sight, only the two of us. As my hand rested on the Jeep's door, my eyes roamed over the cuffs I'd purchased. Was Connor right? Was I making a mistake? Could I trust Marty? I instinctively grabbed the restraints and buried them in my purse before exiting my Jeep.

Marty inhaled a deep breath of night air. "I love the smell of pine." He beckoned me forward. "Come on." He dragged me by the hand through the damp grass, like a hound tracking a scent. "This is the spot," he said, flopping down against a tree trunk. He patted the ground beside him. "Sit."

I looked around for a bench, but there was nothing but the standing timber around us. Beams of moonlight reached down from the starlit sky, weaving their pale golden fingers between the cluster of trees.

He pulled three pint-sized bottles from his jacket before shedding the garment and placing it over the damp grass. "You can sit on my coat."

I kept my purse on my lap. "Do you always keep liquor in your pockets?"

He nodded, wearing a wide grin. After opening the first bottle, he took a generous swallow, sighed, then handed it to me. I wiped the rim with my sleeve, took a tiny sip, and handed it back.

He downed the remainder of the contents without coming up for air. So much for sharing. He dropped the empty bottle on the grass, snapped the lid from the second, and chugged half the liquid. He tipped the second bottle my way. "More?"

Marty's a lush. I didn't even have to try to get him drunk. "I'm good. You go ahead."

In one gulp, he devoured the rest, licking his lips as he finished.

Two bottles! I needed him to be alert, not comatose. "That's an awful lot of alcohol. Are you sure you can handle it?"

He waved me away like a pesky insect. "I know what I'm doing." He rolled his head back and rested it against the tree. "But man, I'm tripping."

There was no way to predict when he might lose consciousness. I didn't wait a second longer to collect on our deal. "We shared a drink, so now I expect you to tell me what you know."

His lips twisted upward as he rubbed his temples. "I don't feel so good."

I sprang to my feet and shook him by the shoulders. "No, no, no! Don't you dare black out on me."

"I did promise to tell you, didn't I?"

"You did," I said, in the most demanding tone I could call forth.

Struggling to keep his eyes open, he muttered, "Well, I don't feel like talking."

"What? Don't think you can break our deal. You owe me."

He chuckled. "I'm reneging, and there's nothing you can do about it. You're a girl—a human. Even totally wasted, I'm stronger, faster, and smarter."

Even with the warmness of the night air, I grew cold—inhumanly cold. Something sinister overtook my soul, pouring rage into my veins. I balled my fists and raised my voice just a hair. "I swear, I'll make you talk."

He belted out more laughter. "Let's see you try."

What a fool I was. He had no intention of telling me anything. Even though Connor implied Marty would deceive me, I still felt empowered to expose him. The restraints at the bottom of my purse begged me to use them and get what I came for. My heartbeat ricocheted off my eardrums, beating faster and faster as I dug into my bag. My hands trembled as my fingers found the cuffs. They shimmered under the soft glow of the moon as I kicked his feet together. Before he even blinked, I locked the irons around his ankles, then scurried up to snap the cuffs into place around his wrists.

He puckered his lips together and blew me a kiss. "Ooh, I like this. Are you going to spank me too?"

I pointed to the sky. "Sunrise will be here before you know it, so start spilling."

"I've got nothing to say, Blondie. Besides, you don't have it in you to watch me fry."

I stood my ground. "I've got no place to go. We can sit here all night. Once you see that big orange ball rise in the sky, you'll start singing like a bird."

He smirked and let out a huff. "Nice try, but you're getting nothing out of me."

I smirked back. "We'll see."

"I'm shaking in my boots."

"Do us both a favor and just tell me what you know."

He focused his gaze off into the distance.

I kept pressing, hoping to break him. "Who did it? Who killed my parents? Was it you?"

He groaned and jerked his head back in my direction. "Will you shut up? You're ruining my buzz."

"You want me to shut up? Then talk."

He glared at me as he struggled with the restraints. "Enough! Uncuff me."

"No."

"Take 'em off. Now!"

"Tell me what I want to know, and I will."

Saliva flew out from his mouth as he shouted, "You're crazy!"

He had a point. My sanity had taken a nosedive. I needed to get my act together, and fast. I'd just wanted to scare him into talking, but clearly it hadn't appeared to be working, and as he pointed out, I was no killer. I blew out an exaggerated sigh and fished the key from the bottom of my purse. As I popped the locks on the cuffs and the irons, I whispered, "I'm sorry."

"Two can play this game," he spat, gripping my wrist and snapping a cuff around it, securing the other around his own. He slipped the key into his pants pocket and said, "I'm gonna finish the rest of my tequila and grab some shut-eye, and when I wake up, you can go."

"Hell no." I yanked my arm backward, pulling him away from the tree. "You're the crazy one if you think I'm just going to sit here all night while you sleep off your buzz."

With lightning speed, his free hand emerged and firmly grasped my jaw. His fingers squeezed my chin, forcing me to lock eyes with him. Mounting pressure pulverized through the bones inside my skull, setting my brain on fire. He put his mouth to my ear and in a low, guttural growl, said, "Either sit tight and keep your lovely mouth shut, or I'll continue to burrow into your brain and compel you to. Your choice."

The searing pain released a slew of tears, which streamed down my cheeks. I struggled to speak each word. "I'll...sit...quietly."

"That's more like it." He shoved my face backward and released me. After snatching up the third bottle of tequila and guzzling it down like water, he settled back into position under the tree.

The intense pain he inflicted silenced me like a submissive child, until he intervened. Bringing my knees up to my chest and hugging them, I shielded my thoughts behind the mental image of a stone wall. Images floated in the space I made there: JJ, my parents, Reynolds, The Vampire Center, and Connor. I zoned out into my own little world inside myself, allowing the physical world to slip away.

The faint chirping of birds brought me back to reality. Heat tiptoed across my flesh. I opened my eyes to the subtle brightness infringing upon the receding night. I jerked my head in Marty's direction. He was still unconscious. I gently nudged him, but he did not budge. I shoved harder. Still nothing. Grabbing onto his shoulders and shaking him as violently as I could, I screamed his name, "Marty!"

His eyelashes fluttered. He rubbed at his eyes, opening them slowly. "What are you screaming about? I thought I told you—"

I cut him off, jutting a rigid finger toward the sky. "Look for yourself."

His eyes bulged from their sockets as he fumbled inside his pocket for the key. It trembled between his fingers as he shoved it into the lock and popped the cuffs. They fell to the ground, unbinding us. He leapt to his feet and managed one step before falling flat on his face. He tried to push up from the wet grass to stand but fell again. "Don't just sit there! Help me."

"You drank waaaaaay too much," I grumbled, slipping my hands under his shoulders and hoisting him up.

Hysterical laughter escaped his lips. "I've been much drunker than this many times before. Something is blocking the use of my powers."

I glanced at the cuffs and irons sprawled out across the grass. "Um, perhaps the cuffs?"

"Maybe...possibly...I don't know! Just get me out of here."

Despite the weight of his body, I was determined not to let him die. "I'm trying. Quit barking out orders."

"Hurry!" he cried as he tumbled to the ground.

My palms grew clammy as I latched onto him, pulling him to his feet. He clung to me like a frightened child—and with good reason. His legs were useless, no better than a ragdoll's. "You're too heavy. You have to help me."

"I can't, you idiot!" he shouted in response.

"You have two choices: help me, or...which is it?"

"I can't move my legs!" he cried, his voice shrill.

I trudged forward, dragging him with me. We gained maybe an inch before his legs buckled, pulling us both down. He pushed past me, scrambling on his hands and knees over the wet earth. He slid back and forth, as if trapped on a patch of ice. Balling his fists and pounding the ground, he released a scream.

I scanned the park for someone, anyone, who could help us. Trees—and the sun's hot rays—fell into my line of sight. The golden beams relentlessly pursued him, plunging onto him and engulfing him completely. His piercing shriek cut through the early dawn. I shivered at its tenor before dashing after him and latching onto his feet. Convulsions rippled through his body as I tugged at his legs, racing backward and fleeing the sun. I couldn't outrun the daylight streaming through everywhere around us.

"Help me," he breathed, his voice raspy.

I didn't know what else to do. I threw my body on top of his, shielding him, but I was no match for the blaze of the sun. Oozing blisters rippled across his beautiful pale skin, turning it gray and then black. His body lay motionless.

I listened for his breathing, but no sound met my ears. Whether vampires carried a pulse or not, I pressed my fingertips to his neck and checked anyway. Nothing. Then a faint pop sounded from his body, then another, and another. He bubbled and sizzled, like bacon frying in a pan.

Standing over him, I scrutinized every inch of his dying body until the instinct to flee stirred inside my bones. I scooted several feet back, just seconds before he erupted, spraying the earth with vampiric black-and-silvery ash. I flinched, stumbled back, and buckled to my knees, letting out a pitiful-sounding wail and hugging my body with my arms, rocking back and forth. I'd never meant for this to happen. I'd just wanted answers. I should've listened to Connor, left The Vampire Center, and gone straight home. Maybe then, Marty would still be alive.

His ashes sparkled in the bright morning light. I panicked and sprang to my feet. As I charged forward to escape the park, the thick blades of wet grass worked against me. I fell hard, picked myself up, and stumbled again and again. Blood trickled from my palms and knees. Grief, sorrow, and regret consumed my heart, strangling my soul. Tears blurred my vision as I raced through the park, weaving through the trees and following the golden rays of sunlight to my Jeep, which waited for me in the parking lot.

When my feet hit the asphalt, I halted, my chest rising and falling as I tried to catch my breath. The world appeared unruffled around me. Shouldn't someone condemn me? Shouldn't the earth open up and cast me into the depths of hell? I waited for the rumbling. None came. I stood alone, staring into the blue of the sky, my mind racing. JJ was missing. My parents were dead. Marty was dead. And I had played a significant role in his death.

CHAPTER 8

An overwhelming sense of dread swept over me as I pulled into the condo parking garage. My hands slipped off the steering wheel and fell into my lap. I sat staring at the concrete wall in front of me, knowing an innocent life had perished and that I could do nothing to bring it back. An urge to burst into hysterical sobs filled me, but how would crying change things? It wouldn't bring Marty back. It wouldn't help me find my parents' killer or discover JJ's whereabouts. Still, I *wanted* to feel miserable—I *needed* to feel miserable and slumped over and rested my head on my hands. I cried for my parents, JJ, and Marty, all at the same time.

Slowly—very slowly—I reclaimed my self-control. As I lifted my head, I caught sight of my puffy red eyes in the rearview mirror. I smoothed my hair and brushed away the tears as I made a commitment to myself to find the culprit behind this tragedy. However, I understood that rational thought was not feasible at this moment. My thoughts were all jumbled up, and nothing made sense to me. I needed to crawl into bed and sleep.

I shoved open the driver's door, as if it weighed a ton, and climbed out, stumbling the several steps required to carry me to the elevator. Jabbing at the call button several times—as if that might make a difference—I kept my eyes glued to the down arrow, anticipating the elevator's arrival. The chime sounded, releasing a bit of my tension. I dashed inside, pushing the button for my floor, and leaned against the elevator wall for much-needed support.

The ride came to a gradual stop, bouncing right before the doors parted. I rubbed my eyes and yawned, lugging my body down the hallway toward my door. Walking into the empty living room sparked frustration. I needed to furnish the damned condo, except for mine and JJ's bedrooms. I shrugged the feeling off, too worn out to care, and headed straight for the bathtub. The hot water ran as I stripped out of my dress and tossed it into the hamper. A blanket of warmth penetrated my flesh, deep down to my bones, as I sank beneath the water. I rested my head against the back of the tub and closed my eyes.

After complete relaxation overtook me, I remembered the restraints and the empty liquor bottles, which lay in the park with my fingerprints all over them. A tingling sensation rippled across my skin. I trembled as I sat upright and opened my eyes. An image of Reynolds hauling my ass downtown played inside my brain. I scrambled out of the tub and dashed into my bedroom. I threw on some jeans, a T-shirt, and sandals. Grabbing my keys, I rushed out of the condo and ran straight for the elevator. The doors had only begun to part when I dashed inside. Floors rushed by as fast as the blood pounding in my throat. The moment it settled on P2, I jetted out, bulldozing over an elderly man with a cane. He cried out and stumbled backward. I grabbed onto his arm to steady him and rattled off, "I'm sorry," before continuing the race toward my Jeep.

I jumped inside and fumbled with the key. It took three tries to land it into the ignition. I shoved the vehicle into reverse and floored the gas pedal. The Jeep blasted out of the garage and barreled down the street, helping me reach the park in less than ten minutes, but I had company—two police cars, accompanied by a sedan, were already there.

I swallowed hard as I thought, *This can't be a coincidence.* They were probably investigating Marty's death; I was sure of it. What if their investigation led them back to me? Those restraints couldn't fall into their hands! I spun the Jeep around, escaped from the main lot, and entered the secondary lot, parking in the far-left corner while closely monitoring the police cars and park pathways. What a frigging mess. How could I have been so stupid as to leave the cuffs and bottles behind? I massaged my temples, trying to come up with a reasonable plan. I couldn't retrieve them—not now. What if a cop saw me pick them up from the ground? *Oh, sorry, Officer, I just happened upon these and decided to take them home with me.* No excuse in the world could've justified such an action. The only alternative was to hang around and see what scenario played out. I drummed my fingertips on the dashboard, waiting, watching, hoping they came back empty-handed.

Maybe twenty minutes later, two policemen walking with Detective Reynolds appeared on the walkway, heading toward their vehicles. I covered my mouth to smother a gasp and then slammed my hand against the dashboard. Did Reynolds literally work every damned case? Adding insult to injury, he carried a plastic bag in his hand.

My insides contorted into knots, and sweat drenched my palms. *He's going to come after me.* But I hadn't killed Marty. I hadn't gotten him drunk. I was the one who'd unlocked the restraints, but the wasted vamp had re-cuffed our hands…even threatened me physically when I'd demanded my freedom. Besides, I had never been arrested, fingerprinted, or broken any laws—well, except for the time I broke into my own house, which Reynolds had overlooked. Ultimately, Reynolds couldn't have possibly known that I was in the park with Marty at the time of his death. I might just be in the clear.

The two policemen exchanged a few words with Reynolds before getting into their vehicles and driving away. Reynolds lingered behind, surveying the park with his hands on his hips. What the hell was he looking for? Why didn't he just leave? Was he waiting for something—someone? He turned toward his car, stopped, and then faced my direction.

Like a criminal, I ducked below the sightline of the window. My heartbeat thumped against the bones of my skull, blocking out all sound. I didn't dare take a breath. What if he recognized the Jeep? What if he came over to peek inside? I had no reason to be there. How would I explain my presence? What could I say? I raised my head just enough to peer out at the spot where he had been standing. The sidewalk was now, mercifully, empty, yet Reynolds' sedan remained. Where was he? Had he made his way back to the park? I didn't wait another second to find out. I ignited the engine and discreetly drove out of the parking lot.

Returning to my empty condo served as a bitter reminder of my family's absence. As I spun in a circle and eyed the bare room, the void inside me swelled. I dropped my keys on the floor and ran upstairs to grab my laptop. Furniture and Beyond offered next-day delivery. Perfect! Within a matter of minutes, I furnished my entire condo with the remainder of the insurance money. If only all the rest of the problems plaguing my life could've been solved so quickly.

CHAPTER 9

I woke up on the floor, still sitting with my laptop resting on my lap. What time was it anyway? I pushed the computer aside, grabbed my phone, and tapped the screen. Six o'clock. My eyes widened in shock. That couldn't possibly be right. The numbers stared back, taunting me...an hour and a half late for my shift at The Vampire Center. *Frigging crap!* I struggled to my feet. With no time to shower or change, I rubbed toothpaste across my teeth with my finger and threw my hair into a wild ponytail before scampering out the door. The damned elevator stopped on every floor before finally turning me loose on P2. I bolted out first, jetting past the crowd inside, ignoring their grunts and groans. I clicked the Jeep's remote the moment I was in range. Having barely settled into the driver's seat, I started the engine and skidded onto the road. I wove in and out of traffic while racing toward The Vampire Center. In under fifteen minutes, I pulled into The Center's parking lot and dashed through the glass door. I slowed my pace and attempted to act as if everything was fine, but I was already late and had no valid excuse. I decided appearing confident and behaving as if it were no big deal was the best course of action I could take. I just hoped Nancy saw it that way as well.

As I approached the front desk, a long line of vampires awaited their check-in. One look at Nancy's face spread a rush of heat across my cheeks. A stern fire burned within her eyes as she crossed her arms over her chest. "You're late."

I cleared my throat and chose to speak honestly. "I—I'm sorry. I didn't get much sleep last night and dozed off in the middle of the afternoon. I promise it won't happen again."

She came out from behind the station, placing a hand on her hip and arching a brow. "I have a three-strike policy. This is strike number one. Two more, and you're out."

The flame of shame intensified, piercing my skin. I wanted to disappear, but I managed to keep my gaze leveled with hers. "I understand."

She dismissed me with a wave of her hand. "Join the others in the storage room. They may still need help preparing for tonight."

Obediently, I hurried off, thankful to put some distance between us. When I entered the storage room, I let the door slam shut behind me. Heads turned, and all eyes were on me. Martha let out a laugh when she saw me. "Your face is as red as a beet. You got the three strikes speech, didn't you?" She didn't wait for me to answer but jerked her head toward the others. "We've all been there. She means it, though. We've lost a few volunteers because of that policy of hers."

Maybe they considered me a part of their team and sympathized with me. I would rather not discuss Nancy's wrath, so I merely shrugged my shoulders and asked, "Can I do anything to help?"

Martha shook her head. "We're pretty much done. Just about to go up to the front."

"I'm sorry," I said in my most heartfelt tone. "I won't be late again."

Jeannie, the older blonde, spoke up. "Like Martha said, we've all been there. Don't worry about it. Come on, let's all go up front together."

The entire group headed for the reception area, where Nancy had just finished up with the first half of the vampire lineup. As we approached the counter, Martha abruptly stopped and seized Jeannie's arm. "He's back," she whispered.

"Who's back?" I asked, looking about.

Melissa twirled the gaudy bracelet surrounding her wrist, and I watched her face turn several shades paler. Lifting her finger, she pointed to the fifth vampire in line. "Him."

The vampire's vacant, cold stare, emanating from his pearl-colored eyes, poured over each and every human in the space as he tapped his black fingernails against his arm. An eerie grin formed on his dark lips when he caught me staring at him. He winked, running his tongue over his razor-sharp fangs before blowing me a kiss.

A chill scurried over the surface of my skin, and I swiped at my arms, trying to banish its presence. I'd never seen a vampire convey such evil in their appearance before. It was almost as if he had climbed straight out of the pits of hell itself. Could *he* be the vampire I sought? I took a voluntary step closer, but Martha tugged on my arm, pulling me back.

"We're going back to the storage room. Come on."

She didn't have to tell me twice. I definitely wanted in on any details about this dark and mysterious vampire. Melissa, Sara, and Jeannie darted into the room like a trio of cowardly lions. Martha nudged me inside, quickly shutting the door behind us, and hurried over to one of the lockers.

"That vampire's trouble," Sara informed me between bouts of biting her nails.

Jeannie neared me and touched my arm. "We're prepared, though."

Shaking my head, I asked, "Prepared for what?"

Martha pulled several backpacks from the locker and placed them on the floor. She eyed us all when she answered, "Prepared for him."

I stared hard at her, searching her eyes. "What are you talking about?"

"A while back, he came to The Vampire Center on several occasions, sitting with the same volunteer each time. Then one day, she just up and vanished, and he stopped coming for transfusions," Martha explained.

"What happened to her?" I asked.

Jeannie sighed. "Most of the staff believes the vampire had nothing to do with her disappearance, that she just left town or something."

Melissa slipped her backpack on, adjusting her beaded necklace afterward. "No one up and leaves without saying a word to anyone."

I narrowed my gaze and again asked, "So what do you think happened to her?"

Martha's cheeks paled, and her voice fell. "We believe he killed her."

Her statement triggered images of the bloodless bodies of my parents behind my eyes. Could this vampire be their killer? I didn't know if I should be terrified or thrilled by gaining such a strong lead.

"I know what you're thinking," Sara said, pointing a finger at me.

No, you don't.

Her eyes bulged slightly from their sockets. "You think we're full of it. You don't know; you weren't there. The police questioned him and let him go; can you believe that? Just let him go, said there wasn't enough evidence."

Had Reynolds been the one to question him? He didn't seem the type who would give up easily, but what did I really know about him? What did I really know about him or the situation? I'd grown up and lived in a world where vampires didn't kill...until now. Protecting oneself from them had never come up in conversation, nor had the possible inner workings of a rogue vampire. "I think you all have a valid point."

"Nowadays, vampires appear to have more rights than humans," Melissa said, spinning her bracelet nervously.

"I think that creepy vampire enchanted all of them, making them believe that girl moved away," Sara insisted. "That's why you can never look into their eyes."

Martha tossed me a backpack and grinned. "That's the reason we made these."

I peered inside and let out a gasp. Several wooden stakes, a silver cross, and a glass vial filled the space inside. This was my personal vampire kill kit. William would've been proud.

"You'll find five stakes, a vial of holy water, and a silver cross," Martha said, as if she hadn't seen me peek at the contents. "If that bloodsucker tries to feed on any of us, we'll shove one of these into his heart." She held up one of the stakes.

Sara slipped on her pack, gripping the straps like a warrior. "We've been wearing them off and on for months, practicing and preparing for this moment. The vampires won't hesitate to see us wearing them."

"No one asked what was inside? Not even Nancy?" I questioned.

Martha gave a firm shake of her head. "Nope. Guess people assumed it was just our personal stuff."

Volunteers sporting backpacks must have roused some level of suspicion. "What about the rest of the staff? No one found it unusual that you wear backpacks during transfusion hours? Why wouldn't you leave them in your lockers?"

Martha raised her voice and snapped, "Who cares? We're telling you no one noticed. Let it go. If you don't want to wear one, then don't."

Give up a kill kit? No way. Especially after losing the silver ankle restraints and cuffs to the police. I needed to reclaim them, and I decided that I would enlist Connor's help to do so. He had the ability to effortlessly enter the police station, conceal them from the officers' view, and then confidently leave. Getting Connor on board was essential, but first, I had to somehow talk Sara into giving him up for one night so I could sit with him. I suddenly saw an opportunity. I could use the sinister vampire in the lobby as leverage. "Sorry, I'm just overly cautious." I threw the backpack on. "I'm in and will be the one to sit with the creepy vampire."

One by one, their mouths fell open, gaping at me as if I'd revealed some incredible, shocking secret.

I held up my finger and added, "On one condition."

Martha waved her hand in a circle. "Spit it out."

I faced Sara and stated my terms. "I get to sit with Connor tonight."

Sara balled her hands into fists and stomped her foot. Shaking her head like a spoiled child, she shouted, "No!"

Martha rolled her eyes and groaned, "Here we go."

Jeannie's lips straightened in a sharp line as she glared at Sara.

Melissa didn't waste any time speaking up. "Claire's willing to sit with this creep and keep us safe. Put your selfish needs aside, Sara. Let her sit with Connor."

Sara's eyes darted from Martha to Jeannie and then to Melissa. Again, she shook her head. "I won't do it." She pointed a rigid finger in my direction. "If he sits with her, I'll lose him."

Melissa put her hand on Sara's shoulder and muttered, "You never had him to lose. Do this for us, please."

Sara's lip quivered, and her cheeks burned a bright red.

"Come on, Sara, please," Martha begged.

"It would mean a lot to me, Sara," I admitted.

Squeezing her eyes shut, she whimpered, "No."

Jeannie exploded. "Quit acting like a spoiled brat! She doesn't need your permission. I propose that we hold a vote, with the majority ruling the outcome."

Sara's eyes snapped open, her glare razor sharp. "Fine!" she shouted. "Sit with him."

Martha pumped her fists into the air. "Yes!"

Melissa clasped her hands together and softly uttered, "Thank you, Sara."

After leaving the storage room, Sara didn't say anything. As I approached the front desk, a wave of nerves swept over me. "Nancy," Martha said. "Claire wants to sit with both the creep and Connor. Sara agreed."

Nancy stopped entering data into the computer and faced us. Crossing her arms and shaking her head, she replied, "Martha, he has a name. It's Stanley."

A laugh escaped my lips as I covered my mouth. What sort of name was Stanley for such a vile vampire? Why not Lucifer or Damon? Those seemed much more suited to the creepy vamp.

Nancy shot me a look. "I expect professionalism from you, Claire."

"Yes, of course." I recovered a stoic expression at once.

"I've got Claire with Stanley and Connor then," Nancy confirmed, typing the information into the computer. She bobbed her head to the right. "Claire, chair eight will be yours tonight. Head back to the transfusion room. Jessica will bring Stanley to you first."

Another giggle slipped out. I couldn't hold it back.

Nancy arched a brow at me. "Really, Claire?"

"No more laughing, I promise," I said, hurrying off to chair eight. I waited for Stanley in the reading chair and fidgeted with my hands. I had no idea how to bring up the subject of my parents' murder. A direct approach wouldn't fly. Subtle might be better.

Jessica's voice broke through my thoughts. "Claire, this is Stanley. Stanley, Claire."

I looked up at him. He tilted his head down, peering at me through shards of his greasy black hair, a wicked grin stretching from ear to ear. My urge to laugh vanished, and goosebumps pinched my flesh. I fought back an involuntary shiver and greeted him. "Hello, Stanley."

His cruel eyes twinkled as they focused on my neck. "Nice cross," he noted before taking his seat.

Fingering my necklace, I answered, "It was my mother's."

He replied only by blowing me another kiss.

Jessica swatted at his hand and issued a warning. "Behave, Stanley."

He shrugged his shoulders. "What?"

"You know what," she responded, shaking her head. She adjusted the flow of his IV and added, "Claire, you are familiar with the procedure. If you need me, just call me."

I kept my eyes fixed on Stanley's face as I answered her. "I will." The retreating sound of her footsteps launched butterflies into my stomach. His eyes locked defiantly with mine as he leaned closer. My ears popped as his brain collided with mine, and pressure mounted throughout my skull. I sat motionless and mute, unable to defend myself or even cry for help. With a flick of his finger, he released me after gathering what he needed. While I glared at him, I slumped against the reading chair and blinked away tears.

He chuckled. "So you consider yourself to be a vampire slayer?"

In a desperate attempt to silence him, I placed my finger to my lips. "Shh! I'm no slayer. I just need information."

He laughed once more, but this time mockingly. "But Marty's dead. In my book, that makes you a slayer *and* a vow breaker."

"Hello. You were in my head," I snapped. "You know I didn't kill him. I tried to save him."

"He wouldn't have had such an unfortunate accident if it hadn't been for you. Would you kill me too, to gain information?"

I couldn't let him rattle me. *Show confidence. Don't play his game.* "I'll say it again. You read my mind; therefore, you know I'm no killer."

He winked at me. "Just messing with you."

I boldly displayed a sneer of annoyance, triggered by his little stunt.

He ignored my irritation and continued. "They need to open a center in the Vampire District. The Center's location is too far. Eats into the too-brief hours of the night."

The thump of my racing pulse filled my ears. "You live in the Vampire District?"

He nodded.

"Then you must know the vampires, Nate and Parker?"

A grimace twisted his perfect features. "I haven't seen those pesky little twits in quite some time, actually."

The urge to leap out of my seat surged through my legs, but I remained calm. "So you do know them?"

"I know *of* them. Skateboarding isn't my thing." He leaned forward and leered at me. "You have a question spinning around inside your head. Ask me."

I promptly accepted his offer without any hesitation. "Did you kill my parents? Do you know my brother's whereabouts?"

He let out an agitated huff and folded his arms over his chest. "Greedy little thing, aren't you? I'll make you an offer. Meet me at the Holy Cross Cemetery at midnight, and I'll give you my answer."

Intrigued, I moved to the edge of the chair and pressed, "Are you saying you know something?"

"I am."

I searched his eyes for sincerity or candor, but only a cold, vacant stare met my gaze. My logical brain screamed, *Don't do it! Don't go with him! Been there, done that. Bad idea. Remember the Marty fiasco?* But logic didn't matter. If there was even a minuscule chance he indeed possessed information about my family, I owed their memory this opportunity.

He grinned as he asked, "Have you made a decision?"

"You could just be trying to get me alone, like Marty did."

"I could be, but I'm not." He nodded toward the backpack. "Besides, you came prepared."

I sat back and regarded him. "Why can't you just tell me right here, right now?"

"Where's the fun in that?"

"So this is some kind of game for you?"

His grin widened, revealing his fangs. "I love to play games, but the present is not one of those times."

Was he playing me? What the hell was he after? I knew I shouldn't meet him alone outside of the relative safety of The Center. "Maybe all you want to do is get me alone so you can hurt me."

A scowl forced its way across his forehead, and he white-knuckled the chair arm. "I honor The Vow."

"That's not what I heard," I fired back.

His body grew rigid, his eyes glinting menacingly. "What exactly did you hear?"

The accusation shot out of my mouth before I thought better of it. "That you killed a center volunteer."

A hideous snarl curled his lips back from his fangs. "I didn't kill her," he spat. "I drank from her, yes, but with permission. She allowed it—wanted it."

"That's breaking The Vow, not honoring it!"

"She wanted it," he said again, raising his voice, but then quickly lowered it. His tone turned almost tender as he disclosed, "She begged me to drink from her. I resisted, but the temptation became too much to bear. The fact that I consumed her blood does not mean I killed her."

"Then what became of her?" I inquired. "Where is she now?"

His expression turned bleak, and he hung his head. "I don't know."

He seemed to genuinely feel sorrow for the volunteer's disappearance. Was it possible the girls misjudged him? Maybe he didn't kill her, and she'd actually left town of her own free will. Creepy didn't necessarily equate to murderer.

When I looked back at him, his lips twisted into a wicked grin. "You remind me of her."

"But I'm not her. I'm here for answers about my family," I reminded him.

The last drop of blood fell from the IV bag to course its way into his arm, causing his smile to disappear. "Will you meet me or not?"

Despite my inability to trust him, the unwavering desire for justice was unaffected by the potential consequences. I took in a deep breath, with which I answered, "Yes."

"I'll wait for you by Jacob Meyers' grave. You can't miss it. A white owl hovers above it."

"Who is Jacob Meyers?"

A sinister glow lit his eyes, and he licked his lips. "My first kill."

I stiffened. Maybe this wasn't such a good idea. Before I managed to stammer out a reply, Jessica appeared to withdraw his IV. "Have a good night, Stanley," she said, releasing him back into the outside world.

He stared at me with a hopeful expression on his face. "I plan to," he responded, before vanishing with vampiric speed.

Uncontrollable tremors swept over me, like those caused by a gripping nightmare.

Jessica's expression became puzzled as she studied me. "You're shivering. He's gone now. It's okay, you made it."

I drew in gulps of air, trying to rid my body of the jitters Stanley had left in his wake. "I'm okay," I said, attempting to sound unruffled.

She knelt down and searched my eyes. "Did Stanley say something to upset you?"

He's one creepy freak, and I think he wants to drink my blood. I forced the thought to the back of my mind and simply stated, "No, nothing."

"You're sure?"

"Jessica, I'm fine. He just gave off a creepy vibe."

She eyed me a moment longer, seemingly weighing the truth of my words. The lines in her brow relaxed gradually. "All right, then. I'll bring Connor back."

As I waited, I kept my eyes fixed upon the polished floor. The minute Connor got inside my head, he would know what had happened to Marty, learn about my plan to get the restraints back, and my plans to meet Stanley. I didn't know how he would feel about the whole situation, but I hoped he would agree to help me. Footsteps approached, and my knee flew into a bouncing frenzy. Connor's combat boots fell into my sightline. Moment of truth. As I slowly raised my head to meet his, I felt my heart stop. His big smile vanished instantly. He blinked, and then his eyes grew saucer-wide. Staring at me, he stumbled backward and bumped up against the side of the chair.

Jessica lunged for his arm and caught him, helping to lower him into the vinyl surface of the chair. "Connor, are you feeling unwell?"

His eyes eventually wandered in her direction. "What?" He glanced back and forth between the two of us and then ran his hand over his face. "I'm feeling a little weak, that is all."

Jessica confidently stated, "I can resolve that quickly." In seconds, she had him hooked up to an IV. "Lean back and relax. You're in good hands with Claire."

He choked out a garbled laugh, cleared his throat, and flashed her a phony smile. "Yes, indeed, I am aware of that."

I sneered at him.

"You should be feeling better soon." She patted his hand. "Just give me a shout if you need anything."

"Will do," he said as he watched her walk away. When she reached the other side of the room, his eyes darted to mine. He grabbed my arm and pulled me close, whispering, "Jesus, Claire, is that what you needed the restraints for?"

I shoved his hand away. "Of course not."

In a smug tone of "I told you so," he stated, "I warned you not to go with him, but you wouldn't listen."

I pressed my lips together in a tight line. "I don't need any scolding from you; I need your help. I know you read my mind, which means you know I didn't mean for Marty to die. I did my best to help him!"

He raised his eyebrows and replied, "Yes, I witnessed everything, detail by detail. Marty's an idiot...was an idiot, but you...I mean...damn, Claire, the alcohol and the silver made for one deadly cocktail."

I rubbed the back of my neck, trying to knead away the building tension. "How was I supposed to know that? Besides, I took them off when he insisted. He cuffed us back together and even threatened me. It all happened so fast, and I fought like hell to shield him from the sun, but it…" The image of the vampire combusting into flames before being reduced to ash flashed through my mind. I curved my shoulders inward and over my chest, then hung my head in shame. "You have to believe I'm incapable of killing anyone."

He lifted my chin and tenderly whispered, "Of course you're not. I believe you."

I clutched at both his hands. "I'm in so much trouble. Reynolds has the restraints, and my prints are all over them. I'm afraid it may be only a matter of time before he catches on. We have to get them back before he finds out it was me."

He squeezed my hands. "Don't worry, we'll figure this out." Arching his brow at me, he added, "But my stealing evidence from the police isn't the brightest way to go about fixing this."

I pulled my hands away and let them fall in my lap. "If you've got a better idea, I would love to hear it."

He winked at me. "I'm a vampire. Leave the figuring out to me."

"What does that mean?"

"Look, I'll fix it, I promise. Don't worry. Now, let's talk about Stanley. I can't believe you're going to do this again."

"He has information about my family. He wants to meet me at Holy Cross Cemetery tonight." I looked away from Connor as I said, "I have to do this. It's for my family."

"No way. Absolutely not. You're smart, but Claire—this is crazy. Have you learned nothing?"

"Probably not. If there's the slightest chance he's telling the truth, I have to meet him." I again said with desperation, "For my family."

"Then I'm going with you," he asserted, emphasizing his point by slicing his hand through the air. "End of story."

The truth was, I was relieved. To have him by my side when I faced the sinister Stanley would be a godsend. I sank into the chair and breathed, "Thank you."

He took my hand, his jade-colored eyes brightening like fireflies. "You don't have to thank me. I want to make sure you're safe."

Nodding, I sniffled back my tears. Despite the uncertainty, there was a glimmer of hope pushing me forward.

"So why Holy Cross Cemetery?"

"I'm not sure. He wants to meet at midnight by Jacob Meyers' grave, the grave of his first kill."

Connor let out a groan. "Wonderful. This just gets better and better."

"What about the cuffs?"

"I've got plenty of time to take care of that little problem. Meet me in front of the cemetery at eleven forty-five." His expression became stern. "Wait for me. Do *not* go in without me."

I traced a line across my heart. "I swear, I won't."

CHAPTER 10

ue to circumstances beyond my control, I walked out of The
Vampire Center's doors a few minutes before eleven forty-five.
With the help of my Jeep's navigation system, I swung into the
cemetery's parking lot ten minutes after the agreed-upon time to meet
Connor. Slipping on my backpack filled with vampire deterrents and
jogging up to the front cemetery gate, I found it vacant. No Connor. I
scanned the street. Empty. Where was he? Had he run into trouble trying to retrieve the restraints? Should I risk calling Reynolds?

I tapped my phone and checked the time. It was precisely midnight. Resting against the wrought-iron gate, I weighed my options—go
in alone, wait a little longer, or go home. Connor had promised to be
there, and I'd promised not to go inside without him. I peered through
wrought-iron slats and into the cemetery beyond. Going in alone was
undoubtedly risky, not to mention stupid. But for me, leaving empty-
handed seemed even more unthinkable. Stanley could have answers.
He could know the killer—and maybe even who might be holding JJ.
More sinisterly, he could indeed be the murderer I sought. I kissed my
mother's cross and whispered, "Dear God, watch over me and shield me
from harm. Amen."

I took a step back and assessed the locked gate. The only way in
was up and over. I scaled the bars like a professional thief, hoisting my
body over the bowed metal. When I reached the jagged top, I ducked
under the tangle of overgrown branches before jumping to the ground
and skimming the perimeter. Dove-colored trees dotted the landscape,
their branches littering the grounds with burnt-orange leaves. A fine
layer of mist blanketed the freshly cut grass, and beams of moonlight
played among the many stone markers. It was kind of beautiful in its
own morbid way and seemed to urge me to march forward.

Zigzagging between the scattered headstones, I combed the cemetery for Jacob's grave. The sound of dry leaves crackling beneath my

shoes followed me along the path. A sudden whoosh and a gust of air directly over my head disturbed the stillness of the night sky.

I looked up to find a white owl gliding through the night sky, as if beckoning me to follow him. Stanley's words echoed inside my head. *A white owl hovers over it.* I rushed forward, trailing the owl, positive he would lead me to Jacob's grave.

The owl glided gracefully to a stop, perching softly atop one of the many tombstones clustered together. He inspected me with his pitch-black eyes and cocked his head. I read the name on the tombstone, *Jacob Meyers.* I stood completely still, my chest rising and falling as the sweat coated my palms. The owl's head jerked to the left, and he screeched. Spreading his magnificent wings and soaring upward, he vanished into the dark night.

"I see you found the grave," Stanley spoke, stepping out from the shadows. His figure shifted to a blur under the golden sheen of the moon. He reappeared in front of me and brushed a strand of hair from my brow with his long black fingernails.

My fear switch flipped on, and a slew of goosebumps raced over my arms. It took all of my will to push my shoulders back and stand tall, hoping he bought my smokescreen of confidence.

He purposefully snickered. "You're trembling. I know you're scared, so drop the act."

Keeping my gaze glued to him, I removed the backpack and hugged it against my chest—my last line of protection. "With good reason."

He bobbed his head toward the backpack. "Are you going to use your bag of nasty tricks if I misbehave?"

I pulled the backpack even closer, holding it like a shield. "Yes, if I have to."

"Thanks for the warning."

"Hey, I came like you asked me to. Give me *some* credit."

"All right, all right! And in return for your bravery, you expect information."

"Yes."

He licked his hideous lips. "First, I desire a taste of your blood."

My muscles tensed, preparing for fight or flight, while a shiver ran down my spine. I stepped backward and unzipped the pack. "That wasn't part of our agreement."

His eyes glowed brightly as he pursued me. "I don't recall making any deal whatsoever."

A frantic impulse to run shot through my brain, but there was no way I could outrun or outsmart him. My only option was to threaten him. My fingers latched onto a wooden stake. I whipped it out and pointed the tip at him. "Stay away from me, or the stake ends up in your heart."

He slammed a fist against his chest, taunting me. "Go ahead, stake my heart."

In an instant, I saw my dead, bloodless body flash before my eyes. A wave of anger overpowered my fear. I was so desperate to find answers about my family that vampire lies had lured me twice now. I clenched the rough wood under my fingers, my knuckles turning pale white. "I don't want to hurt you, but I *will* stake you."

"But I like you."

Angling the stake in his direction, I shouted, "Do you have information or not?"

He held up his hands in surrender. "Calm down. I'll give you a hint. Your search lies with the living, not the undead."

I struggled to make sense of what he said. I didn't have patience for riddles. "Are you saying the killer was human?"

"Allow me a taste of your blood, and I'll tell you."

"I would rather never learn the truth than let you drink my blood!"

A low, deep growl rose in his throat. His pearl-colored eyes darkened into pitch-black sockets of emptiness. Arching his shoulders, he shot upward, disappearing into the sky above. A single thought dominated my brain...*run*. I bolted forward, racing away from Jacob's grave.

Stanley plummeted out of the sky, crashing on top of me and pinning me to the ground. The impact knocked the wind out of me, leaving me gasping for air. A sharp pain shot through my shoulder as the weight of his body pressed down on me. With adrenaline coursing through my veins, I thrust the stake into his chest, missing his heart. Drool dripped from his fangs onto my face as he growled. "I'm going to enjoy gorging on your blood."

I screamed and dug my nails into his face. "You will *not* taste my blood!"

He roared with laughter, stating confidently, "Oh, *yes*, I will."

Hands gripped Stanley's shoulders, yanked him off me, and sent him hurling through the air. He flew several yards before crashing headlong into a stone marker. Rising to his feet and staggering a couple of steps, he swayed and collapsed to the ground. My gaze darted away from Stanley to the pair of striking jade-colored eyes hovering over me. A sob escaped my throat as I choked out his name. "Connor."

He pulled me to my feet and shoved the backpack into my arms, shouting, "Run!"

I didn't hesitate to obey and scurried in the opposite direction. Running madly toward the front gate, I weaved between the trees and trampled over leaves and grass. My freedom, my salvation, was the wrought-iron gate. As it came into view, a few feet away, an avalanche of tears rained down my cheeks.

My adrenaline powered me up and over the gate. As soon as I hit the ground, I scampered to my feet and kept running, but I hit a giant crack in the cement. Tumbling forward, I fell hard. The jagged concrete ripped through my jeans and sliced open my skin. The sharp sting left me paralyzed as warm blood seeped through my clothes and stained the sidewalk. I had to get up; I had to run, but I couldn't move as I sat cradling my knees and stifling the wail rising in my throat.

A cricket chirped somewhere off in the distance, and then the snap of a branch behind me fueled me to leap to my feet, regardless of pain. I whirled around and thrust a stake in front of me, ready to protect myself. Only darkness surrounded me. I didn't wait around to find out what or who made that sound. Screams of pain flew from my mouth as I bolted toward the parking lot, focusing my eyes on the warm glow of the streetlight. It called out to me: *You're almost safe. Run. Run like hell!* As I drew closer, the keys slipped through my sweaty fingers, falling to the ground. The attempt to latch on to them stung every nerve in my body, and I screeched loudly like Jacob's owl.

Throwing open the door, sharp twinges of pain gnawed at my flesh. Gingerly, I guided my injured legs into my Jeep and slid onto the driver's seat. For the briefest of seconds, I let my head rest against the steering wheel as I closed my eyes. As I screamed, my hand clenched into a fist, and I slammed it against the dash.

The force of the blow seemed to drive out some of the pain—enough so I could turn the engine over. I gunned my Jeep and sped down the street, looking in my rearview mirror for any sign of Stanley. The road appeared vacant, but I didn't trust my human vision. I ran all the traffic lights, driving at speeds just as lethal as the bite of any vampire. I didn't care. I just wanted to reach home as quickly as possible.

As soon as I arrived at the condo parking garage, I scanned the dimly lit structure with a narrowed gaze, in search of nocturnal creatures hiding in the shadows. The beat of my overexcited heart thrummed inside my ears. Was I safe? Was I alone? While easing the door open, my eyes darted in every direction. Nothing. Still, I pulled the vial of holy water from the backpack and gripped it in the palm of my hand, listening to the buzz of the overhead lights.

I sprinted to the elevator, bawling, and punched the call button, my brain trying to block the excruciating pain. Once inside the safety of the four thick silver walls, I released a sigh of relief. The elevator jerked upward, carrying me home. *Almost there. Almost safe.*

The doors parted, and I staggered out, focusing on the things I needed most: aspirin, a long hot shower, and sleep. I dropped the vial into the backpack as I turned the corner to my unit. Too exhausted and debilitated by pain to lift the pack's weight, I dragged it across the floor by the strap. When I reached my unit, I spotted Connor leaning against the door.

My heart fluttered at the sight of him. He'd just saved my life. I owed him everything, but with each step forward, my pace slowed. A frown burrowed across my forehead. Again, he'd found me, but I had never told him where I lived.

"Relax," he said, holding up his hands. "I followed you from the cemetery. Your unit number popped into your head as you boarded the elevator. I raced up before you."

"You could've just ridden the elevator with me."

"You're right, I could have."

I threw a sneer at him. "You were supposed to meet me at the cemetery. What happened to that part of the plan?"

"And you were supposed to wait for me."

"*You* didn't show up."

He smirked as he answered, "I got sidetracked at the police station. Seems you have a record."

"Breaking into my home isn't a crime."

"Maybe not, but you're just lucky they didn't print you, or the little matter of retrieving the restraints would've been a lot harder to resolve."

I rushed forward and latched onto his arm. "Were you able to get them back? Did anyone see you? Do you have them with you?"

"Well, aren't we full of questions?" He shrugged his shoulders. "Things got complicated."

"Complicated how?"

He swept his bangs out of his eyes before continuing. "I had to improvise."

"I don't like the sound of that."

"Hang on, I'll explain." His eyes traveled along the rip in my jeans. "But first, I need to heal you." He pricked his finger, drawing his blood forth, and bent to rub it across my knees. "There, good as new."

At his touch, the stinging pain vanished. My tensed-up muscles relaxed. "Oh my God. Thank you."

He flashed a proud grin. "You're welcome. Oh yeah, I also have an update on the Marty incident. The police haven't learned his identity yet. At this point, all they know is that a vampire died in the park. However, the discovery of the restraints nearby leads them to suspect murder."

I slumped against the wall. "I can't believe this is happening."

"We'll get through this. Don't worry."

I swallowed hard and gave him a hesitant nod. "So, how did you improvise?"

"You can trust me to carry out such simple tasks." He made a brushing-off motion with his hands. "Easy peasy."

"I only trust myself."

"Yet you enlisted me to retrieve the cuffs. I think that implies an element of trust. Besides, I saved your life. You know, for a human, you certainly do get into a lot of trouble."

My recent circumstances have been unlike most people's. I had to navigate challenges many others would never encounter. In fact, normalcy had abandoned me the moment I'd arrived at the airport. The vampire, or vampires, responsible for my loss had changed everything for me. I looked at him and huffed. "I wonder why that is? Maybe because some frigging monster ruined my life."

"Relax. I was kidding, sort of," he said, placing his hand on my shoulder.

"Just tell me you got the cuffs, please."

He released me and crossed his arms. "The police station was overrun. There were simply too many people to control. Besides, the restraints were already logged in as evidence. Removing them would've been a risky move, and I deviated from our original plan." He smirked. "They won't find your prints or anyone else's for that matter. I wiped them clean."

"I know I keep saying this," I laid my hand on his forearm, "but thank you."

He lightly stroked the top of my hand and smiled. "No need to thank me. I happen to enjoy being a hero."

He genuinely seemed to care about me. I leaned against him, allowing the comfort in his touch to soothe my loneliness. Although I would never again see my parents, there was still a decent chance I might find JJ. The moment when JJ's big blue eyes held my attention once more couldn't come soon enough. He had a unique ability to make everything seem right. I recalled a memory of him standing in my bedroom once, his hands full with a cookie dough ice cream container and two spoons. Plastering a goofy smile on his face, he had handed me a spoon and said, "Ice cream repairs everything."

"Not this time, JJ," I said half-aloud.

"What was that?" Connor asked.

I pulled away from Connor and turned toward my door. "Nothing. It's late...you should go."

"Let me stay so I can make sure you're okay."

"That's not necessary. I'm a big girl."

His eyes lit up like fireflies again, as if I'd affected some sort of reaction in him. "But I want to get to know you better." Running his combat boot over the floor, he added, "I have lots of great boyfriend-like qualities."

"Connor—"

He interrupted me and spread his arms wide. "I'm incredibly handsome, charming, and witty for starters."

I let out a laugh, but I quickly swallowed the humor. "Right now, my family has to come first. I don't have time for anything else."

He brushed his lips across my cheek and whispered, "I'm quite persistent. I'm pretty confident I'll win you over."

He vanished, leaving me standing alone, palms sweating and butterflies swarming inside my stomach. There was some irresistible quality about Connor, drawing me to him. I couldn't seem to shake my attraction to him...but did I even want to?

"Claire." A familiar male voice sounded inside the quiet corridor, disrupting my thoughts.

Reynolds headed up the hall toward me. *What the hell is he doing here at this hour?* After Connor's little intervention trick, Marty couldn't have been the reason, but something had led Reynolds to my doorstep. Could his visit pertain to my parents or JJ? A spark of hope filled my chest as I took a step toward him. My shoe contacted an object in my path. Catching sight of the backpack at my feet set off a silent alarm inside my head. The backpack was filled with vampire slayer gear. What if he asked what was inside? What if he wanted to search it? *You're overacting. Get a grip; he has no reason to search a backpack.*

Plus, why would he? Slipping my hand under the strap, I swung the bag over my shoulder in the most nonchalant manner and tucked it behind my back and out of sight.

"I went over to your parents' house," he said. "I found out that you sold it. After a little investigation, I made my way over to The Vampire Center. It seems I just missed your shift. They gave me your address. Please excuse the lateness of the hour, but I figured you would be up since your shift ended not too long ago." His gaze swept over me, and his thick brows came together. "What happened to you? Are you okay?"

I shifted back and forth on my feet, my brain trying to come up with a reasonable excuse for my damaged appearance. Pointing to my ripped jeans, I muttered, "Went for a jog and tripped on a crack in the sidewalk." Inwardly, I cringed. *So not convincing. Who goes jogging in jeans, and at midnight no less?*

He pulled a leaf out of my hair and examined it. "Do you always jog in jeans?"

I laughed and threw up my hands. "Laundry's backed up because of the move. Had to improvise."

He shook his head and cracked a smile. "I believe you think fast on your feet."

Steering the conversation away from me, I asked, "Any leads on my parents' case or luck finding JJ? Were you able to question Nate and Parker?"

His expression grew long as he shoved his hands in his pockets. "Unfortunately, the answer is no to both."

I sagged against the wall, closing my eyes.

"Don't worry, we'll find the killer and JJ too," he promised, his tone thick with optimism. "I won't give up until we do."

Opening my eyes and fixing my gaze on him, I thought hard about his words. My heart truly wanted to believe him, but I couldn't let groundless optimism cloud my judgment. We were dealing with vampires who openly opposed The Vow. I may never have the luxury of closure.

"But that's not why I'm here," he said, locking his eyes on mine.

Oh crap! "Then why?"

"I'm following a lead."

I nearly choked on my breath. *Stay calm. He couldn't possibly have known you were with Marty.* "What kind of lead?"

"One tied to a dead vampire found in the park." He removed his hands from his pockets and laced his fingers. "Know anything about that?"

A cold brick of panic landed on the floor of my stomach. *He knows!* Maybe Connor only thought he had wiped the restraints clean. Maybe Reynolds had recognized my Jeep in the park. Was this some kind of manipulation on his part to get me to confess? Every detail about Marty's death lingered inside my brain, begging to come out. I ignored my thoughts and eyed the detective. I could play his game, too. I splayed my fingers across my chest. "Me? What makes you think I would know anything about that?"

"We found a set of silver cuffs at the scene. I traced the serial number, and they belonged to Detective Miller. The detective stated that he had traded them in at Cops-R-Us. I had a delightful little chat with the store clerk. Seems a pretty young blonde purchased them. Paid cash."

The room started to spin, and I wanted to throw up. The last thing I needed was for him to see me panic. I anchored a hand on my hip, gathering my strength of will. "Well, if you're implying I purchased them, you're wrong."

He rocked back and forth on his heels, seemingly unconvinced. "Maybe not. Can't say for certain. The store surveillance camera crashed the night before the purchase, and our crime lab couldn't get clear prints."

Despite my internal turmoil, I maintained a composed demeanor. "And I'm the one you suspect. Lucky me."

He shrugged his shoulders. "I'm a detective. I piece things together. Your situation provides a motive, don't you think? Besides, I recall seeing a Jeep similar to yours in the park that morning."

"You're way off on this one, Reynolds."

His focus shifted away from me and down the hall. He squinted as his gaze drifted toward the ceiling. "What the hell?"

Reynolds gripped my arm and shoved me to the floor. "Stay down!" he shouted. He drew his gun and aimed it at the ceiling, squeezing off three rounds.

Bullets whizzed overhead; the gunshots rang inside my ears. Who was he shooting at? *Oh God, please, don't let it be Connor.* I raised my head and followed where the shots led. Greasy black hair and pearl-colored eyes filled my vision. A gasp flew from my mouth. Stanley had hunted me down to finish what he'd started. I jerked backward, my body smacking against the wall as I crouched down and witnessed Stanley blowing me another kiss.

Reynolds fired off another set of rounds. Shells flew, raining across the carpet and bouncing like Mexican jumping beans. Stanley blurred from corner to corner around us, dodging bullets and cackling with delight.

He came to a standstill, that cold, blank stare of his claiming his pallid face. His eyes altered into a glowing blood-red before an inhuman hiss flew past his lips. He descended from the ceiling, diving straight for me. Reynolds fired—a bullet struck.

An expression of utter shock twisted Stanley's brow, and he sank to his knees. His pale flesh erupted with dark-gray patches, devouring his body and sucking the life right out of him. He sizzled, popped, and then exploded into a powerless pile of silvery ash.

I cradled my knees and looked away. Another vampire died because of my involvement. Suddenly, after years of peaceful coexistence, vampires began to murder humans and vice versa.

My neighbors' doors burst open. Clad in bathrobes and pajamas, they spilled into the hallway with widened eyes and mouths gaping. They swarmed Detective Reynolds. Their shrill chatter filled my ears.

"Look, vampire ash!"

"He shot a vampire!"

"Why did you kill him?"

"What happened?"

"Are we in danger?"

Reynolds flashed his badge and shooed them away. "Relax. Everything's under control, folks. There's nothing to see here. Go back inside your homes."

The crowd didn't budge.

He approached them with his hands out, waving them backward. "Come on, folks, back into your units, please."

In slow motion, they crept back into their homes and shut their doors. Reynolds returned to me, lifting me up and off the floor. "Are you okay?"

I opened my mouth, but no words escaped.

Reynolds peered over his shoulder at Stanley's remains, and he slowly shook his head. "In all my years on the force, I've never seen a vampire attack a human. We may have a more serious situation on our hands than I initially thought. The Vow appears to be falling apart for some unknown reason." He turned to me in disbelief. "Thank God for silver-plated bullets. Without them, we would both be dead."

I shivered at the implication of his words. Could he be right in thinking that The Vow was disintegrating? Was an uprising of rogue vampires in the works? Had Stanley been one of them? Was he my actual parents' killer, and trying to throw me off track by telling me to search among the living for their murderer? Had he taken JJ's life as well? Unfortunately, I would never know. The answers died along with the sadistic vampire, leaving me with two options: continue my search as if the killer was still out there and my brother was still alive, or accept that Stanley was the killer of both my parents and my brother. I shuddered at that thought. I could never accept that, never. I had to keep searching as long as I kept breathing.

CHAPTER 11

Dying vampires haunted my dreams, exploding into silvery ash over and over again. I couldn't help them. I couldn't save them. My lashes fluttered, ushering me into wakefulness and ending the vicious cycle. I bolted upright before flopping back down, exhausted, on my pillows. I lay in bed, completely awake, focused on the ceiling as my brain struggled with the aftermath. Marty's and Stanley's deaths set me on edge. I trembled and twitched, unable to relax, and my heart pounded with anxiety. The memories of their final moments played on a loop in my mind, a haunting reminder of my helplessness. Sleep seemed an impossible escape as I lay trapped in my thoughts, yearning for peace. I needed my parents. I needed my brother.

The doorbell chimed. I glanced at the clock—8:00 AM. *Who in the world? Oh crap, the furniture delivery.* I climbed out of bed and threw on a pair of black floral-print pants with a crop top and sandals before hurrying to open the front door. "Coming," I called to keep them from giving up on me.

Inside an hour, modern and vintage pieces, combined with brightly colored accents, filled the previously bare interior of my entire condo. The furniture gave off a comfy vibe, as if the pieces had traveled everywhere with me. The best part was having something to run my eyes over besides empty walls and floor space. One recent accomplishment I could feel good about, and at this point, I would take any triumph, no matter how small. The only things missing from my life were closure for my parents' murder and the whereabouts of JJ. I didn't have a clue how to achieve either of those. I curled up on my new couch, grabbing an accent pillow and hugging it to my chest until the sun went down.

I blew off The Center, calling in sick. I needed some alone time and to be near my parents. Perhaps I couldn't reach them as I used to, but the best option would be to sit in front of their graves and talk in hopes that their spirit forms would hear me.

In the field outside the cemetery, I stopped to handpick a bouquet of wildflowers, my mother's favorites, to adorn their graves. I parked my Jeep at the end of a long row of trees. Thousands of stars twinkled against the midnight-blue canvas above. Fresh, crisp air, like the kind left behind after a rainstorm, filled my lungs. A blanket of green grass filled the space between the checkerboard of flat square markers—its vibrant scent wafting through the air. Flowers decorated select graves, while others lingered bare and forgotten. Following the trail to my parents' graves, I ascended the hill.

I sat between them, offering up the bouquet and kissing the raised letters on their plaques. The hole their deaths punched through my heart grew a bit larger, its ragged edges of sorrow spreading through my limbs. I ached all over for their touch and their kind words of encouragement. I hung my head, tears spilling down my cheeks as I let my mother's soothing voice play inside my head, giving me the strength to speak. "I'm in trouble," I said. "JJ's missing. I'm lost without you. I don't know who to turn to or where to look. I need your help. Please, if you can hear me, help me."

I waited for a reply. None came.

The brittle snap of a tree branch disturbed the peaceful night. I jerked my head in the direction of the sound, and my gaze landed on a man standing among the trees. The night breeze lifted the hem of his long dark coat. He strode forward, approaching me, stopping just short of my parents' graves. The gleam of moonlight illuminated his colorless face and aquamarine eyes, exposing his true nature—a vampire.

My heartbeat spiked, and I pushed to my feet to confront him. "What am I, some kind of vampire magnet? I can't go anywhere without running into one of you."

He tucked his dark-brown locks behind his ears and laid his hand over his heart. "My vampiric hearing couldn't help but deliver your plea to me. I've come to offer my assistance."

This couldn't be a coincidence; he and I were in the same place at the same time, and he harbored a fervent desire to play the hero. After my experiences with Marty and Stanley, I knew better than to trust a vampire. "Why offer assistance to someone you don't know?" I challenged him.

"Why would I have to know you to help you?"

"Please," I said sarcastically. "Take your charity and leave. I'm not interested."

"Not all vampires are evil, my dear. When I was still human, I was a priest. I still practice to this day."

"A vampire priest? Intriguing. Heard any good confessions lately, like, 'Hey, I killed this girl's parents?'"

He laughed lightly before his demeanor became quite solemn. "No, I must say I have not."

There was something both intriguing and unsettling about the transformation of a man of faith into a creature of the night. I couldn't help but wonder what events or temptations led him down this dark path.

I bobbed my head toward a bench at the top of the hill. "Wanna sit and chat?"

A warm smile lit his eyes. "I would like that. By the way, my name's Jonathan. People who have known me over the years have come to refer to me as *the priest* and most simply call me *Priest*.

"Mine's Claire." I didn't need a priest—especially not one who was also a vampire. "I'll call you Jonathan if you don't mind."

"Very well, Claire. Pleased to meet you."

I didn't return the sentiment.

We sat at opposite ends of the wooden bench, staring at one another. He folded his hands in his lap and broke the silence. "I sense the weight of death on your heart."

I cracked a smile and cocked my head. "Got inside my brain, did you? What a surprise."

"No, of course not," he professed. "I would first require your permission to read you. Your body language conveys what I sense."

"What?"

"As a priest, I've seen it many times: the clenched jaws and restlessness, the fear behind the eyes, accompanied by the guilt buried deep within the soul."

"Fair enough," I admitted. "Okay, here's the thing. A vampire murdered my parents."

His aquamarine eyes softened, but he didn't speak a word. I studied him, the way he sat so still and patient, the warmth in his expression, but underneath all the virtue had to be something self-seeking—he was a vampire, right? He probably had an agenda. I wasn't about to trust him. "JJ," I continued, "my brother is missing. I want to find him, and I want justice."

His eyes widened before swiftly returning to their benevolent state. "These are horrible crimes you speak of."

Was the flare in his eyes a brief flicker of acknowledgment? Had I struck a nerve? "Yes, they are."

"If a vampire did indeed murder your parents, it is unlikely he or she would've left a witness alive," he stated matter-of-factly.

"Are you saying JJ's dead!" I exclaimed.

He reached out to touch my arm. "No, no, that's not what I meant. Forgive me, I'll rephrase. Your brother may be in league with the vampire."

"What, like a hostage or something?"

"A human is taken only when they wish to be transformed."

I shivered and gripped my arms tightly. My mind conjured up images of Nate and Parker. Could they be responsible for all of this? But JJ had loved them like brothers, so why would they kill our parents or turn him? And just where had they disappeared to? None of it made sense. Reynolds' rogue vampire theory carried more logic behind it. "If that were the case, JJ would've contacted me by now. He would've let me know he was safe. He wouldn't let me suffer like this."

"I'm only surmising. Vampires are selective when creating a fledgling. Your brother would've had to agree to be turned."

A new line of questioning threaded through my brain. "Being a priest, you must hear many confessions."

"I hear my fair share, yes."

Again, I asked, "So, has there been any talk about a murder? About a local human couple who were drained of blood in their home?"

"I'm afraid not, but then, many vampires operate outside my circle of influence, ones who choose to bend The Vow to suit their desires."

I narrowed my gaze as I asked, "What do you mean by bend?"

"Evil vampires still exist among our numbers. They hunger for human blood obtained by the hunt."

I rose from the bench and blurted out, "They hunt and kill people for their blood?"

With the same calm demeanor, he replied, "They do hunt, but they don't kill. That is what I meant by *bend* rather than *break*." A gleam flashed in his eyes. "But I may have something to aid you in the search for your parents' killer. A map."

"What kind of a map?"

"I am offering you a map that pinpoints the locations of evil vampires' tombs. Despite the obvious presence of these tombs scattered throughout the graveyard, humans would never discover them without the map."

"How will that map help me?"

He smiled broadly. "It points to their resting locations."

I shrugged my shoulders. "So."

"One of those evil vampires is most likely the one you seek."

I slowly lowered myself back onto the bench and searched his eyes. "Why would you jeopardize your kind's possible incarceration from someone you just met?"

He chuckled and waved away my skepticism. "I have no use for the map. For you, it may be a vital clue. I was once a man of God, helping all those who sought Him. Tonight, I choose to help another soul in need, if you should decide to accept my help."

I erupted into laughter. "I'm not buying your saintly act. What's your angle?"

He remained calm; not even an eyebrow twitched. "I have no hidden agenda. I'm merely offering the map if you believe it can help you.

You will, however, need to keep it protected due to the sensitive nature of its contents. Days after The Vow came into being, I hid it inside my church."

"I can't protect it. I'm only human, remember?"

He rose to his feet, bowed his head, and politely stated, "Then I shall leave you." He paused his retreat to face me once more. "If you should change your mind," he said, placing a key in my palm, "the map is hidden inside My Lady of Grace, beneath a broken altar tile."

I closed my hand around the cold piece of metal as I regarded him. Showing up at my parents' graves, revealing a secret vampire map, and giving up the key to its hiding place all seemed far too convenient. There *must* be an ulterior motive behind his actions.

"Good luck with your quest," he said before vanishing into the night.

Common sense gave way to the map's allure, but was this a trap or an opportunity? I wonder what my vampire-hunting ancestor, William, would do in such a situation. There was no doubt in my mind that he would go to the church and retrieve the map. That settled the matter. I would do what I believed he would do. Before sprinting to my Jeep, I threw my fist in the air in celebration. When I reached my Jeep, I found Connor leaning against it.

Wearing an overly confident smile, he asked, "What did Priest want?"

I ignored his question, asking one of my own. "How do you keep finding me?" I nudged him aside so I could unlock the door and teased, "You're starting to take on the role of stalker."

"I'm not a stalker." He paused and cocked his head. "Well, technically, I am. I *am* a vampire. We're notorious stalkers." He became increasingly serious and gestured toward me. "*You* didn't show up at The Center, so I went looking for you. I found no response at your condo. Obviously, my next stop would be a graveyard. It appears that graveyards are your preferred hangout spot. And bingo, here you are, hanging out with none other than Priest. What were you two talking about?"

"You were spying on me?"

"More like harmless eavesdropping."

"Then you already know what we were talking about."

"True. I do indeed."

"Why ask?"

"It seemed like the human thing to do."

"But you're not human."

"I like to pretend I still am."

I gazed at him, unable to contain my amused smile. He *was* rather humanlike.

He came closer, his eyes narrowing as they locked onto mine. "Trouble seems to follow you wherever you go. So Stanley ended up as vampire dust?"

A chill ran through me, and I slipped my hands into my jacket's pockets. "He came back to kill me. Thank God, Reynolds was there. But the worst part is I believe Stanley knew something about what happened to my family, and now he's dead."

In a soothing tone, he added, "Someone has to know something."

"Like the vampire Jonathan." I opened my palm. "He gave me this key. Kept rattling on about some secret vampire map."

He furrowed his brow as he stared at it, then asked, "Do you want my opinion?"

"I do."

He stomped his combat boot into the ground and replied, "Toss the key. Forget the map. It could get you killed."

I knew there were risks with such a map, but weren't they mine to take? "But what if the murderer's location is really on this map? It could lead me to them."

He flicked a finger against my forehead. "Is there a brain in there? Haven't you lived through enough near-death vampire encounters?"

"I know it seems I'm not being smart about things."

"You think?"

"You could come with me and protect me." I winked at him. "Or I could drive home and grab my trusty vampire backpack."

He jerked up the zipper on his jacket and rolled his eyes in a disbelieving manner. "This isn't a joke, Claire. And why didn't you bring the damn thing with you tonight? You should have glued that thing to your back."

"Of course it's not a joke. I know that. I wasn't expecting to run into your kind yet again."

He raised a single brow at me. "My kind?"

"Yes, and speaking of vampires, I think the map's worth checking out."

"You're not going to let the matter go, are you?"

"Absolutely not."

He sighed. "I didn't think so. Well, I can't have you going alone. You're accident-prone. You need my help." He nudged me out of the way and slipped into the driver's seat. Pointing to the passenger's side, he said, "Get in. I'll drive."

I crossed my arms and tapped my foot impatiently. "Did I say you could drive?"

He winked and patted the seat. "Come on, get in."

I huffed loudly to communicate my displeasure before climbing into the passenger seat.

"Where to?" he asked, all smiles.

"Don't get too excited, and you already know since you were eavesdropping. Our Lady of Grace on Fifth, downtown."

He rubbed his hands together. "I like it. A vampire map hidden in an ancient church."

"Just drive."

"Very well."

He started the engine and pulled onto the street. Watching the white lines rush by on the street set my mind adrift. Connor made a valid point. Both my previous vampire encounters had turned deadly. With the assault still fresh, every breath ached. Maybe I needed a sounding board. "Can I ask you a favor?"

"Shoot."

I stuck out my trembling hand. "Look at how on edge I am. I feel like...like I'm drowning. I don't know how to stop it."

He took one hand off the wheel and offered up his palm. "Then why are we hunting down a vampire map inside a creepy old church?"

"Because..." Angry tears threatened to fall, and I swiped at my eyes. "Because the killer has to pay."

"But you can't keep accusing random vampires." He glanced at me with kind eyes. "You're too close to this. It's clouding your judgment. You should let the police handle this."

"I can't."

"Yes, you can."

I laid my head in my hands and heaved an impatient sigh. "No, I can't."

"Why should the responsibility fall on you? You cannot take on the world of vampires. For a human—even a slayer in training—it's impossible. Isn't that obvious?"

His argument made sense, but no matter how stubborn I was or how stupid I was, I had to continue to fight. "The police have no leads. Maybe JJ's time is running out. Isn't that obvious to you?"

In a gentler tone, he said, "I can't begin to imagine what you're going through. Your family must have been your entire world, so if you can't surrender this struggle, allow me to assist you. I can gather information from places you cannot reach." His jade-colored eyes brightened. "You do realize I'm beginning to care about you, right?"

Part of me wanted to believe him, to feel the warmth of his words. But another part remained guarded, reminding me he was a vampire after all. "You don't even know me."

His astounded expression lifted his brows. "But I *do* know you. You're smart, fearless...and beautiful. Despite your convincing tough exterior, your overwhelming sense of compassion is tearing you apart. Family's everything to you, and you would sacrifice your life to save your brother's." He winked at me. "Shall I go on?"

"You have an unfair advantage. You can get inside my head, but I can't do the same. I don't know your last name, how old you are, where you live, or if you have a job…"

He smiled. "I rather like being inside your head."

"I'm not playing around here. Tell me something about who you are."

"Okay, okay! Hmm, well, the last name's Scott. I was turned at the age of twenty-three. I live in an apartment down in the Vampire District. Don't work; don't need to. I come from a wealthy family. Is that enough detail for you?"

"That's surface stuff. I want something deep."

He leveled off the sarcasm, his expression growing serious. "Before the institution of The Vow, I lived in utter filth, and being a vampire, mankind considered me a hideous fiend. My family's money could've helped my situation, but at that time I refused. I mostly hid in the shadows and slept in tombs or coffins. My maker was my only companion, and compassion was not his strong point." He forced a smile. "Satisfied?"

I gave him a curt nod. "Yes. Thank you."

"Don't mention it." He nudged me and grinned. "Now, back to you."

He was somewhat annoying, wholeheartedly narcissistic, and overly persistent, yet my heartbeat quickened every time we were together. "Stop focusing on me, and let's worry about finding the map."

"What if there is no map? Did you ever think about that possibility?"

"Don't say that. Don't even think it. We'll find the map…we have to."

He glanced over at me. "You do realize the situation could be a setup?"

I didn't need him to point out the obvious. I was well aware. "Yes. The priest, the map—it's all too convenient."

"We need to be prepared for anything, and you're not going in alone. I'll stay by your side." Slowing the Jeep, he pulled it to the right and parked against the curb. "We're here," he announced as he turned off the engine.

I clutched nervously at my mother's necklace and shifted in my seat. "My heart's already pounding like crazy."

"I'll have your back, so try not to worry."

My gaze traveled over the gray-stone exterior of the church. The arched stained-glass windows resembled pages from a child's coloring book, full of irregular shapes exploding with a kaleidoscope of vibrant hues. Marble steps led up to the giant mahogany door for which I held the key. An image of Indiana Jones popped into my head. How would he go about retrieving the map? Would I end up solving complicated riddles or facing overwhelming obstacles as he had in the movie?

The passenger door opened, and Connor extended his hand. A smirk claimed his lips as he said, "Come on, Indy. Let's go find us a vampire lair map."

I gestured with my finger. "Stay out of my head."

A twinkle of glee flashed in his eyes. "You know that's wishful thinking on your part, right?"

I let out a groan. "Whatever." I looked away from him and focused on the front door.

As he ascended the first step, he waved me forward. "Let's go."

I joined him on the steps and then opened my hand to examine the key. The rapid thud of my heartbeat drowned out the world around us. Uncertainty pulsed through the veins beneath my skin. What if the map fell short of my expectations?

Worse yet, what if Connor was right and there wasn't a map to find? What if we were both falling into a carefully planted—almost blatantly obvious—trap?

Connor gave my shoulder a gentle shove. "What are you waiting for? Open the door."

I turned and glared at him. "You're really starting to annoy me."

"You worry too much. Think of it like being on a scavenger hunt."

I paused and looked heavenward, as if contemplating asking for divine help. "Hmm, what should we do if you turn out to be one of the vampires alluded to on that map?" I teased.

His eyes deepened a shade. "I assure you I'm not. Yes, I did my fair share of killing, but only to feed. I've never been evil, not even in the beginning, and I'm certainly not now."

The determination creasing his brow and the intensity in his eyes seemed to represent he meant every word. Therefore, I chose to believe him. "All right, but you can't treat the situation like a game. You said so yourself, remember?"

"I did, but merely to put you at ease. Now, open the damn door."

My hand trembled when I slid the key into the lock. The door creaked, opening no more than a crack. Connor gave it a rough push, exposing the entryway to the church's interior. Streetlamps shone through stained glass, casting a rainbow of colors across the walls. As I crossed the threshold, my footsteps echoed all the way up to the high arch of the ceiling. We were about to search a house of God to locate a map that pointed out evil vampires. The entire situation felt deeply unsettling. As I held my breath, I pushed forward until I was standing in front of the marble altar.

"Your face is even paler than mine," Connor said with a laugh.

"To be honest, I'm seriously freaked out."

When he turned my body toward him, a look of certainty burned in his eyes. "If anything should happen, know I'll protect you."

"Thank you," I whispered.

He flashed a charming smile as he whispered back, "You're welcome."

We stood inches from each other in the center aisle, gazing into each other's eyes. He brushed a strand of hair from my forehead, his touch setting my body afire. *I'm not ready for this.* I backed away. "The map. We have to find the map."

He didn't seem to have taken offense to my diversion. "Lead the way."

Angels of gold and ivory stood at either side of the altar, bearing basins of holy water. Their peaceful expressions and the manner in which their heads tilted toward one another suggested a genuine affection between the two. Just beyond the angels, the marble tiles came into view. The chipped tile stood out plainly from the smooth perfection of the others. I stood there staring, not being able to look away, as if one blink would make it disappear. A sudden rush of blood swam into my brain, causing me to stumble back a few steps. Connor steadied me and then hooked his arm under mine as we approached the cloak-and-dagger tile.

I knelt to the ground and ran my hand over the tile's jagged edge. "This has to be the one."

"Now what?"

"Let's see if I'm right." I grabbed the broken border and pulled. It didn't budge. "We need a chisel or something to loosen it. Can you see if you can find one?"

He smirked. "We're in a church, not Home Depot. I'll just smash it."

"Smashing the tile could damage the map." I looked around as if the answer was somewhere nearby. "Let's think about this for a minute."

His gaze remained fixed on me. "God, you're beautiful."

"Seriously?" I pointed at the tile. "We're here to retrieve the map. Focus."

"I'm focusing on you."

He got a smile out of me, and I playfully pushed him away. "I'm serious. Either help me or go wait in the car."

He huffed. "Has anyone ever told you you're exceedingly difficult?"

"Connor," I paused and sighed. "My parents are dead, and my brother is missing. I can't think about anything else. Are you going to help me or not?"

His smile vanished as he quickly set his sights on the tile. "Yes, of course I'll help. I'm sure I can pry it loose."

"I'm worried about the map being damaged."

He glanced at me and shrugged. "I don't see any other option at this point."

"Okay, but pull gently."

His fingers gripped the ragged edge, and he pulled slightly. A small piece broke off and flew across the floor. "I need to get in a better position." He lowered himself onto his elbows and shoved a finger under the tile, jostling it back and forth. "This sucker's glued on tight." The tile protested with a resounding crack, a large chunk of it whizzing past his head. He managed to duck out of its way.

I sighed loudly. "Oh, just break the damn thing."

"Gladly." He balled his fist and sent it smashing down on the tile. The pop of shattered stone exploded inside the peaceful church, spraying the air with a thick cloud of dust.

I waved away the dense powder as I bent over the tile, searching the floor beneath it. "I don't see a map. Do you?"

"I do," Connor shouted. He snatched something out of the indentation in the floor. A moment later, he held up an old and discolored plastic bag. "Here you are, my dear," he said, graciously handing the bag over to me.

Carefully, I ripped a corner to open the bag and gently pulled out the map. Pressing it over my heart, I shouted, "The vampire map is mine!"

"Unfold it. Let's see who's on the damn thing."

My hands trembled as I gingerly expanded the parchment and spread it out on the floor before us. Images of hundreds of tombs embellished the surface of the old paper, each labeled, some identified by name and others by a set of numbers and a location. One tomb in particular captured my attention. I lightly brushed a finger across the words "she knows" inked beneath. Reading the address, I committed it to memory—*Pine Lake Memorial Park, Crypt 33657*. My eyes found Connor's as I rattled off, "What do you think that means? She knows what? Do you think someone wrote it there as a clue to the identity of my parents' killer?"

He shook his head. "I think you're grasping at straws. That note could mean a thousand different things, none of which may have anything to do with what happened to your parents. Besides, the map is ancient and was obviously buried here way before the day your parents were murdered."

Excitement, emotion, and hope overpowered reason and pushed it out of my brain. "Maybe the priest wrote the message and wanted me to see it."

"He only gave you the key a little while ago. You think he had time to pry up the tile and write this message on it? Plus, if it was him, the glue would've been fresh, making that tile much easier to pry loose. That thing was hanging on for life! You're too close to this and not thinking clearly."

"Well, something that cryptic—no pun intended—is at least worth checking out. The cemetery mentioned on the map isn't far from here. We have time to go there now."

"Claire, put the map away." Connor's tone sounded strained.

I didn't look his way. I was unable to pull my gaze away from the map now that I'd found it. "I just started looking at it. Why would I put it away?"

He gripped my chin and turned my head so I faced the front door. "*Hide* the map," he instructed under his breath.

A deep, jarring voice invaded the stillness of the church. "Barbie and Ken appear to be stealing our map."

Goosebumps exploded across my arms, and I shivered in their clutches. A pair of lifeless, dark-brown eyes peered at me through strands of thick, unkempt hair. The vampire drew his crimson lips back to expose long, narrow fangs. I scrambled to my feet and inched closer to Connor, tucking the map into my pants.

Connor put his lips to my ear. "Looks like Priest did indeed set you up. Stay at my side."

I tried to absorb the meaning from his words, but a second vampire blocking the door demanded every ounce of my attention. An inhuman gleam blazed forth from the hollow craters resting on either side of his nose. He tilted his head, fixating on me with devilish orbs as if he meant to eat me alive. My legs tensed with the urge to run, but I stood frozen in fear by Connor's side.

The first vampire stepped in front of me, curling his finger toward his chest. "Hand over the map."

I held a guarded hand over the map and pressed it against my stomach. No way was I handing it over to that freak. I needed a way to escape with the map still in my possession, like a distraction of some kind. The streetlight flickered through the windows, its rainbow of colors shimmering over the surface of the holy water. The reflection was almost like a signal from God himself. My gaze followed the warm glow cascading down the side of the altar. Nestled inside and tucked away into a corner lay a wooden crucifix. My gaze bounced back and forth between the holy water and the wooden cross, feeding my brain a dangerous distraction.

A thin layer of cold sweat coated my skin. Running a finger over my mother's necklace, I mouthed the words, *Watch over me,* before bolting forward and seizing the crucifix and stashing it inside my jacket. I shoved Connor out of the way and thrust both hands into the basin of holy water, splashing all the water into the air and dousing the first vampire. A hissing noise, like a tea kettle on the verge of boiling, rose from the surface of his exposed skin. The stench of burnt flesh polluted the church. Flailing his arms, he ran in circles, squealing in a high-pitched tone.

A second scream sounded, but distant and faint. Had it come from the second vampire? I whipped around and faced the front door. He remained at his post, arms crossed, chin held high, watching the events play out with a slight smirk, seemingly amused by the pain inflicted on his hysterical comrade. Who had screamed? I turned in a circle, scanning the space around me. Where was Connor? Had I unintentionally drenched him with holy water as well? Panic burned inside my chest as my gaze darted around wildly, searching for him, and I caught a glimpse of his combat boot behind the altar. I dashed over to where he lay motionless on the floor, his face and hands charred. My stomach clenched, and guilt consumed me. *I did this to him.*

The first vampire sailed over the altar and pounced on me, knocking me to the ground. His razor-sharp fingernails flew at my face, but I ducked, and he struck empty air. I sent my knee smashing into his gut with enough force to knock him off-balance. He quickly sprang to his feet, tackling me and snapping at my neck with his fangs. There was only one choice I could make: either to save my life or to take his. I gripped the crucifix inside my jacket, and with every ounce of human strength, I flung it upward, burying it deep inside his undead heart.

A loud grunt spilled from his lips as he collapsed on top of me. I shoved him away and scurried backward. Unbelievably, he staggered to his feet and lunged at me. Why the hell wouldn't he die? Maybe he came equipped with nine lives, like a cat. Growling out a warrior cry, I charged forward and thrust the crucifix deeper, watching it disappear inside his body. His chest split wide open, expelling his gift of immortality. A pitiful groan-rattle passed his lips as he faded away. His body crumbled to vampiric ash and littered the church floor.

The soft whoosh alerted my ears, signaling that the second vampire had abandoned his post. I didn't have time for fear. Adrenaline flooded my bloodstream, coursing new strength into my body. I dove for the crucifix resting in the middle of the first vampire's remains. A blur flashed before my eyes. I swung the crucifix savagely and struck only air. The second vampire grabbed me from behind, tightening his arms around my waist. His icy breath stung the back of my ear as he snarled, "You will kill no more of my kind."

The throbbing rhythm of my blood conveyed a resounding message. I needed to survive and fight. I couldn't let him win. "Yes, I will... at least one more," I declared, hurling the crucifix at his chest.

He flicked it away with one finger and seized a chunk of my hair, jerking my head backward. A pinching sting scurried over my scalp as the strands were stretched to their limit. I cried out, grabbing my hair with both hands and snatching it from his grip. He latched onto my throat instead, pressing his blackened lips against my face. His incisors lengthened into lethal switchblades as he ran his tongue along my neck. The scent of death and decay carried sickeningly on his breath. Bitter bile filled my mouth, and the irresistible urge to spit came over me. I did just that, spitting directly into his face. He only laughed wickedly, the unnatural shimmer of his eyes fading to pitch black. His unclean lips spread as he said, "What a treat you will be."

He wanted to drain my blood to the last drop, but my will to survive grew a thousand times stronger. Kicking my foot into his side, I broke free and lunged for the cross. He caught me by my ankles and yanked me upward, swinging me around and around, before releasing me and letting me plummet.

I fell face-first, spiraling toward the altar. The church whizzed past me in a blur. I tried to latch onto something, anything, to break my fall, but my hands clutched at empty space. I struck the floor, spinning toward the wooden pews. My back slammed into the bench, and I ricocheted off its rough surface, my body skidding to a stop in the center aisle. Sharp pain gripped my core as stinging heat spread into my limbs. I grew cold—numbingly cold. My consciousness slipped, muddling my surroundings into the advancing darkness.

****

Excruciating spasms jarred me awake. There was a dull, throbbing pain in my left arm, and the muscles felt stretched and strained, as though they were pulled in different directions, rushing blood into my fingertips and making them tingle. The feeling of weightlessness I experienced was like floating on a gentle breeze as my feet dangled in the air.

A hissing sound came from directly above me. My gaze darted upward. I wasn't floating; I was hanging! The vampire's bony hand gripped my upper arm as he hovered at the highest point in the church's arched ceiling. Fear crept up my throat. *He's going to drop me again and let me fall to my death.* I scrambled to come up with a plan. *Weigh him down. Force him to land.* The spasms surged up my spine, sending a piercing shriek into my mouth. Clenching down on my jaw, I suffocated the urge to release it. I needed the element of surprise as I latched onto his ankle with my free hand. That seemed to catch him off guard as he loosened his grip, allowing me a brief moment of victory to wrench my other hand free and circle it around one of his knees. He dropped down a notch or two, hissed at me again, and then dug his nails back into my arm. The power behind the pain weakened my grasp, forcing my hand to slide down his knee toward his ankle. *Dear God, please, don't let me die.* At that moment, I lost all concern and let out a high-pitched screech.

"Stay still," Connor ordered as he hovered next to me—his body completely healed. But the vampire holding me captive was his focus.

"Help me!" I screamed at him.

"Hang on. I'll come back for you." He flew past me, with his arms plastered to his sides and his feet angled downward, soaring with preternatural speed.

"Connor, no!" I cried. "He'll drop me!"

He glanced down at me, his eyes burning with certainty. "Trust me."

The vampire clung to my arm and I to his leg, our unnatural embrace seemingly vital to our survival. He whirled around to confront Connor, taking me with him. My legs whipped out from underneath me, flailing uncontrollably and awakening the agonizing twinges in my back. The pain splintered off into a thousand knives, impaling my spine. I wailed as tears streamed down my cheeks. "Connor!"

The vampire lashed out at Connor with his free hand, connecting with the right side of his head. A fiendish scowl distorted Connor's handsome face, and he unleashed a deafening roar, exposing his lethal incisors. His appearance chillingly overshadowed the gut-wrenching pain. The Connor I knew vanished, and this one slashed his fangs across my captor's throat, slicing it open to the bone. A waterfall of blood gushed from the vampire's wound as gray patches rippled across his perfect, youthful flesh. The vampire glanced down at me, a devilish smile touching his lips. He blew me a kiss before releasing my hand.

For one fleeting second, I floated, suspended in air. Then, gravity seized me, engulfing me completely and propelling me toward my demise. I squeezed my eyes shut and prayed, "Dear God, have mercy on me. Save me. Let me live, please!" Arms encircled my waist, bringing the spinning to a halt. My prayers were answered.

Connor touched us softly down upon the church floor as he cradled me in his arms. Gazing into my eyes, he sighed in relief. "That was far too close."

"I'm so sorry," I whimpered. "I didn't mean to burn you with the water. I thought I pushed you out of harm's way."

"I should've ducked and helped you out, but you went all slayer on me and caught me off guard." He scrutinized me thoroughly. "You definitely have William's blood flowing through your veins."

"Well, I had to do something."

He shifted his focus. "Your arm, it's bleeding."

"What?" I examined the red stain soaking through the sleeve of my jacket. "That vampire scratched me."

Connor reached for my wounded arm as he set me gently on my feet. The second I supported my own weight, excruciating pain brought me to my knees. Every breath triggered another spasm, and the bitter taste of bile rose in my throat once more. I clutched my back and cried out.

He knelt beside me, his voice rising. "What's wrong?"

"My back. It hit one of the pews when he threw me. Something's not right."

He scooted behind me to have a look. "There's blood. I need to lift your shirt."

"Okay, but hurry. It's stinging...bad." The edge of my shirt lifted away from my skin. The cold air seemed to numb the pain, and I could breathe a little easier.

"Jesus," he blurted out.

"What?" I strained to look over my shoulder. "Tell me what you see!"

"There's a piece of wood embedded in your back. I've got to get you to a hospital."

I latched onto his arm. "No! No hospital. We can't tell anyone what actually happened, and I'm not a good liar. I'll screw it up. We broke The Vow, and I'm a repeat offender. They'll call the police, and with my luck, it will be Reynolds. I'm already in enough trouble as it is."

"We all broke The Vow tonight, but..." He gestured toward the two mini-mountains of silvery ash. "...they're dead, and we're very much alive, so you might have a good point. We have no one else to back up our story." He pursed his lips, eyeing my wound, and shook his head. "No matter what, though, that's gotta come out."

"No hospital."

He picked me up and set me down on one of the pews. Sitting close to me and applying pressure to my wound, he insisted, "It's bad, Claire. You need a doctor."

"No hospital!" I shouted forcefully.

"Then I'll heal you myself, but I can't just smear blood on it like I did with your knee. You have to drink my blood."

"Drink? No way."

"It's the hospital or my blood. Make your choice."

A hospital bed, handcuffs, and Reynolds were all elements of the least desirable route. This was definitely not the path I wanted to take. I groaned. "Fine, you win. I'll drink your blood."

"Claire, this isn't a battle of wills. I'm trying to save your life yet again."

"I know, I know. I'm sorry, but drinking blood...geez. I mean, I've never done it."

"It'll be okay, I promise." He speared his wrist with his fangs and lifted it to my lips. "Drink."

"How do I know when to stop?"

"You'll know."

I believed him when he said his blood would heal me, but would it change me as well? Would I feel different? Would I still be me? I searched his eyes for the answer.

He took my hand and squeezed it. "There's nothing to be scared of. It won't change you. It'll just heal your wound. Now, drink."

As I touched my lips to his wrist and sucked in a stream of his blood, my heartbeat hammered against my eardrums. Warm copper fluid flowed past my tongue, rushing down my throat and spilling into my veins as it sought the foreign object. With every swallow, the splinter shifted—a wet, sticky gurgle escaping my wound as it inched its way out of my body. At the small of my back, I felt a strange tugging sensation that erupted with a loud pop. The splinter of wood ejected and bounced across the floor. The gaping hole fused closed as if invisible stitches were sewing my flesh back together. Little by little, the crushing pressure subsided, slowly fading away, as did the smarting pain. I let out a deep, gratifying sigh and stopped drinking.

He smeared his blood over the holes in his wrist, healing them. "Better?"

I wrapped my hand around his forearm. "Thank you so much, and once again, you saved me. Words alone aren't enough but thank you."

His eyes danced with the beautiful and bright fireflies once again. "You know, a kiss might be a better way to express your gratitude."

"We discovered the secret location of an ancient map, killed two vampires—in a church no less—survived nearly dying ourselves, and you want a kiss?"

A sheepish grin played across his face. "Pretty much."

I nudged him with my shoulder before lightly kissing his cheek.

He frowned. "That's not really what I had in mind, but I suppose it'll do...for now." Pointing to the remnants of the vampires littering the floor, he added, "We should leave. Others may come to check up on their progress. Make sure you have the map, and let's ditch."

The worst-case scenario flooded my brain—one of the vampires taking the map during the struggle and reducing it to ash, along with the rest of his body. I clutched at the waistline of my pants where I'd stuffed the parchment. The old paper crackled beneath my fingers. I uttered a soft, "Thank you, God," then latched onto Connor's arm again. "You're right, we should get out of here."

He held up my keys. "You've had a rough night of it, so I'll drive."

"I think you just enjoy driving...Or mine scares you?"

He chuckled while helping me to my feet and slipping his arm around my waist. "Perhaps...or maybe it just makes me feel chivalrous."

I let him lead me out of the church and back to the Jeep, even though I was quite capable of walking on my own. He settled back behind the wheel and started the engine, glancing at me in such a way as to fill my stomach with butterflies. "So, you do like me," he boasted.

"Stay out of my head," I protested.

He leaned over and kissed my cheek. "I can't."

Playfully, I pushed him away. "Cut it out and drive."

He snickered. "Yes, Miss Daisy."

"I need to close my eyes and get some peace and quiet just for a bit."

"Go right ahead. I know the way to your condo." He reached into the glove compartment. "Parking garage remote's in here."

"My parking space is on the second level, number 238. Or did you already know that too?"

"I did not."

"See, you don't know everything."

He pressed a finger to my lips. "Shh, no talking. Peace and quiet, remember?"

"Hmph." I waved him away before settling farther into the seat and closing my eyes.

It seemed only moments had passed when he tapped me on my shoulder. "We're here."

I rubbed at my eyes. "Did I doze off?"

"Indeed, your snoring was as loud as that of a bear."

"I was not snoring."

"Kidding." He ran around to my side and opened my door, offering me his hand. "Glad to be home?"

"For sure."

While waiting for the elevator, I rested my head on his shoulder, but on the ride up, we stood a short distance apart. As the elevator doors opened, he clasped our fingers together. Silence accompanied us to my unit, but not awkward silence. Rather, it was the kind of content that happens when no words need to be said.

Turning the key, I asked, "Would you like to come in?"

He swept his hand through his bangs and smiled. "I would like that very much." I held the door open, and he took a step forward, stopped, and cocked his head, reminding me of a dog who'd heard one of those high-pitched whistles. "A man just got in the elevator. Your unit number is in his thoughts."

I shooed Connor inside. "Ten to one, it's Reynolds." Shutting the door, I gave the front room the once-over. All clear. There is no visible evidence of vampire gear.

"Detective Reynolds?"

"Yes, he's investigating my parents' case. He's also the one hounding me lately. He persists in bringing up the issue of the cuffs, despite your efforts to erase my fingerprints. He recognized my Jeep in the park."

"Did he see you or just your Jeep?"

"I believe it was the Jeep, but Reynolds traced the cuffs back to Cops-R-Us. The store clerk told him a pretty blonde girl purchased them."

Connor winked at me. "Well, you are pretty."

I rolled my eyes. "I'm serious. I have to get him off my back."

"Let me handle it."

A brilliant plan began to take shape inside my head. "Your being here is perfect timing. Having a vampire as a guest in my living room could potentially throw him off."

"I'll do you one better. I'll enchant him and plant information in his brain."

"That won't mess with his head, will it?"

"It's harmless, I promise. He'll never suspect a thing."

The doorbell rang.

"Do it," I blurted out, waving him toward the couch. "Sit down. Oh, and take off your jacket."

Another chime sounded.

In a soothing voice, he said, "Relax, and answer the door."

I took a calming breath and swung the door wide open. "Reynolds, showing up at all hours is becoming a regular thing with you."

He looked as though he had pulled an all-nighter. Dark circles resided under his eyes, and his tie hung loose around his neck, the top button of his shirt undone. He merely nodded at my less-than-welcoming greeting and gestured toward the entryway. "May I come in?"

I stepped aside and waved him in. Reynolds stopped abruptly as soon as he saw Connor. A deep frown settled between his thick brows.

"Reynolds, this is Connor. Connor, Detective Reynolds."

Connor rose and offered his hand. "Pleased to meet you, Detective." He glanced at me. "Claire tells me you're working her parents' case."

Reynolds' expression relaxed a touch. "Yes, I have been."

Connor approached me and took my hand in his. "Any progress?"

Reynolds seemed fixated by our clasped hands. "Nothing new." He shook his head, as if attempting to regain his focus. "I'm here tonight about a different case."

What was it this time? The restraints? Marty? Stanley? "So to what do I owe the pleasure of your visit?" I asked, pouring nonchalance into my tone.

"The case from the park I mentioned to you before."

A gust of air lifted my hair when a blurred form dashed past me. I blinked and found Connor standing next to Reynolds with my map in his hands.

What the hell was he doing? An accusation crept up into my throat and lodged itself there. I couldn't afford to make a scene and stifled my displeasure, forcing a smile in the officer's direction instead.

Connor's gaze intensified as he locked eyes with Reynolds. "A man running through the park dropped this," he told the detective in a tone that left no room for argument. "The map belongs to the killer from the park."

Transfixed, Reynolds nodded, taking my map into his hands. When Connor released Reynolds, the beautiful jade color returned to his eyes, but the damage had already occurred. Reynolds blinked, shook his head, then folded the map, slipping it into the inside pocket of his coat. "What did the man look like?"

Connor blatantly lied, saying, "He sprinted right past us. From what I can recall, he was tall, stood at least six feet, and was wearing a long coat—black, I believe." He turned to me. "Right, Claire?"

I bit my tongue and nodded.

The muscles in Reynolds' face twitched as he jotted across his notepad. "Which park? What time?"

Connor fed him more lies. "Green Forest Park. We were sitting on the benches next to the fishpond at around eight or so."

Reynolds headed for the door, then stopped. "One more question."

I dug my nails into my palms. To hell with his questions. I wanted him to leave already. A pent-up scream was pushing its way out!

"Marty, the vampire you mentioned? The one who may know something about your parents' murder? He was reported missing. Records from The Vampire Center state you sat with him on the night he disappeared. Do you recall what time he left?"

I stood statue-like, staring at him. *Why? Why does this keep happening to me? It's happening because I'm letting it.* As I dug myself further into the mess, I found it more and more difficult to escape.

"I remember that night," Connor said, snapping his fingers and drawing me out of my trance. "Claire and I left The Center together. I saw Marty drive off on his bike." He pursed his lips and rolled his eyes up to peer at the ceiling. "Maybe around midnight or so."

Reynolds didn't move an inch, his gaze locked on me, searching my eyes.

I slowly nodded and forced the words out of my mouth. "Yes. It was about midnight."

Reynolds tapped his pen against his pad. After several minutes, he nodded before opening the door. "Claire, I'll be in touch."

After he had closed the door, I waited, giving Reynolds time to advance toward the elevator before I turned to Connor. "Is he out of earshot?"

"Yeah, he's in the elevator now."

I barreled toward him, unleashing a scream. I jabbed my finger into his chest. "You gave him *my* map. Why? I trusted you."

"Don't be mad...I can explain."

"Mad? I'm not mad. I'm furious! Like the brand of anger people feel when they see red." He reached for my hand, but I slapped it away. "Don't touch me."

He thrust himself in front of me. "I did it to protect you."

"No, no, no. You should have planted a seed in Reynolds' mind instead of offering up the entire garden.

"Claire, the map is dangerous. It almost got us killed. I gave it to him to protect you and to get him off your back like you asked."

I ignored the last part of his statement. "*You* decided for me." I clenched my fists. "That map was mine! You had no right to just give it away."

"Whether you believe me or not, that map was going to get you killed. I had to get rid of it."

His betrayal broke my soul. I sank to the floor and dropped my head into my hands. "Get out. Leave me alone."

He knelt next to me but didn't dare to touch me. "I can't leave you like this."

I couldn't stand the sight of him and scooted to the far corner of the room to escape. "I was a fool to trust you. You need to go. Leave now!"

His voice grew frantic. "Claire, please, I need to stay. Let me help you."

I glared at him. "I hate you right now. I don't want your help."

A pained expression overtook his face. "Don't say that."

"I need space. I don't want you hovering over me. Just go."

"Damn it," he grunted as he slammed his fist against the floor. Without another word, he left.

Holding myself together, I clung to my body. I failed miserably in my attempts to gather information. Despite my best efforts, I failed to hang onto the map. I was a horrible vampire hunter. William was probably rolling in his grave with shame. The message in his journal seemed simple: hunt, expose, destroy. I encountered so many obstacles. Just as I was on the verge of giving up, the thought "She knows" suddenly crossed my mind. I sat straight up and blurted out, "Pine Lake Memorial Park, Crypt 33657." I didn't need the map. I'd memorized her location. Come morning, I had a vampire to hunt.

CHAPTER 12

Early morning rays of sunlight drenched the treetops at Pine Lake Memorial Park. Inside the maze of graves, daylight wove between the branches and spilled over the freshly cut grass. With my mother's cross around my neck and my kill gear hidden in my backpack strapped to my back, I faced the towering crypts head-on. An overgrowth of vines crawled into every crevice, penetrating the aged stone. Their roots burrow deep, dislodging bricks and creating fractures in the once-sturdy structure.

Countless tombs stretched out before me in a daunting fashion, but I only cared about one—hers. She is the one who possesses knowledge. Despite Connor's words, I held onto the hope that she had some connection to my family. Trekking down the path, I surveyed the five-digit codes engraved over each doorstep, searching for hers.

As I patrolled the fifth row of tombs, a dull ache thumped against my temples. How could I continue this monotonous task of reading numbers? Had I already passed hers—overlooked it perhaps? As I twisted my head left and right in an attempt to relieve my headache, I caught a beam of light ricocheting off an ancient crypt inscribed with the words "Seek the truth within." Dirty footprints led up to its entrance, and the door stood slightly ajar. I squinted and focused on the number—33657. I blinked and read it once more. 33657. I'd found her!

I stood motionless, listening to my pulse throb inside my ears. A flutter of uncertainty brushed the walls of my stomach. I needed a solid plan. Marty and Stanley had both gained the upper hand, and I'd made serious mistakes. This time, I had to remain calm and in control of the situation—I had to become William. I glanced up and down the pathways to make sure I was alone. No one stood around me. I stepped into her doorway.

My hands trembled as I pushed the door fully open. It led me into a windowless, pitch-black chamber. The scent of rotting death and dried blood assaulted my senses. The urge to gag tickled at the back of my throat. I smothered the reflex, not wanting to utter a single sound. Maintaining the element of surprise might offer me a slight advantage. I kissed my mother's cross and quietly unzipped the backpack.

As my eyes adjusted to the darkness, I noticed a metal-framed coffin adorned with bronze roses pushed up against the right wall. It was breathtakingly beautiful, and the magnificent craftsmanship stirred my emotions. I kneeled before the elegant box and ran my hand over the embellished lid before slipping my fingertips underneath. The lid rose instantly, and inside lay a flawless porcelain doll. Her dark, coiled locks rested against a white velvet pillow, and her pale arms lay crossed above her chest.

In an instant, her eyes flew open, and I saw two glistening sapphires glaring back at me. Her scarlet lips curved wickedly, revealing her pointy blades of death. She floated upward and hovered over me, waving her finger. "It's rude to break into someone else's home, you know."

I leveled my gaze with hers and affirmed, "I only came for answers."

She landed and placed her face inches from mine. "What kinds of answers?"

"About my family."

Her sapphire eyes deepened in shade. "I don't believe your intention to be so benign. I honor The Vow, but I can't say the same for you, what with that bag of tricks you're carrying."

"They're only for my protection," I assured her.

A chilling laugh escaped her lips. "Do you think I would afford you the luxury of protecting yourself?" She tapped my cross. "And the little trinket around your neck won't save you either."

Stay in control. Challenge her. "Maybe, maybe not."

Her perfect brows came together and then relaxed. "Silly human. You could never escape me, should I wish to catch you."

"If I intended to run, I wouldn't have entered."

Her eyes widened before quickly narrowing. "Then ask me your questions."

Confidence flowed through me as I spoke. "A map came into my possession, which led me to your tomb. Do you know what the words 'she knows' mean? They were written by your crypt on the map."

Her wicked smile returned. "It means you're a fool."

"So then, you don't know?"

"No, I don't. But do tell me, does your blood taste as sweet as your brother's?"

The urge to charge straight at her flashed through my mind, but I quickly thought better of it and instead reached for my pack. I held a wooden stake in front of me and demanded, "Did you kill my brother?"

"Why would I kill my lover?"

I jerked my head backward, blinked, and shook off the shock. She wouldn't waste her time with a boy. "You're lying."

"Maybe, maybe not." She mimicked my words back at me.

As I uttered my words, I lost all control. "He could never love someone like you."

A malicious leer spread across her flawless face. "Someone like *me* can destroy someone like *you*."

I'd seen that look on a vampire before—eyes glazed over, hungry for blood...*my blood*. I lunged for the door, my free hand skimming over the metal latch. She darted in front of me, knocking the stake from my other hand and blocking my escape. I fought back, sending my boot flying into her ribcage, but she seized my ankle, flipped me upside down, and dragged me across the floor and hauled me inside her coffin. With my body pinned beneath hers, she ran her tongue over my throat, releasing the sting of her cold breath onto my flesh. I kicked and scratched, screaming as loudly as I could. Nothing fazed her. Then, I thought of my mother's necklace. With speed, I gripped the cross and shoved it against her cheek.

A shriek erupted from her mouth as she bolted from her coffin and threw me across the crypt. As my head struck the wall, the scene in the church resurfaced. This time, Connor wasn't there to save me. She lunged forward, ready to attack me once more. Her arms cradled me, bringing me close to her parted, icy lips. Her pointed fangs pierced my flesh and embedded themselves into the side of my throat. The copper scent of my blood filled the vault as it flowed into its new host. My limbs grew heavy, too heavy to lift. The sounds grew muffled, and my vision blurred. The once strong thump of my heart diminished into a pitiful whisper. I wasn't ready to die. I screamed for my life!

The crypt echoed with a loud whoosh as the door burst open wide and struck the wall. The sun's rays poured into her crypt, encircling her in a deadly embrace. An exasperated hiss emitted from her after tossing me aside and flying upward with remarkable speed. In a dark corner of the ceiling, she found refuge from the sun. In the final moments before my eyes closed, Detective Reynolds picked me up from the moldy floor and carried me out of the crypt.

CHAPTER 13

When I opened my eyes, a sterile white hospital room surrounded me. My body lay limp within the confines of a hospital bed. A bag filled with ruby-red blood trickled into a long clear tube, feeding into my vein. My eyelids felt heavy...too heavy, and they fought to close as I struggled to stay awake, but the darkness returned.

The next time I opened my eyes, I had no idea how much time had passed—minutes, hours, days? I couldn't be sure. The assault flashed in my memory—her deadly fangs piercing my neck. I grabbed my throat, feeling layers of gauze bandages surrounding it. I shunned the image and pulled the covers up to my chin. *How am I not dead? But, thank God, I'm not dead.*

A loud snore hit my ears, and I flinched. It was only Detective Reynolds. He was asleep at my bedside, his head propped against a pillow on the back of the chair. My gaze drifted past him to find Connor sleeping face down on a small cot, his feet hanging off the end. Lying back against the softness of the pillow, I moaned at the tenderness of my wound and closed my eyes. I should have listened to Connor. My life had become so complicated. I needed to remember I was human—powerless and easily expendable. I couldn't continue on this destructive path. Everything I'd done changed nothing. JJ was still missing, and my parents' killer still breathed free air. I had to let it go.

Reynolds stirred before running his hand over his face and then glanced at me. He sprang out of the chair and blurted, "Thank God. I'm going to find your doctor. I'll be right back."

Connor bolted upright in a similar fashion and turned his head in my direction. The warmth of fireflies shimmered in his eyes. Before I drew my next breath, he stood by my side, holding my hand. "I thought I'd lost you."

I squeezed his fingers. "You can't get rid of me that easily."

"You almost died, Claire."

A nervous tremor swept over me, and I shuddered from his words. Wanting to avoid the unpleasant truth in his words, I changed the subject. "Can I have a glass of water, please?"

He grabbed a pitcher from a small table nearby and filled a glass with water. With a furrowed brow, he handed it to me. "You need to take this vampire hunting thing more seriously."

Obviously, he wasn't going to let go of the reprimanding. I squeezed his hand as I took the glass. "You're right, and I will."

"Then no more slayer stuff, okay?" his voice was on the verge of pleading. "It's exhausting chasing after you, and that hospital cot is about as comfortable as a rock."

I genuinely liked him, but more so, I needed him. "I rather adore you chasing after me and sleeping in uncomfortable places just to remain at my side."

A charming smile touched his lips. "Is that your way of telling me you love me?"

"Wow...slow down. Let's start with like."

"Like's good."

"But I do owe you an apology," I said, using my most heartfelt tone. "You were right. The map almost got me killed. I should have listened to you. I'm sorry."

"You're alive. That's all I care about."

"Thank you for caring about me."

"Oh, and just so you know, Reynolds brought your Jeep back from the cemetery. It's safely parked in your garage."

"What about my backpack? Did he find it? If Reynolds has it, I'm in serious trouble!"

"Relax. I read his mind. Nothing in there about a backpack."

Before I could comment, Reynolds returned with a woman clad in a white coat and wire-rimmed glasses resting low on her nose. A large clip held her red hair away from her freckled face. She leaned over me, shining a light into my eyes. "Claire, I'm Dr. Walsh. How are you feeling?"

"A little tired."

"That's to be expected. You lost a lot of blood, and vampire bites can be somewhat complicated, as we rarely get a chance to treat them."

Her eyes glanced at the bag hanging by my bedside. "If your lab results come back normal, we can stop the transfusions. You're lucky to be alive. The detective here is a real hero."

Reynolds shoved his hands in his pockets and shrugged his shoulders. "Just doing my job."

Dr. Walsh peeled the bandage away from my neck. "Looks like the antibiotics are doing their job. No signs of infection."

Reynolds eyed my neck and asked, "What about rabies?"

I rolled my eyes. "Really?"

Tilting her head, the doctor appeared to be considering it. "An infected animal transmits rabies. As far as I know, vampires don't carry the disease."

"It's still a bite," Reynolds said.

Connor crossed his arms over his chest and groaned. "It's impossible for a vampire to be infected with rabies...or any other disease for that matter."

Dr. Walsh placed a hand on Reynolds' shoulder. "There you have it, straight from the horse's mouth." She approached the doorway and then turned to face me. "Claire, get some rest. I'll check in on you later."

As she exited the room, Reynolds called out, "What about vampire transformation?"

She waved away his comment, shaking her head as she kept walking.

Reynolds studied me carefully. "A vampire bit you. How do we know you won't turn into one?"

Connor shook his head and sighed. "If it were that simple, a surplus of newly turned vamps would be running rampant through the city." He gestured towards Reynolds. "You need to brush up on your vampire statistics."

Reynolds huffed. "Why don't you just enlighten me?"

Connor didn't hesitate to educate the detective. "It's relatively straightforward. A human must first agree to be turned. The vampire drains their blood, and then the human drinks from the vampire to be reborn as their fledgling."

Reynolds bobbed his head. "Makes sense." He glanced at me, then back at Connor. "Hey, I need to speak with Claire. Would you mind giving us some privacy?"

Connor turned to me.

"It's okay. I'll be fine."

Connor leveled a stern glance at Reynolds. "Go easy on her. She's been through a lot." He kissed my cheek before leaving us alone.

Reynolds sat in the chair and pulled it closer to the bed. Before he could say anything, I spoke first. "You want to know why I went to her crypt, don't you?"

"Yes."

"The map Connor gave you had a cryptic message on it. 'She knows' was written on the map by the location of her crypt. I went to see what she knew."

"That's my job. Who's the cop here, me or you?"

I heaved a sigh. "You."

"You're lucky I had the same gut feeling. What if I'd waited a day or two to investigate her crypt?"

His *what-if* turned my stomach. I shivered and sank deeper inside the covers. "You saved my life. I'm eternally grateful, but what about my family? Who's finding justice for them?"

He pointed a rigid finger at himself. "I am. Putting away the bad guy is what I do. You need to remember that."

I twisted the blanket between my fingers. "But I know things you don't."

"Like what?"

"Before she tried to kill me, she told me JJ was her lover."

Reynolds nearly fell off the chair. "What?"

"See what I mean? I know I'm in the wrong, but how would you have learned that? You need to find out if what she said is true."

Reynolds' shoulders slumped forward. "The vampire abandoned her crypt. I don't have a shred of evidence to go on. Hell, I don't even know her name. Tracking her down won't be easy."

"You have to try. Promise me you will."

"I told you, I *never* give up."

CHAPTER 14

A week's time out of the hospital seemed to cool my need for retribution, or possibly the deadly vampire encounters and the scar left behind on my neck that kept my slayer compulsions at bay. I even put the volunteering on hold. A vampire sitting in my chair and tempting me wasn't a good idea. For now, I sat around my condo, staring at the walls and obsessing over the doll-like vampire being JJ's lover, but the idea of the two of them as lovers was ridiculous and farfetched. However, as a suspect in my parents' murder case, she satisfied most, if not all, of the criteria. Heck, she could've even been responsible for sending both Stanley and the two vampires from the church after me. Apparently, The Vow held no meaning for any of them. The chime of my doorbell interrupted my thoughts. Each night at seven o'clock on the dot, Connor paid me a visit. Tonight, it seemed, would be no exception.

I pushed off the couch, stretching and yawning as I opened the door. There he was, combat boots and all. His eyes traveled down my pajamas, then back up to my face. He drew his brows together. "You're wearing pajamas. What's wrong? Are you sick?" He didn't wait for me to answer, scooping me up and carrying me to the couch. He propped me up with some pillows before stepping back and staring at me. "You look pale. I'll get you some orange juice."

"Stop fussing. I don't need any juice. I'm just a little tired, is all."

"I can't stand seeing you like this." The brilliant glow in his eyes dimmed, reminding me of a used-up fluorescent bulb. "I have to do something. Let me take care of you."

I pulled him down to sit beside me and rested my hand on his knee. "Some orange juice would be wonderful."

He sprang to his feet and jogged to the kitchen. "One glass of OJ, coming right up." The refrigerator hummed as he opened its door. "Hey, I've been doing some digging, asking around about JJ."

I jumped off the couch and ran into the kitchen. "Did you find anything?" He handed me the glass, and I abandoned it on the counter. "Well, did you?"

He offered a thumbs up. "I did. There's a vampire who says he has information about your brother."

I crossed my arms and huffed. "Like I haven't heard that one before."

"This is different. I know the vampire well. He is traditional, unpredictable, and dangerous, but if we adhere to his rules, he will provide us with the necessary information."

"Hmm, I don't know. My conversations with vampires have never ended well."

He placed his hands on his chest. "I'm a vampire, and we're doing just fine together."

"That's different." My love for my brother made me ask, "Who is this vampire anyway?"

"Name's Gabriel. He owns a club called The Cave. We have a history together."

"Good history or bad?"

He tilted his head slightly. "A little of both."

My need-to-know switch flipped on, and I demanded, "I want details."

"It's complicated."

I conjured up my most stubborn glare. "I've got time."

"Later. So, are you in? Want to go talk with him?"

"First, explain. What aren't you telling me?"

He fixed his eyes on mine as he said, "I've lived a lifetime more than you. There are many skeletons in my closet. I don't feel comfortable sharing some of them with you."

"You can't scare me away. I *want* to know."

"Some things are better left unsaid."

"When you want to know something about me," I pressed my fingertips to my temples, "you just get inside my head. I can't do that, so you need to give me something...something of substance."

"I see your point." His eyes darkened as a painful expression overcame him. "Very well. Before The Vow, blood controlled me. My every thought revolved around who to kill, where to hunt, and when to feed. I left trails of dead bodies behind, baiting more than a few slayers to come after me. As long as I ensured my survival, I didn't care who I fed upon." He released a sigh. "Is that more along the lines of what you wanted?"

I held him in my gaze, moving closer—so close that our bodies touched. "Yes, and thank you for confiding in me."

His brows pulled inward as he regarded me. "That doesn't frighten or upset you?"

"You're not that person anymore."

"There's one other thing I should tell you," he said, rubbing at his jaw. "Gabriel, the vampire I'm taking you to see, is my maker."

An excited quiver shifted through me. "Really?"

"Yes," he answered, his tone guarded. "We parted ways after The Vow came into effect. We experienced a significant disagreement. Gabriel sees following The Vow as a weakness, favoring humans while repressing one's natural vampiric nature. I, on the other hand, wanted to surround myself with mankind and bury the most brutal aspect of my vampire instincts."

I took his hand and squeezed it. "You're anything but weak, Connor."

He forced a smile. "In Gabriel's eyes, I'm a waste of his immortal gift."

"Well, he's wrong."

"You humans are quite adoring. Gabriel doesn't know what he's missing."

I nudged his shoulder with mine. "So let's go have a chat with him."

"Okay, but no slayer stuff tonight, agreed?"

I ignored his request and hurried into my bedroom to change. I dressed quickly in jeans, a T-shirt, and a sweater coat. After pulling on a pair of boots, I rejoined Connor in the front room.

He snatched my keys off the hallway table and bounced them in the palm of his hand. "I'll drive."

"Do you even have a car?"

He tapped the tip of my nose with his finger. "I have no need for a car since I can fly. With you along for the ride, however, the Jeep it is."

"Whatever. Let's just go."

We made our way to the elevator, and my thoughts returned to JJ, stirring up morbid theories. If he had become a vampire, who was his maker? The vampire from the crypt? And where did that leave me? Would he still consider me his sister or just another warm body to feed on? I clutched at my sweater, pulling it tighter around me.

As the elevator descended, Connor wrapped his arm around my waist. "Are you all right?"

"I just need to know JJ's safe."

"Hopefully, Gabriel can shed some light on the truth."

"Hopefully."

When we exited the elevator, Connor hurried to my Jeep and opened the passenger door. As I stared straight ahead, he got into the driver's seat and started the engine. All my energy went toward my brother, but was I ready to learn his fate? "Wait," I said, placing my hand on his arm.

"What's the matter?"

"What if the news is horrible? What if..."

"Don't torture yourself with what-ifs."

"He's the only family I have left."

"And we'll find him."

"What if he doesn't want to be found? What if he's chosen an immortal life?"

"You don't believe that."

"Then why hasn't he reached out to me?"

"I can't answer that." His gaze softened. "But remember, whatever the outcome, you've got my shoulder to lean on."

"But you're immortal. I'll age, and then whose shoulder will I lean on?"

He laughed. "Whoa, you just jumped far into the future. That conversation doesn't have to take place for years."

"What does that mean?"

"It means that there's no rush. Besides, the present isn't the time or the place to get into that discussion."

"But I want to discuss it." I twisted in my seat. "I'll age while you'll stay frozen in time, and that contrast makes me anxious about any future we may have."

He flexed his fingers before gripping the steering wheel. "You don't get it. I've fallen in love with you, Claire. So it doesn't matter to me whether you're twenty or fifty."

I stammered to get words out of my mouth. "Wh-Wh. What did you just say?"

He laughed again. "I said I love you. I love everything about you. You're strong, independent, passionate, brutally honest, carelessly impulsive, and absolutely gorgeous." He paused. "The main reason is your blue eyes. They penetrate to the deepest parts of me, right down to my soul, and fill me with this incredible warmth, making me feel human again. I'm not going anywhere. You and I are forever."

Although my mouth was open, I was unable to utter a sound.

"Speechless?"

I found my voice and corrected him. "Forever isn't a part of my world, Connor."

"It could be."

I jerked backward. "Are you considering turning me?"

With a gentle voice, he replied, "Not today or tomorrow, but in time. With your permission, of course."

How dare he make such an assumption? A vampire had completely upended my life, taking away my parents and possibly even JJ. "You can't just blurt out something like that, especially after everything I've been through."

He fired back, "You wanted to go there. I asked you to let it go, but no, you had to press."

"And thank God I did. Now I know your true agenda—turning me."

He pressed his lips together in a hard line, and his voice rose as he said, "I don't have any agenda, hidden or otherwise. I'm not scheming behind your back. Is it so difficult to believe I just care about you and want to be with you?"

"You can't expect me to be grateful for the transformation just because I am a willing participant in *your* story."

"I don't even know what the hell that means."

"It implies that I'm not prepared to give up my human life, bid farewell to sunlight, and abandon everything I know," I threw at him.

As he spoke, he clenched his teeth. "Of course, I know about all the sacrifices. I've been there, lived through it, and I learned to adjust to the person I became. Besides, as you pointed out, what kind of future could we have if I didn't turn you? And yes, I do realize that I'm being selfish."

I scooted as far away from him as I could, bumping up against the door. "I'm done with this conversation. Just drive!"

After putting the Jeep into reverse, he floored the gas pedal, blasting out of the garage without saying a word. His eyes remained glued to the road without so much as a glance in my direction. I had every right to be upset, but what right did he have to be angry? He wouldn't even look at me, treating me as if all of the problems were my fault. How could he just sit there so calmly and quietly? He needed to explain himself, or at the very least, apologize. I threw my hands up and yelled, "I can't believe you!"

After swerving off the road, he slammed on the brakes, inhaling and exhaling slowly before speaking. "I didn't mean to horrify you, disgust you, or piss you off. All I meant to say was that I didn't want to live without you."

My anger remained unrelenting despite the warmth of his statement. I turned away from him and rested my head against the window, refusing to respond. My attention remained on the scenery outside the window as he groaned theatrically. The Jeep surged forward as it gained speed and turned onto a winding road. After descending its steep slope for some time, we finally reached the bottom of the hill. Taking a sharp right, he entered a parking lot facing the ocean.

The moon hung low in the star-kissed sky. When I opened my door, the low rumble of crashing waves greeted me, and the salty air cleared my head. Connor strode along the sidewalk, heading toward a lone structure claiming most of the street. Connor's swift stride separated us, yet I maintained my own pace, patiently approaching the building without pursuing him. My gaze roamed over the intricate detail of the rock siding making up the structure and the massive boulder-like door guarding the entrance. It was a fitting entrance for a club named The Cave. The door must have been on a sensor, as it rolled open at Connor's approach. A dim glow flickered from inside the doorway.

"Are you coming?" he asked, looking over his shoulder.

"Yes, of course," I answered, catching up to him and crossing the threshold together.

Torchlights illuminated the narrow, barren hallway as we entered. A spiral staircase led to the lower floor, where a multitude of voices drifted upward, mingling together and too many for me to count. As I peered over the railing, silhouettes hid in the muted lighting below, taunting my gaze. Would these vampires honor The Vow? Was I in danger?

"You're safe here. No one will harm you, I promise."

Connor took my hand and escorted me downstairs and into the club. Although I believed he would protect me, I remained skeptical. He was just one vampire, but what if several surrounded me, wanting a taste of my blood? When I reached the bottom of the stairs, I let go of his hand to cling to his arm, realizing how exposed I was. Even with Connor's presence, an uneasy feeling lingered, reminding me how fragile my humanity was in a supernatural world. "I don't know, Connor," I said. "This place is full of vampires. It's starting to freak me out."

He cupped my face in his hands. "Look me in my eyes," he instructed, his tone adamant.

I didn't hesitate.

His orbs transformed, becoming bright. The brilliance held me spellbound, slowing the beat of my heart and the flow of my breath. A drug-like state of euphoria settled into my body, eliminating stress and tension. Everything around me altered into a shining web of beauty.

He broke our gaze. "I apologize for enchanting you, but I need you in a calm state right now, and that was the fastest way to get you there. Are you ready to continue?"

"So ready."

Gray-toned walls were illuminated by floating lights from the rocky ceiling. Blood carafes garnished the lacquered bar tables, releasing an intense odor of salty-sweet blood. Many patrons were wearing elaborate jewelry and piercings, and their flawless marble flesh was covered in dark clothing. Although they were not humans, these beings were drinking blood, conversing, and relaxing, like humans. They were creatures of the night. In the dim light, their eyes glimmered, constantly aware of what was going on around them, observing every movement in the room with predatory grace.

I shivered as an unsettling chill swept over me. The air around me was suffocating as I sensed their eyes darting in my direction, hungry for the blood I carried within. I moved closer to Connor and whispered, "They're looking at me like vultures."

"Stay focused on me," Connor instructed, turning my head to face him. "All vampires can employ the same methods I used to calm you. However, if vampires combined their efforts, the level of sedation and influence would be significantly more potent. These vampires can cloud your mind, making it impossible to discern the truth from manipulation." He locked a protective arm around me and steered me in the opposite direction of the hungry flock and toward the chrome-accented bar.

A vampire with tattoos painted all over his pale skin slid off a barstool and slapped Connor on the back. "Well, if it isn't my long-lost pal, Connor." Stroking his fingers over his braided goatee and squinting at me with his stormy-gray eyes, he cocked his gleaming bald head in my direction and pointed a finger at me. "And you must be Claire."

Connor moved his hand to the center of my back. "Claire, Gabriel. Gabriel, Claire. She's the girl I told you about."

A grin spread across Gabriel's face, revealing blood-stained fangs. "Aren't you a pretty little thing?" He nodded at a table to his right. "Let's sit and chat." He led us to the table, which was away from the chatter surrounding the bar. Pulling a chair out for me, he said, "Please, sit."

A female vampire brought a carafe of blood and two glasses to the table, as well as bottled water for me.

Gabriel sized me up with his oddly colored eyes. "So, you're the blonde who's been running around town chasing after vampires." He chuckled. "I pictured a lioness, but you're no more than a mouse." He raised his brows. "A beautiful mouse, but still only a mouse."

I huffed. "I'd hardly categorize myself as a mouse. Could a mouse survive four vampire attacks? I think not."

"And feisty too." He glanced at Connor. "I see why you're so taken with her."

Connor drummed his fingers on the table and spoke with an edge to his tone. "Then you can also understand why I want to help her. Tell us what you know about her brother."

Gabriel leaned back in his chair and hooked his arm around the back. "What's the hurry? Let's catch up first. I'm curious to hear how you two met."

Connor leveled a stern gaze at Gabriel. "We're not here to play games. Get to the point."

Gabriel held up his hands in surrender. "I'm not playing games. Loosen up, Connor. Have a glass of blood." He glanced at me. "You don't mind, do you, Claire?"

Before I could answer, Connor retorted, "Some other time."

"That's right. I forgot. You prefer to settle for The Center's blood. I vividly recall our hunting days before The Vow clouded our memories." He barked out a laugh. "You were quite a resourceful bloodhound back in the day."

"He respects The Vow," I interrupted, casting a scolding gaze toward him. "Do you?"

Connor grabbed my hand and murmured in a tone of warning, "Claire, don't."

Gabriel narrowed his eyes at me. "What do you know about it? You didn't live through it as one of us. We lost our rights and freedom. Some resent that. I'm one of them." He spread his arms wide, a satisfied smile animating his face. "That's why I created The Cave. The blood I serve doesn't have to be fed through a tube."

"You're right. I can't speak from experience, but I do know The Vow allows both species to coexist. You don't hunt us, and we don't hunt you."

Gabriel exploded with laughter. "That's a case of the pot calling the kettle black, don't you think?" He leaned across the table. "You hunt. You kill. You broke The Vow."

Oh, he was good, attempting to push all the right buttons to get a rise out of me. He wanted to play games. I'll play along. Leaning back in my chair, I mustered up my most smart-assed brand of glare. "An eye for an eye."

Connor jumped in, steering the conversation back to JJ. "Look, you agreed to share your information about her brother. Can we stop the pissing match and get down to business?"

Gabriel jutted a finger at me and raised his voice. "You can't trust her. She'll choose her brother over you. Put your life in danger to save him."

I clenched my hands beneath the table as I too raised my voice. "I would not."

Connor pushed his shoulders back and held his chin high. "I trust her."

"You're blinded by your feelings for her," Gabriel accused. "She did douse you with holy water, did she not?"

I stared unbelievingly in Connor's direction. "You told him that?"

"Yes, but he's misinterpreting it," Connor clarified.

"We're brothers," Gabriel asserted. "Blood brothers. He feels pain; I feel pain. Something a human couldn't begin to comprehend."

I glared at Gabriel. He employed nasty tactics, trying to make us turn on one another. "I understand more than you know."

Gabriel stared me down with an even weightier scowl than I'd given him. "He's your link to the vampire world. How far will your search go without him? Maybe you're just pretending to care for him so he will aid you in finding your brother. I'm confident you're using him."

Uncertainty flashed in Connor's eyes as he directed his gaze in my direction.

I tossed my hands in the air and protested, "You can't honestly believe him. He's making up this crap to plant a seed of doubt." I intertwined our fingers. "I care about you, and you know it."

Gabriel raised his brows and grinned. "Let's test her devotion. See how real her feelings are."

"Go ahead, test me," I challenged.

Gabriel looked over our heads, centering on something or someone in the background, then executed a sharp nod. The next instant, a pair of gloved hands ripped Connor from his chair, coiling a silver chain around his neck and twisting it tightly into a noose. A piercing wail, one that sent shivers down my spine, erupted from Connor's mouth. Gray streaks scuttled beneath his immaculate ivory flesh, devouring him from within.

My mind raced, screaming at me, *Get the chain off him!* I shot out of my chair, knocking it over in my haste, and shoved my fingers underneath the links, tugging at it as hard as I could.

Gabriel yanked me backward and barked out an order, "Sit down."

Connor's head dropped to his chest, and his arms fell limp at his sides, but the shrillness of his screaming continued. I cringed with every shriek. The gloved vampire pushed open a door behind the bar and vanished inside with Connor in tow. His muffled screams echoed on, torturing my ears. The sting of tears burned behind my eyelids as I locked my gaze on the door and blinked away tears.

"Look at me," Gabriel demanded, a tinge of delight coloring his tone.

I turned and met his eyes with a cold, hard stare. "Bring him back, you crazy freak."

He shook his head and chuckled. "Humans. You never cease to amaze." The sudden harsh cast to his brow ushered in a new seriousness to his words. "You're in no place to make demands."

I folded my hands on top of the table and sharpened my tone. "Get to the point. Tell me what you want."

He folded his arms behind his head, rocking back and forth in his chair. "A no-nonsense gal—I like it. Very well, I'll make you a deal. No, let me rephrase; I'll give you a choice."

"I'm not playing with Connor's life."

He let the chair come to rest on the floor and regarded me in a haughty manner. As he drummed his fingers on the table, he stated, "You can choose to save Connor from a slow, horrible death or hear the information I have about your brother. What'll it be?"

I bolted to my feet and jabbed a rigid finger in his face. "Bastard! That's cruel and unfair. You can't make me choose between two people I love."

Connor stopped screaming. Goosebumps prickled across my skin as my gaze cut to the door. Why had he stopped? "Please, tell me he's not dead."

He snickered. "He's alive...barely. In another fifteen minutes, it'll be lights out. Better hurry and make your choice."

In the face of Gabriel's words, I closed my eyes and imagined Connor's overconfident yet charming smile. It was his fiery eyes that always warmed my heart. How he constantly swept his hand through his bangs was adorable. Did he ever take off his leather jacket and combat boots? He was always there for me. He had slept in my hospital room, gave me his blood, and saved my life a few times. If I had to save one of them, Connor was the one present, and poor JJ might already be dead. I blurted out, "Connor. I choose Connor."

"Excellent choice," he murmured, wearing a pompous smirk. He clapped his hands and shouted, "Bring him back!"

The door opened, and two vampires emerged. Each held one of Connor's arms, dragging him across the floor toward the table—the chain still wound tightly around his neck. Gray patches covered his skin, and his head hung forward, swaying limply back and forth. All traces of life appeared to have vanished from him. My hands flew to my mouth and I smothered a horrified gasp.

Gabriel glanced at me and said, "Relax, he's not dead." He faced the vampires and pointed at the chair next to me. "Put him there and remove the chain."

The vampires set Connor in the chair and removed the chain from his neck. Connor slumped forward, his head striking the table. I gently lifted his face to discover a dark and vacant stare left behind in his once bright eyes. "Connor," I said softly, "stay with me." He blinked, and sparks of recognition came to life. I glanced in Gabriel's direction and demanded, "Now what?"

"Five pieces of silver are imbedded in his neck. Human blood will flush them out. Offer him your blood."

I didn't flinch or hesitate and turned to Connor. Stroking his cheek, I urged, "My blood is yours. Take what you need."

Connor's voice was above a whisper. "No, Claire. I can't."

I cupped his face with my hands, and as if we were the only two people in the room, I said, "It's my turn to save you now."

His breaths were shallow, and he forced out each word. "Might—not—be—able—to—stop. Can't—live—with—that."

"I can't lose you. I trust you with my life. Connor, please, you must drink."

"I love you," he breathed, cradling my head in his hands. His soft lips touched my neck, spreading to allow the tips of his fangs to press into my skin. Only for a moment did my breath catch in my throat, then it flowed freely. I trusted my instincts. He wouldn't harm me.

He bit hard, stabbing my vein. Stinging pain shot up my neck—the most painful blood draw ever. A scream swelled inside my throat. He tugged, pulled, and sucked on my neck. Burning pain spread through my flesh as he gorged on my blood. My vital fluid willingly jetted from my veins and into him. Shouldn't one of the pieces have ejected from his body by now? As if I possessed telekinetic powers, a chime responded with the metal bouncing onto the floor. I fought the impulse to thrust my arm up in victory as four more needed to fall. Another clang sounded off to my left. *Number two.* I sat still, straining to hear numbers three, four, and five strike the ground. A double ping signaled the fall of numbers three and four, as they broke free from his skin simultaneously. The final piece fell, rolling across the floor. I'd passed Gabriel's test. I collapsed against Connor, exhaling a deep breath of relief, but he refused to release his hold. He'd only tightened his grip, drinking with vengeance.

Maybe he didn't realize that all five had come out and he was in the clear. In a steady, calm voice, not wanting to let doubt filter through, I said, "Connor, it worked. All the silver pieces have been removed. You can let go now."

He ignored me, releasing a muffled growl. Pulling me farther into his heated embrace, he sank his fangs deeper into my flesh.

My mind raced, searching for a way to reach him. Random words popped into my head, but nothing substantial. I blurted them out anyway. "Stop! This is *my* blood. I trusted you. Let go...now!"

He broke the hold, but only briefly, before latching onto me again, his fangs embedded in the flesh of my neck, though he did not drink.

Were my words getting through? I had to keep trying. "Connor, can you hear me? The silver's out. You're safe." His raspy breath moistened the base of my throat. My ears picked up on the rapid pounding of his immortal heart against mine. What could I say to distract him, to bring back the Connor I loved? Tell him! My voice cracked with emotion. "I love you, Connor."

He loosened his arms and sat very still. The loud panting tapered off to an even rhythm. Dislodging his fangs and pushing away from me, he met my eyes. A boyish smile claimed his lips as he asked, "Did you say you love me?"

My gaze wandered over his healed ivory flesh, which appeared a thousand times more striking than before. I blushed and confirmed, "Yes, I love you." My heart pounded in my chest, echoing the vulnerability and excitement that now enveloped me as if baring my soul had stripped away all my defenses.

The fireflies returned, lighting up his jade eyes. "You saved my life."

"Just like you saved mine."

He punctured his finger and pressed the bloody tip to my neck. "I love you too."

Gabriel scooted his chair between us and teased, "Aw, how touching."

Connor gripped Gabriel by the shirt and shouted in his face. "You almost killed me, you asshole."

Gabriel laughed, pushed Connor away, and smoothed out his shirt. "Come now. I knew she would cave. Worst-case scenario, had she refused, I would've grabbed a human off the street to heal you."

Connor shoved his chair backward and slammed his fist into the table, cracking it. "Unbelievable."

Gabriel shrugged half-heartedly. "Well, I couldn't have her weakening my bloodline. I had to be certain of her intentions."

"It's all so simple for you," I shouted at this infuriating vampire.

Gabriel huffed. "It's never simple."

The veins in Connor's forehead surfaced and pulsated rapidly. "What you did to me—to Claire—was unspeakable, yet you sit there so smug."

"My actions may appear unreasonable," Gabriel explained, "but until you create immortal life, you will never understand the dire need to protect it. I could never put you in danger."

"Claire would never hurt me," Connor stated with conviction.

Gabriel fingered his goatee. "Now, I am sure of it."

"Vampires slaughtered my parents and possibly kidnapped my brother," I enlightened him. "Yes, I went to extreme measures to learn the truth, but I would do nothing to bring harm to Connor."

"We've established that. Let's move on."

"Does this mean you'll still provide me the information about JJ?"

Connor glared at him. "After the stunt you pulled, you'd better start talking."

Gabriel rolled his eyes at Connor. "Relax. Don't go all Rambo on me. Yes, I'll tell you. So let's get right to it. Your brother came to my club several months ago."

Connor reached for my hand.

I wasn't ready to trust him yet. "What makes you so sure?"

Gabriel tilted his head, eyeing me. "Well, he's blonde and blue-eyed like you."

"You'd better have more proof than that."

"Be patient; there's more. He looked to be about sixteen or seventeen, somewhat withdrawn and quite restless—not controlled like you."

"JJ's seventeen," I confirmed. "But the rest of your description doesn't sound like him."

"That's the boy I observed. He also carried a notebook, clinging to it as if it were his firstborn child. He bobbed his chin toward me. "And your name was scribbled all over it. If he wasn't your brother, he had a raging obsession with someone named Claire."

Gabriel's statements didn't add up, but he didn't seem the type to hold anything back. "Was anything else written on the notebook?"

A knowing grin spread on his lips. "Equations. Notes. Weird stuff."

Connor spoke up. "Be more specific."

Gabriel paused before responding. "The equations appeared to solve a problem. What, I'm not certain. He was definitely obsessed with vampires. He said our blood cured everything, and he wanted to become one."

That certainly didn't sound like JJ. Hanging out with vampires every day made him immune to their charms, even more so than the average person. I didn't buy it. "Why do you say that? What proof do you have he wanted to turn?"

"He wasn't shy about asking the vampires in my club to turn him. Came back night after night."

A chill overtook me. Did I really not know my brother? None of those descriptions sounded like the JJ I'd grown up with and loved. "Did he succeed?"

He ran his hand over his chin and tugged on his goatee. "Vampires have a code. No crazies. Your brother wasn't quite right."

His words lingered in my mind for a while. "What do you mean when you say that something wasn't quite right?"

Gabriel fixed his eyes on Connor. When their eyes met, an unspoken message seemed to pass between them. Connor nodded at Gabriel. "Tell her."

"He was off in his own little world, talking to people who weren't there, babbling on about formulas and other gibberish. No vampire would touch him," Gabriel stated flatly.

A sick feeling rolled around inside my stomach. What had happened to him during the years I'd spent in college? And what of the female vampire who claimed they were lovers? I had to see if Gabriel knew anything. "I met a vampire who claimed she'd tasted JJ's blood. Said they were lovers, but she never mentioned any bizarre behavior."

Gabriel threw his head back and bellowed with laughter. "You speak of Victoria." Keeping his laughter in check, he continued. "You invaded her crypt, offering up your thoughts freely to her. She read you like an open book."

"No," I challenged. "She mentioned JJ, not me."

Gabriel leaned forward, placing his hands on the table. "Are you daft? I said she *read your thoughts*. Victoria played you and lied to gauge your reaction. She does love a good game of cat and mouse."

"So you're saying she's *not* with JJ?"

"I'm saying...she's never met your brother."

"What?"

"Focus on the positive," Connor encouraged. "Now we know Victoria didn't turn him."

I couldn't let it go. "But what about the map? 'She knows' was written beside her tomb. It had to mean something."

"They're just words," Gabriel told me. "Priest and I go way back. The map is his most prized possession. Why he would offer it to you baffles my imagination."

A twinge of anger quickened my pulse. "I believe it's pretty simple. He plotted my murder."

"Why would he do that?" Gabriel asked.

Connor cast an exasperated stare his way. "Come on, you know he set her up."

"But why would he do that? What reason could he have?" Gabriel wondered.

"That's what we need to find out," Connor pointed out.

Gabriel leaned over the table, his gaze intense. "Maybe he only wanted to help himself to Claire's blood."

"He showed no interest in feeding off me."

"You don't know him like I do. Being a former servant of God, he struggles with the need to rob humans of their blood. He employs other vampires to carry out his nefarious tasks and gather the blood on his behalf."

"You're way off base on this one, Gabe. I was there, remember? Those vampires were after a lot more than a little blood."

"I think not," Gabriel said, unyielding regarding his theory.

I slumped in my chair. Another dead end. Were unknown forces conspiring against me? Why was there so much deception surrounding my parents' deaths and my brother's disappearance? Every lead seemed purposefully hidden to prevent me from discovering the truth. "You're saying Victoria had nothing to do with this, and the priest used the map to steal my blood, right?"

Gabriel nodded calmly. "That's precisely what I'm saying."

"No. There's got to be something more."

Gabriel scoffed. "You're a human and can be easily tricked."

Connor let out a disgusted snort. "Like you have it all figured out. You're surmising at best. Besides, we're not here to discuss the map or Priest. Do you have any other information that might help us find her brother or not?"

"That's all I know. He stopped coming to the club. I guess he got tired of hearing the word *no*."

"You said JJ didn't measure up to your code, but *how* off was he?"

Gabriel shifted his hands in the air like a balancing scale. "Middle-of-the-road crazy."

JJ was my brother. I knew him to be a highly intelligent, if not eccentric, geek. All this speculation meant nothing, yet a tiny sliver of doubt crept into my heart. Now more than ever, I needed to find him. But I knew I couldn't do it alone. I needed help, but not of the vampire persuasion. I needed Detective Reynolds.

CHAPTER 15

Two days later, I sat inside the precinct, waiting to see Reynolds. Oddly enough, he had reached out to me about a new lead in my parents' case. Connor was at The Vampire Center and promised to join me afterward. I crossed and uncrossed my legs a hundred times as I watched the clock. The minutes crawled by: seven o'clock, seven fifteen, seven thirty. At nearly seven forty, he pushed through the double doors. "Claire, come on back. We're in the last room on the right." He pointed to an open door at the end of a short hallway. A sense of emptiness overwhelmed me. Regardless of the nature of the news, I remained composed. "I asked Connor to meet me here. Can you ask someone to bring him back when he arrives?"

"This doesn't involve Connor. When he gets here, he can wait for you in the lobby." Reynolds placed his hand on my shoulder and guided me into the room. He pulled out one of the chairs for me. "Have a seat."

The tabletop held scattered files, JJ's cell phone, the vampire map, and a set of keys. Several storage boxes, a computer monitor, and some video equipment occupied the far-left corner of the room. I eased myself into the chair, my eyes poring over the items. Could the files conceal any clues? Why display JJ's cell phone among them? Had Reynolds found out what the keys unlocked? What relevance did the map offer to the rest of the items? "Why is all of this here?"

Reynolds placed his hands on the table's edge and shook his head. "This case has baffled me like no other in my career. I've gone over it and over it, and I always come back to the beginning. Do you know why that may be?"

"No, but I'm sure you're going to tell me."

He laughed. "You're right."

He moved his chair around, opposite mine, and flipped open one of the files, fanning out the pictures of my parents' dead bodies. I flinched and looked away. "How can you be so cruel as to show these to me?"

He put his hand on my arm. "I know it's hard, but I need you to look, please."

My hands trembled as I forced my gaze to fall back over them.

He pointed at the puncture wounds. "Why so many bite marks?"

He was right. There were too many. "Anger? Aggression? Extreme hunger?"

"I did some research." He drummed his fingers on the table. "There's one thing all vampire cases have in common." He sat back, allowing the tension to build. "Two puncture wounds per victim—no more, no less."

I scooted to the edge of my chair and leaned forward. "Then why so many on my parents?"

"I've asked myself that very question over and over, arriving at two conclusions. Firstly, more than one vampire was involved. It made me consider your brother's friends as suspects for a while." He rubbed a hand over his chin. "I rejected that theory and will explain why later, and secondly, your parents were not killed by a vampire."

My hands fell into my lap as I stared at him. After all this time, how could he drop a bombshell like that on me? "You assured me a vampire had killed them."

"Well, now, I'm saying that theory doesn't add up."

I shuddered and turned away, near tears. Because of my obsession over my parent's killer being a vampire—Connor, the priest, Gabriel, Victoria, the two unknowns from the church, Marty, and Stanley—they had all suffered or died, and for what? "Oh God," I murmured.

"Is there something you're not telling me?"

I lifted my head and glanced his way but said nothing.

"I believe there is." He pulled out his notepad. "I've been keeping track of your odd behavior. You broke into your parents' house, neglected to turn in your brother's cell phone, likely played a role in the park incident, led me on a perilous journey using a vampire map, and infiltrated a vampire crypt equipped with weapons intended for vampire hunters. And those are just the transgressions I'm aware of."

Dear God, he'd kept notes on me and had found the backpack! My brain scrambled to rectify the situation. "Yes, I screwed up. I believed that I could handle this case independently, but I was mistaken. I need your help, and that's why I came here."

"No, I asked you here."

"Yes, but I'd already planned to call you, I swear. It's about JJ. Before he disappeared, he was seen at a vampire club called The Cave. Apparently, he was begging vampires to turn him."

He sat back, shaking his head in disbelief. "Was he turned?"

"The vampires wouldn't touch him."

"Why's that?"

It hurt to say it out loud. After a long pause, I forced the words from my lips. "They thought he was crazy."

"Is he crazy?"

"Not the JJ I know. We need to locate him."

"We'll find him. Don't you worry. I also have new information about your brother, which is part of the reason why I called you in."

I gestured to the clutter on the table. "Does it have something to do with this stuff?"

"Yes." He picked up the keys and pointed to the one with the red rubber coating. "I know you said you didn't recognize these but look again. Maybe something will come to you."

I squinted, examining it. "No, nothing."

"It's a key to a storage unit in Mount Laguna, registered to your parents."

"Mount Laguna? I don't—I never knew about any storage unit."

He nodded in the direction of the boxes and equipment in the corner of the room. He said, "I found these in the unit. The boxes are full of journals and video memory cards dating back to 1990. The last recording was shortly before your parents' death." He pointed to the computer. "I've got the first memory card loaded. Shall I hit play?"

"Uh, yeah, of course. I want to see."

Reynolds tapped the remote. A snowy-white haze filled the screen. The camera adjusted focus until two blood-covered vampires materialized. Each vampire, bound to chairs by silver-plated chains, slumped forward, their bodies motionless. Countless wooden stakes penetrated their skin, causing dark blood to accumulate around their bare feet. One whimpered while the other remained dead silent.

I stiffened and gripped the edge of the chair. This video couldn't belong to my parents. They wouldn't keep anything so vile. Reynolds must have been mistaken. The camera jiggled as if someone had bumped it, and then a male voice shouted, "Vile creatures such as you do not deserve to share my world. You're nothing more than cockroaches without wings. Look at me when I speak." A female snickered in the background.

Dear God. His voice. Her voice. No, God, it can't be!

The point of a silver blade plunged into the whimpering vampire's chest. His bloodcurdling scream pierced my eardrums. An eerie silence followed, prompting another squeal of high-pitched laughter. Hands blocked the camera lens, shifting the angle onto a bare wall. Footsteps sounded as a man and woman came into view. I struggled to breathe. It was my mother and father! They thrust their fists collectively in the air and yelled, "Death to all vampires."

My trembling hands covered my face, but I couldn't look away. Who had my parents really been? For all the twenty years of my life, they'd kept me in the dark as to their true nature. Had it all started with William, passed down in our blood? Our legacy? Well, it certainly wouldn't be mine. I glared at the screen and shouted, "Turn it off."

Reynolds killed the image and rubbed gently at my shoulder. "I'm sorry, Claire. I had to be certain you didn't know."

I clutched my stomach, nauseated, and slowly shook my head. "I didn't know. I feel sick. Can I have some water, please?"

"Of course. I'll be right back."

After he left the room, I broke into sobs. They had been laughing about killing those poor creatures, even taking pleasure in the act. How could they have been so horrible, so ruthless? The Vow had meant nothing to either of them. They had willfully defied it. Even William had hoped for a truce. Had JJ known? Had the knowledge destroyed him, or actually driven him mad? Could it be the reason he'd vanished? *Oh God, was he a vampire murderer too?*

"Claire." Connor said my name so tenderly, it sent my heart into a wild flutter. Desperate for a hug, I rushed into his arms. He pulled me into his embrace and stroked my back. "I'm here."

I glanced at Reynolds and whispered, "Thank you."

He had a six-pack of Coke under his arm, which he put down on the table. Shrugging his shoulders, he said, "He was making a scene in the lobby. This was the only way to shut him up." Reynolds pointed to the cans. "Thought this might be easy on a queasy stomach more so than water."

"Thanks."

Connor searched my eyes. "Are you okay?"

I rubbed my arms, trying to brush away the horrible, sickly chill. "I'm...I'm...I don't think there's even a word to express what I'm feeling right now. My parents never discouraged JJ or me from having relationships with vampires. Geez, I mean, Nate and Parker were constantly over at our house, and they even slept over some weekends and everything. It doesn't make sense. It's like they led double lives or something."

Connor peered over at Reynolds, his eyes glowing. "You've been busy collecting evidence. Maybe you can shed more light on all this?"

Reynolds gestured at Connor. "Don't get inside my head, or I'll throw your ass out."

"Very well. How does any of this involve Claire? Why show her such a morbid video? Was it simply to horrify her?"

"I've already explained myself to Claire." Reynolds gestured to the soda. "Let's all relax, have a drink, and discuss the case."

Connor popped a lid and took a couple of sips. "I do love a tasty can of Coke every now and then." He set the soda down and pointed to the boxes. "How many videos are there?"

"Hundreds, easy," Reynolds replied.

Connor noted, "That's equivalent to hundreds of deceased vampires."

Reynolds nodded and added, "For each vampire, there are multiple journals full of detailed notes."

I gripped my mother's cross tightly with my fingers, resisting the impulse to throw it across the room. "In 1990, they would've been around my age. That's quite a young age for them to hold such distorted beliefs."

"The documenting of their kills started then," Reynolds corrected. "I believe there were earlier kills before they became so...detail-oriented."

I rubbed my forehead, hoping I might wake up from this nightmare.

"Claire, do you object to me showing Connor the pictures of your parents? I need a vampire's opinion."

"That's actually a fantastic idea. Show him."

Reynolds flipped open one of the folders and passed it to Connor. "What do you see?"

He studied the photo, leaning in closer and furrowing his brows. He tilted his head left, then right. "Something's wrong."

"Go on," Reynolds urged.

"There are too many bite marks. Stranger still, some holes appear to be larger than others." He shook his head with conviction. "These bites were not made by a vampire."

Reynolds snapped his fingers. "Exactly what I thought."

"Who killed them then?" I demanded.

"I've got a theory, but hear me out, Claire, before you react."

I pressed my lips into a flat line, eyeing him. What was the detective up to now?

"We have to re-examine the evidence to consider how it might relate to your brother."

I slammed my hand against the table. "You're not pinning this on JJ. We don't even know what's happened to him. He could be hurt or abducted...or worse, and now you want to arrest him?"

Reynolds kept his voice composed and emotionless. "Calm down. I didn't say anything about arresting him. I just want to speak with him to find out if he knows anything."

"He's just a kid," Connor offered up.

Reynolds sighed. "I get that. He could've been frightened and gone into hiding. Maybe he doesn't know where to turn, but I do have evidence that suggests motive."

My throat went dry, and I struggled to keep my voice from cracking. "Connecting JJ?"

Reynolds didn't respond right away. A pained look clouded his eyes, and he laid his hand on my shoulder yet again. "Nate and Parker were your parents' final victims."

I sagged in the chair, the edges of my vision blurring. My parents had killed JJ's best friends. JJ was missing. Stanley had told me to look to the living. Reynolds had his suspect—my brother. I just needed to get to him first.

CHAPTER 16

The following night, I stood in front of the entrance to The Cave. Gabriel was the sole source of information that could lead me to JJ, who could potentially have ties to the murderer of our parents. Finding justice for my parents was not a priority for me. I wanted to abandon their memory. They'd fed me nothing but lies my whole life and had turned out to be hideous monsters who'd tortured and killed vampires. Nonetheless, I still held love for them deep down inside my soul. I wouldn't be able to rest until I'd found their killer.

After the stunt Gabriel had pulled, Connor would've never agreed to my returning to The Cave, especially alone, but it was a no-brainer for me. Hopefully, Gabriel wouldn't make my second visit to The Cave as chilling as the first. JJ had spent time with these vampires, even seeking to become one of them. Maybe a vampire, or several, might remember something—anything—to help me find him. I knocked on the door a few times, but it remained closed. It didn't open automatically for me as it had for Connor. I ran my fingers over the rough surface, searching for a sensor or some hidden trigger to grant me access. The hinges let out a faint creak as the door rolled wide open. I shuffled back a step. Had I triggered something? It didn't matter. This was my admittance ticket.

"Wait," a male voice called out from behind me. "A vampire must escort you inside."

Two male vampires dressed in black glided toward me. Their dazzling, diamond-like eyes shimmered in the darkness. The first entered the club without so much as a glance in my direction. The second, and taller of the two, stopped just inside the doorway. The magnificence in his eyes took on a blinding glow. Was he attempting to enchant me—lure me? I threw up my hand, shielding my eyes and blocking the power of his stare.

"Ouch," he retorted. "I'm not used to being rejected." He chuckled. "You can put your hand down. I got the message. I'll still take you inside if you'd like."

Hesitantly, I peeked through my fingers. His eyes remained subdued, so I dropped my hand. "Thank you. I'm actually looking for Gabriel."

He waved me in, and the door closed behind us. "He rarely leaves the bar. I'm sure you'll find him there." He tipped his head to me before vanishing down the stairs.

I hurried along the hallway illuminated by torches, feeling a surge of butterflies in my stomach. I reminded myself of why I'd come—for JJ. Growing up, we'd always had each other's backs. In seventh grade, a multitude of boys flocked around me, seeking my favor. Such behavior had made the other girls jealous and cruel. I was once rummaging through my locker, grabbing books for class, when ice-cold water doused me from head to toe. Soaking wet, I'd gasped aloud, stumbling backward and dropping my books into the wet puddle on the ground. When I'd whirled around, three girls came into view, squealing with laughter. They had begun chanting, *Drowned rat, drowned rat, drowned rat.* Humiliated, I'd bolted from the school, run all the way home, and collapsed onto my bed, sobbing.

Later that day, JJ entered my room and handed me his favorite GI Joe figure. "Don't cry, sis," he had said. "General Hawk will protect you." His sentiment and the expression on his little face came back to me in my darkest moments when I needed to soldier on. Now, it was my turn to protect JJ, and Gabriel was going to help me—whether he liked it or not.

As I descended the dark spiral staircase, cold air swirled around my warm flesh. Purposely, I blew out my breath, and it danced before my eyes. Did the deadly chill radiate off a much larger number of vampires than had been present for my previous visit? Was the blood I carried inside me in jeopardy? Perhaps it was, but I hadn't traveled this far only to retreat. I needed answers about JJ. Dwelling on the danger wasn't a luxury I could afford. I bravely ascended the stairs two at a time, fortifying my resolve as I ventured into the perilous environment below.

Weaving through the swarm of immortals and dodging thirsty stares, I followed the sheen of the chrome bar, which led me to Gabriel. He occupied the very spot where I'd first met him. Deep in conversation with a lanky vampire sitting next to him, Gabriel ignored me completely. I inched closer, standing right in front of him so he couldn't miss me. Still, he refused even a brief glance at me.

I wedged my body between the rude vampire and his friend. "Gabriel, I need to speak with you."

His shoulders slumped. "For the love of God, who let you in?"

"Please. It's important."

He let out a groan. "Not interested. Now go away and get out of my club."

"At least hear me out...please."

"I think you have me confused with Connor." Boredom claimed his expression. "I care about neither you nor your brother."

"That's obvious," I fired back.

He brushed his fingers over his goatee and smirked. "Where is our boy, Connor? Does he know you're here alone?"

"Of course he does." I did my best to sound convincing.

He angled his body toward me, lifting a brow. "Sure, he does."

Lying to a vampire seemed an impossible task. I groaned in defeat. "Okay, fine, you know he doesn't have a clue. I came anyway because I desperately need your help."

He emphasized his words. "Again, not interested."

"You care for Connor." I attempted a bit of reverse psychology. "He's your family, and you would do anything in your power to protect them, right?"

A light flickered in his eyes, and then the heartless vacancy returned. "Save your speech for someone who cares."

I clenched my hands, wanting to strangle him. "Look, my brother's in trouble. I have to protect him, and you have to help me."

"No, I don't."

"Please! I'm begging you."

He shoved his finger into his face. "Look here. Do I look like I care? Go home."

I didn't budge, standing my ground. He *was* going to help me. "Then do it for Connor's sake."

His stormy-gray eyes narrowed, crystallizing into ice. "Connor's infatuation with you is none of my concern."

"I'm fighting for my brother! I just want to ask some questions."

"You're confusing me with someone who cares."

My heart pounded in desperation. "I'm not asking you to care. I don't need your compassion. Just let me ask my questions, and I'll leave."

He heaved a loud sigh. "Jesus, you're like the Energizer Bunny. You just don't quit. Look, even if I wanted to help, I don't know where your brother is."

His walls seemed to be coming down, and I felt myself gaining ground. "You could let me chat with the vampires who spoke with him."

He shrugged listlessly. "Vampires come and go. It's not like I keep a guest log. I don't know who spoke to him."

"JJ came into *your* club," I pressed. "You must know something."

"Is that so, Claire?" he challenged. "Why should I know anything about your brother? He was of no importance to me. I don't keep track of everyone who walks through those doors."

"But you're a vampire. You have a photographic memory." I tapped my temple and raised my voice. "Think."

He rolled his eyes and waved me away. "I've already told you what I know. Should I make something else up?"

My chin dipped toward my chest. Where else could I turn? My options were running thin. Sobs swelled inside my chest, making my shoulders quiver.

"If you're thinking about turning on the waterworks, save it. It's annoying and serves no purpose."

Maybe that was it! Maybe if I cried my eyes out, he would give in. I threw everything I had at him, exaggerating every sob, blubber, and wail, letting my built-up emotions spill from my eyes in front of him.

"Enough," he grumbled. "You win. Stop that dreadful noise. I have an idea."

I pressed my palms to my eyes, swiping at my tears. "Okay."

"I have to show you. Come with me." His giant strides led him behind the bar and to the ominous door Connor had vanished behind the other night.

I skidded to a stop, and with a firm shake of my head, I objected, "No way in hell am I entering your torture chamber."

A fit of raucous laughter burst forth from him as he pushed open the door. "It's just my office."

Clinging to the doorframe, I peered inside. The room was outfitted with nothing more sinister than a large desk, some chairs, a file cabinet, a computer, a printer, and a fax machine. I relaxed slightly and followed him in.

"Now sit down and listen."

I sat in one of the chairs, facing his desk. "I'm listening."

"The surveillance equipment monitors the entrance. Your brother and the vampire who escorted him in were likely captured on camera. We'll start there." He eased himself down in front of the computer, his fingers flying across the keyboard. "I'm almost positive he showed up just after the first of the year. I'll upload footage as far back as December to be certain." He rose to his feet and waved me over. "Just hit the forward and back arrows to move through the frames."

"And if I find him, what then?"

"We'll cross that bridge when we come to it."

I gave him my most engaging smile. "Thank you for helping me."

He eyed me up in a less-than-friendly manner. "If providing you with access to the tapes helps me get rid of you, then it's worth it to me."

"You care. I can tell."

"Think what you will," he said, heading for the door.

"Gabriel?"

"Now what?"

"Did JJ ever approach you asking to be turned?"

"He did."

"You told him no?"

"You already know the answer to that."

"How did he react?"

He shrugged half-heartedly. "Angry. Defeated."

I ached for JJ. I couldn't imagine what he had been thinking or what he might have been going through. I wished I could've been there for him and wrapped my arms around him and assured him everything would be okay—even though our lives may never be again. "Did you read his mind?"

He straddled a chair in front of me and stared at me. "I get why you're asking, but do you really want to go there?"

"I do. Tell me."

"Darkness, rage, formulas."

"This is the second time you mentioned formulas. What formulas?"

He shook his head. "Your guess is as good as mine."

"I need your help so I can find him."

"Start with the footage."

"And then?"

"You're putting me in an awkward position. What does Connor say about all this?"

"I told you, he doesn't know I'm here. What came between the two of you anyway?"

His tone turned bitter when he spoke. "When a vampire turns a human and offers them the gift of immortal blood, there's an unspoken bond forged. You're family, forever. He was *and still is my brother.* We hunted, killed, and fought together, always together..." He tightly clenched his jaw. "...until The Vow. On that day, he broke our bond and rejoined mankind." He sneered at me. "He has always harbored a fondness for you humans."

"You act as though you were never human yourself."

"It was the happiest day of my life when I left my human existence behind, so yes, I've forgotten all about those days of inferiority, but not Connor. He chose to abandon the vampire way, and I resented him for that."

"And now?"

He stared silently for a moment before answering me. "It's lessened somewhat, but yes, a touch of it remains."

In Connor's defense, I said, "He believes you think him to be a waste of your gift."

His eyes widened. "Waste? No. My blood made Connor a powerful vampire."

I took his hand and gave it a squeeze. "I know what it's like to lose family. You should tell him how you feel."

A hint of compassion flickered in his eyes. "Maybe someday I will." He stood quickly and retreated. "Stop pestering me and get busy searching."

He left the room and shut the door, leaving me to my search. I sat staring at the computer and muttered "Please" inside my head before giving the forward arrow the first tap. Figures emerged, some as glowing silhouettes and others as dim, solid forms. Was that body heat distinguishing the vampires from the humans? That would explain why the door didn't open for me. I leaned closer and squinted at the screen. The only illumination in the frame came from a distant streetlamp. Faces were pixelated and fuzzy. Spotting JJ among the blurry mess seemed an impossible task. I could effortlessly navigate past him without noticing anything. I scolded the defeatist attitude inside my head. Failure wasn't an option. I would find him—I *had* to find him.

Twenty eye-straining minutes later, I lost focus. Images melded together, making everyone look the same. I pushed away from the monitor and rubbed my eyes. The task was a lot harder than I'd thought it would be, but then, nothing in my life has come easy lately. Law enforcement surveyed footage all the time. Maybe Reynolds knew of some sort of shortcut, but I was sure any help he offered would come with a lecture, which I neither needed nor wanted. Maybe I just needed a break. I stood up, stretched my arms overhead, and walked around the room. My stomach let out a savage growl, reminding me it needed more than just breakfast. I'd poured every waking minute into my quest to find JJ. Stopping to eat hadn't crossed my mind until now. I'd get something to eat later. Facing the computer screen once more, I picked up where I'd left off.

The office door creaked, and footsteps entered the room, but my gaze remained glued to the screen, scrutinizing face after face. The smell of bacon and toasted bread filled my senses. I caught a glimpse of hands placing a sandwich and a glass of iced tea on the table. "Gabriel, did you bring me food? How sweet. I knew deep down you cared." I pointed at the screen and asked, "Isn't there a way to make the video clearer? Peering at fuzziness is giving me a headache."

"Maybe if you adjust that setting to your right?" Connor suggested as he twisted my chair around and forced me to face him.

Warmth crept across my cheeks as I asked, "What are you doing here?"

He rubbed the back of his neck as if it pained him. "I'm here to save your ass. I know you think you're indestructible, and I've come to the conclusion rationality isn't one of your strong points, but..." He paused and pursed his lips. "...coming here alone was one dicey move."

I flipped my hair over my shoulder and rolled my eyes. "Whatever. The Cave was my only lead."

He mimicked my eye roll, but much more theatrically. "You could've at least told me."

"You would've said no."

"I probably would have, but we're both here now, so what's your plan?"

I reached for his hand. "Help me find JJ."

"I already told you I would, and I meant it, but there can't be any more secrets."

I placed my free hand over my heart. "Promise."

He gestured toward the sandwich. "Eat your BLT while I check the footage for your brother."

"But you've never met JJ. You won't know who to look for."

"He has blonde curly hair, blue eyes, a slim build, and a goofy smile. I've seen him inside your head a hundred times."

"Perfect description. That's him."

"A skinny blonde kid won't be hard to miss." Again, he gestured toward the food. "Eat."

I picked up half the sandwich and took a bite, but my gaze refused to wander away from the monitor. "I can eat and watch."

Connor adjusted the track and zoomed in on the faces. "Much better," he said with pride. "Now we can actually see something."

I gave Connor a worried glance. "What if I missed him already?"

"If we don't find him, we'll double back."

I took another bite and washed it down with the tea. "Did Gabriel call and tell you I was here?"

He smirked and returned his focus to the screen. "Vampires don't call each other. It's more of a mental summoning, but yes, he did."

"What did he say?"

"He said, 'Your girlfriend's a pain in my ass. She's at my club. Come fetch her.'"

I almost choked on my sandwich. "Am I a pain in the ass?"

He leaned over and kissed my cheek. "Yes."

Nudging him away, I said, "Not funny."

"It's one of the things I love most about you." He narrowed the gap between us by leaning forward. "And one of these days, I want a *real* kiss."

"Again with the kissing."

"It's a thing couples do to express their affection."

I exaggeratedly dropped my jaw. "I had no idea."

"I'm serious," he said, resting his hand on my knee. "I would gladly wait a lifetime for you, Claire."

My pulse sped up as warmth flooded my body. Amidst all the chaos, he gave me hope, devotion, and tranquility. He quickly became someone I deeply depended on, and my feelings for him grew significantly.

The possibility of forever wrapping itself around my heart in an un-yielding way. "You don't have to wait a lifetime. I'm already with you."

A sheepish grin spread across his face, and the fireflies flared to life across his irises. "So forever is possible?"

"Perhaps," I answered a thread above a whisper.

He leaned in to cover my mouth with his, kissing me in a soft sort of way and making my whole body shiver with pleasure. The palm of my hand brushed against the keyboard. When I looked up, a speck of curly blonde hair flashed onto the screen. "Stop!" I shouted, leaping to my feet.

"What?" he demanded in a panicked voice. "Did I do something wrong?"

I nearly smashed my face against the monitor in response. "Oh my God," I gasped, tracing JJ's hair with my finger. "It's him. That's JJ."

Connor ejected from the chair, standing next to me and staring at the monitor. "What? You're sure?"

I didn't answer. I couldn't. I dug my fingernails into my palms so hard, pain radiated through my hands as I fixated on the vampire standing next to my brother on the screen—the priest.

CHAPTER 17

That psycho priest has JJ. I just know it," I said, my gaze darting between Connor and Gabriel. "I got too close to the truth, so he sent his gang after me to take me out."

Gabriel shook his finger at me. "You need to calm down. Priest willingly accepted my invitation to join us here, but one glimpse at the crazed look in your eyes, and he'll clam right up. Is that what you want?"

A nervous laughter escaped my mouth as I waved him away. My fidgeting and skyrocketing heartbeat were telltale signs of trouble, especially to the keen senses of a vampire. And I knew the minute I looked into the priest's deceitful eyes, I would lose it. Attempting to release some of the pent-up energy, I shook out my hands and paced back and forth. "He didn't screw with *your* life, so don't tell me to calm down."

Gabriel stepped in front of me, blocking my path. "Hey, this is my show. I can determine whether Priest is on the up-and-up. The last time I checked, you don't, so if you actually want to find out what he knows, then you'll get your shit together."

Connor guided me away from Gabriel and into a chair. "Claire, Gabriel is right. We need to keep our composure. Let us handle Priest. If he's concealing anything, we'll uncover the truth through any means necessary."

I massaged the dull ache growing at either side of my temples and threw an accusatory glare at Gabriel. "He brought JJ into your club. He fooled everyone. He possesses a remarkable skill for deceiving everyone. What's to stop him from getting away with it again?"

Gabriel merely huffed and walked away from me.

Connor leveled his eyes in line with mine. "We won't let that happen, I promise you."

Gabriel smirked. "I promise too."

"You claim to know him," I shot back, "mouthing off about how you and the priest go way back, yet the all-powerful Gabriel had no idea he was using your club to solicit teenage boys."

"I'm not his personal secretary, you know. His comings and goings, along with the identity of who he might have brought into my club, are none of my concern, and I'll remind you, neither is your brother. He is only of importance to you."

Clenching my jaw, I grinded out my words. "You've made that perfectly clear. Aren't you the least bit curious to find out why the priest came to my parents' grave on the night I was there? Isn't that a little too convenient? And why did he give me the map? Just to send vampires after me to kill me?"

"I'm not curious." Gabriel gave a nod toward Connor. "But he is."

"I truly am," Connor confirmed.

"Kiss-ass," Gabriel teased him before continuing. "Don't worry your pretty head, PITA. We'll get the answers we need," Gabriel said with confidence.

I narrowed my eyes. "PITA?"

"Pain In The Ass," Gabriel clarified, his body shaking with laughter. He then composed himself and ironed out his expression. "Seriously, though, we will get the answers we all need."

"Jerk," I muttered, just loud enough for his vampire ears to catch. But despite Gabriel's confident manner, I wasn't buying his story. He and Connor were far too sure of themselves when it came to the priest's motives. Did they know something I didn't? "The two of you are making this sound far too easy."

The vein in Gabriel's forehead throbbed, and he flared his nostrils, reminding me of an angry bull. "Priest is not coming here to engage in idle chatter. He understands that I will demand honesty from him, and he is committed to delivering it."

"The priest is not just going to waltz in here and confess," I pointed out with an exaggerated gesture of my hand.

"I didn't say anything about obtaining a confession. We don't know for certain whether he's guilty of anything. And call him Priest, not *the* priest."

Was he serious? "Fine, *Priest*. He's too thick in the middle of things not to be guilty of something. He could be my parents' killer. He tried to kill me. He could have JJ. Maybe he even turned JJ."

Gabriel plastered his customary smirk on his face. "I'll make sure to ask him all those questions when he gets here."

His words sent heat rushing through my body. Was my suffering a game to him? "Do you always have to be such an ass?"

Gabriel ignored me and faced Connor and said, "She's going to be a problem if she can't keep her emotions in check."

I sprang out of the chair and blurted out, "Don't even think you're doing this without me."

Connor sighed and stepped between us. "Knock off the bickering, both of you." He glanced at Gabriel. "And she stays."

Gabriel pointed at me. "Look at her. She's foaming at the mouth like a rabid dog. One look at Priest, and she'll come undone."

"Foam? Come on, stop being so melodramatic."

Connor came to my defense again. "She's okay. I trust her. She just needs some closure. If it were you, wouldn't you want the same?"

Gabriel shook his head in dissent. "What's brewing inside her has nothing to do with resolution, and you know it. I wouldn't be surprised if she came packing a stake or cross under her jacket."

I ripped off my jacket and patted myself down. "Satisfied?"

"She's itching for a fight, Connor. I say we enchant her before he arrives."

"Absolutely not," I protested.

Connor took my hands and gave them a squeeze. An expression full of kindness took over his face. "You are wound pretty tight. It might be for the best."

I wrenched my hands away and took a step back. "No. Please, don't. I'll keep my cool, I swear."

He shifted his eyes back and forth, seemingly unable to make a decision. He pressed his lips together, then muttered, "I don't think you can keep your cool."

"Connor, this is my brother we're talking about." I pleaded my case as if on trial. "He's all the family I have left. I need to participate in this conversation with a clear mind, not overwhelmed by vampire enchantment."

Gabriel blurted out, "Enchant her already."

Connor cupped my chin, forcing me to look into his eyes. A feeling of panic ripped through me. "Stop!" I shouted, pushing him away. "I said no. You can't just force this on me, damn it."

A pained look creased his brow. He turned to Gabriel. "She's right. I can't force her."

I rattled off a sarcastic, "Why, thank you."

Gabriel opened his mouth—no doubt to throw some snide remark my way or call me another name. A knock on the office door banished whatever ill comment had crept into his throat. "Yes?" he called out.

The bartender poked his head inside and announced, "Priest is here."

"Send him back to us," Gabriel requested, his tone commanding.

The bartender replied, "Will do," while keeping the door slightly open.

I looked at Gabriel and promised, "I can do this."

"You'd better keep your cool," he warned, "or I'll enchant you myself—with or without your consent."

"Understood."

Connor stood next to me, offering his reassurance. "Focus on me. I'll keep you calm and safe."

"I'm not afraid."

"That's what worries me," Gabriel said. "You'll just blurt out whatever comes to mind without caring about the consequences."

With my gaze fixed on the door, I groaned, "For the last time, I said I'll behave. Just make him tell the truth."

"I have every intention of doing just that," Gabriel said with a wink.

"Leave it to us," Connor said, stroking my back.

The door inched open, and Priest entered the room.

A floodgate of hatred spilled into my veins as I watched him casually take a seat on the opposite side of the table. Calmly folding his hands in his lap, he acknowledged each of us with a nod, not saying a word.

Gabriel grabbed a chair and straddled it. "You brought trouble into my club. I want to know why," he demanded in a voice that even frightened me.

Connor pulled two more chairs over so we could sit with them as well.

"I had my reasons," Priest answered.

Gabriel leaned in closer, his eyes morphing into intimidating slits. "You would rather not play that game with me."

Priest didn't flinch. In fact, he locked his gaze with Gabriel's. "Are you threatening me?"

"I am," Gabriel confirmed in a cold tone.

Priest broke eye contact, his self-control shifting as he reluctantly surrendered. "I suppose it would be in my best interest to comply."

"I suppose it would," Gabriel agreed.

"May I start from the beginning?" he asked.

"Please do."

Gabriel's warning to get what he wanted was no surprise to me, and I most definitely felt grateful. Without him, I wouldn't have gotten one iota of information out of the vampire who may have taken my brother.

"Before The Vow..." he began, releasing a dramatic sigh.

I scrunched up my face. What the hell? JJ and The Vow had nothing to do with one another. I shot a questioning look at Connor.

Gabriel held his eyes shut as he said, "We don't need a history lesson. Furthermore, it's long past midnight. Get to the point."

"That is precisely what I'm trying to do," he stated.

A stone-faced stare stripped all the empathy from Connor's expression. "What you're doing is trying our patience."

Gabriel waved a finger at Priest and added, "I know stalling when I see it. Either get to the point or we'll force it out of you."

Priest clenched his jaw and glared at my two companions. "I'd planned quite the narration for your enjoyment, but if you must have the condensed version, that's perfectly fine."

Oh, to hell with it. I wasn't about to sit there and listen to a bunch of nonsense. "How do you know JJ?"

He perked up and beamed, grateful for the distraction of a human, perhaps. "Hello again, young Claire. It's a pleasure to see you again. As for your brother, well, you know, I counsel young vampires at my church, and—"

"My brother is not a vampire."

He sighed, seemingly put off by my interruption. "If I may continue, Nate and Parker, both of whom I counseled, brought JJ to my church and introduced us. They wanted JJ to know about every aspect of their lives. They kept no secrets from him."

I eyed him and considered his words. Had JJ's best friends turned him? Had that been my parents' motive for murdering them?

Priest continued. "Most importantly, they wanted to prepare JJ for his life as a vampire."

"Why wouldn't I, his sister, know? He never confided in me." I said, seeking confirmation.

"He did want such a life," he insisted. "He idolized Nate and Parker and desired their immortality."

"But as I said, he never mentioned any of this to me, and we were close. Told each other everything."

"How do you tell someone you love about your plan to leave your humanity behind?" he reasoned.

"You just say it," I blurted out in frustration.

"Finding the right words is not always so easy," he said in reply.

"He figured out a way to tell you, and you're not even part of his family."

"Nate and Parker confided in me, but only so I could offer guidance to JJ."

Connor put a hand on my shoulder as he asked, "Did JJ's parents know he wanted to turn?"

"It's possible," he answered, "but given the circumstances, I highly doubt it."

Gabriel leaned back in his chair and yawned. "Who cares? Fast forward and get to the point, Priest. So far, this has been of no value to me."

I glared at the arrogant vampire. "This isn't about you." I turned back to Priest. "What circumstances are you talking about?"

"Your parents—"

Gabriel cut him off, returning an icy-cold glare back to me. "It's about me when my club's involved. Everything else is irrelevant."

"You self-centered bastard. JJ *is* relevant."

"Not to me."

Connor turned my face toward him. "Ignore Gabriel. This *is* about JJ, and we all know that." It was his turn to shoot a disapproving glare at his maker.

"If it's any consolation to you, Claire, JJ adores you," Priest said, returning my focus to him.

Connor remained skeptical as he asked, "If you knew JJ cared about Claire, why did you come after her?"

"I had to."

Connor loomed over Priest. "Care to elaborate?"

He didn't hesitate to respond. "A vampire was killed in the park. I knew the sins of their parents. I had to seek her out."

Gabriel's gaze briefly centered on me before returning to Priest. "Sins of their parents? What the hell is that supposed to mean?"

"Nate and Parker succumbed to their death at their parents' hands. Many vampires did," he revealed in a relaxed tone. "Claire and JJ's parents were underground vampire slayers. I thought she might be following in their footsteps. That's why I went after her."

Gabriel whipped his head around to face me. "I read your mind the night Connor brought you into my club. There was nothing about slayer parents." He bared his fangs and growled, "Did you hide this from me intentionally?"

"No," I assured him. "At that point, I had no idea who my parents really were."

"Keep your cool," Connor said, shielding me with his body. "I was with Claire when Detective Reynolds sprang the news on her. She literally just found out."

Gabriel eyed me before turning back to Priest. "You wanted to know if she'd taken over for dear old Mom and Dad."

I wanted to ignore his insulting remark, but it only magnified in my head, and I couldn't shake it. I answered before Priest could. "Of course I didn't. I love Connor for Christ's sake." I softened my voice. "I would never do such horrible things to anyone."

"But slaying's in your blood," Gabriel challenged.

Connor faced Gabriel and assured him. "She's not a killer. End of story."

Priest rose from the table, walked its length, and faced us. "I, too, came to the conclusion she may have followed in her family's footsteps, so I deceived her and sent vampires to do away with her."

Gabriel raised his brows. "Are you sure that's all? I think you were after her blood as well."

"My only objective was to eliminate a potential slayer."

Connor leaned back and crossed his arms. "I'm not buying it. You spoke to her. You knew she wasn't a killer, yet you chose to move forward with your plan. Why?"

Gabriel propped his head up with his fist. "Who cares? Let's move on."

Priest carried on as if Gabriel hadn't said a word. "*You* knew she wasn't. I did not. She hungered for revenge. I assumed she was a slayer."

"Here's a thought." Connor sighed. "You could've just read her mind and saved us all a whole lot of trouble."

"I'm conflicted about invading the private thoughts of humans," he admitted.

"Hmph! But taking her life didn't bother you?"

"I have no issue with taking out a slayer."

What an ass! He'd nearly killed me over an assumption. I threw a defiant stare at him. "Except I'm no slayer."

He offered up a sincere expression. "For that mistake, I am sorry."

The need to repeat my words swelled inside me, fighting to get out. I wanted to make a statement—prove who I was. "Jonathan, I'm just a human girl. I don't have any unusual powers. I'm not a slayer. I just wanted justice for my parents' deaths and to find my missing brother. That's all."

"The truth is clear now. However, that night I found a daughter mourning over her parents' graves and believed you would continue their legacy, which would include seeking vengeance."

"Of course I was grieving. I knew nothing of their crimes." I pointed an accusatory finger at him. "But you didn't even try to figure out my true intentions. You acted without cause."

"You must understand, I needed to reclaim the balance, the order. The Vow threatened to disappear forever. The burden of eliminating the threat, which I believed to be you, weighed heavily on me.

I clasped my hands so tightly, my knuckles turned white. "I wasn't a threat. I wanted my parents' killer in jail and for JJ to come back home. Your ignorance almost cost me my life."

A solemn look swept over his face. "I made a grave error in judgment. Apologies aren't enough, I realize, but it's all I have to offer."

"You can offer up Victoria. Tell me what her role is in all of this."

Priest raised his brows. "Why do you ask about Victoria?"

"Just answer the question."

"Victoria is a friend. I assure you, she had nothing to do with my actions."

"Then why did you write, 'She knows,' by her tomb on the map?" I didn't give him a chance to respond. "What does that mean anyway? Were you trying to send me some kind of message?"

He frowned. "Why would you think the message was meant for you? Yes, I wrote those words, but only for myself, to remind me she knew about my map."

My voice grew quiet, my resolve crushed. "I wanted...no, *needed* it to mean something more, like a clue of sorts, maybe pointing to my parents' killer."

Gabriel smirked, barely able to contain himself. "See, I told you Victoria played you."

"You're so annoying." I shot him my most exasperated glare, but he only chuckled.

Priest returned to his chair. "Please, I must continue—your parents murdered Nate and Parker."

"Old news, Priest," Gabriel said, a hint of impatience lacing his tone.

"Hold on, I'm getting there. JJ and vampires were inseparable. He surrounded himself with them. Your parents couldn't have that, not with their set of beliefs," he explained.

"It's all so baffling," I said, shaking my head. "They never discouraged us from forming relationships with vampires. They did the opposite; they encouraged us." A shiver ran down my spine. "God, did they do it to lure more victims in?"

"The more a parent tells a child not to do something, the more the child desires to do it," Priest said, as if he were a psychologist. "But your parents tried a different approach. They manipulated you and JJ to fulfill their dark desires, and unfortunately, Nate and Parker suffered the consequences."

Could he be right? Had our parents controlled that very aspect of our lives? I couldn't recall a single instance when they had forbidden contact with vampires. My mind ran through the past, and I couldn't recall any manipulation. To prove they used us to access vampires would have been impossible. I needed closure. "You're saying our parents used me and JJ as bait, but I can't believe that. They loved us. They wouldn't use us like that."

Compassion softened Priest's stern brow. "Sadly, JJ witnessed firsthand what your parents were capable of."

The reality of his words hit hard, and a cold numbness spread over my body. "JJ watched Nate and Parker die, didn't he?"

"Yes, he did."

I closed my eyes and shuddered. "When did all of this happen?"

I felt Connor's arm surround me.

"The first week of February, at your parents' cabin," he revealed.

The video of the bare room containing the two bloody vampires played inside my head. "What cabin?"

"The one in Mount Laguna."

"They never told us about any cabin." I wondered if Reynolds knew a cabin existed. Did one of the mystery keys open the door to that cabin?

"Your parents took the three boys up to the cabin for the weekend. Obviously, JJ had no idea he was leading Nate and Parker into a deadly trap."

"He told you all of this?" Gabriel asked, sounding much less bored.

"The night Nate and Parker died, he came to me, distraught and filled with rage. He begged me to kill your parents."

I gasped and latched onto Connor's arm. "What?"

"I refused, and my denial infuriated him. Afterward, he demanded I turn him."

I couldn't speak. I simply sat there with my mouth open.

Connor faced Priest and asked, "Did you?"

"I did not," he responded.

Gabriel scowled. "So you brought the kid to my club to help him solicit vampires?"

"I did no such thing. I brought him to The Cave with the intention of showing him the realities of the lifestyle, hoping it would deter him."

"But that's not what happened," Gabriel pointed out. "He propositioned every vamp in my club."

"He came to me for an entire month, begging to be turned. He was changing, becoming more and more withdrawn. I tried to help him."

"Your plan didn't work out so well, did it?" Gabriel fired back.

"I couldn't get through to him. He seemed," sadness permeated his voice, "determined to succeed."

Gabriel dismissed Priest's statement with a wave of his hand. "What gave you the right to allow that boy to solicit vampires at my club?"

He pounded his fist on the desk, splintering the wood. "You weren't there, Gabriel. None of you were. He fell into despair, on the brink of losing control. I had to do something."

Guilt and regret swept over me when I realized what I had done. I was filled with remorse for doubting someone's intentions before knowing all the facts. Priest was right. Having not been present, I couldn't condemn the one person who tried to help him.

Connor wasn't as forgiving. "Bringing him to The Cave only heightened an already perilous situation."

Priest let his shoulders slump forward and nodded his agreement. "You're right, but at the time, I thought I was truly doing the right thing."

"Do you know where he is now?" I asked, hoping for a solid lead to help me find him.

"I haven't seen nor heard from him in quite some time. He was staying at the cabin, rambling on about not being able to leave Nate and Parker."

I stood, determined. "Take me there. I need to see for myself."

Priest rose and placed a hand on my shoulder. "He's not how you remember him."

"Whoever he may be now, he's still my brother."

"The night after your parents were killed, he came to me, gripping your picture in his hands. He clung to it like a child clings to his favorite blanket."

The empty spot on my parents' dresser flashed in my mind. "I'm all he has left. Maybe taking my picture was his way of hanging onto family."

Priest's face grew long, and his voice leveled. "He's lost his way, Claire."

Gabriel stated something similar, but still I asked, "How do you mean?"

"Nate's and Parker's deaths—the incident changed him. He was obsessed with making things right."

Connor, Gabriel, and Priest all turned their eyes on me. I shook my head at them. "Why are you all staring at me? What's going on?"

Connor lightly stroked my back but didn't speak. Gabriel looked away. Priest was the one who filled me in. "Your parents murdered Nate and Parker, his best friends. Afterward, JJ begged me to kill your parents, but I refused, and no vampire would turn him. He wanted revenge. Do you see where this line of reasoning leads?"

I slanted my body away from him. "You can't seriously believe he would do such a horrible thing."

Priest clasped his hands in front of him and bluntly stated, "In all likelihood, JJ killed his own parents."

The floor seemed to drop under my feet. I stumbled backward into Connor. His strong arms came around me, holding me tight. How could any of these statements possibly be true? No! I refused to believe it. My love for JJ swelled inside me, a painful ache I needed to heal. I pushed away from Connor and stood on my own, my head held high. "You're wrong, and I'm going to prove it."

CHAPTER 18

The following evening, Connor and I sat in my Jeep just outside The Cave, waiting for Gabriel and Priest. Grayish clouds floated past the cream-colored moon, distorting its haunting glow. The jet-black sky retained a touch of violet and seemed to mimic my emotions. In the aftermath of losing everything I believed in, I felt abandoned and misguided. As it turned out, our parents were killers, for which JJ might have delivered the ultimate punishment. Certainly, I was not blameless. Because of my obsession with finding their killer, I lost all sense of reason, causing harm to innocent vampires and not-so-innocent vampires alike. The past few weeks have brought me back to reality. JJ has to find his way back now. Our first step was to find him. The plan was to search for him at the scene of the crime—the cabin in Mount Laguna.

"Sometimes things aren't what they seem," Connor said, stroking my hair and bringing me back to the present.

"Sometimes they're worse."

"Don't think—"

The Jeep's doors opened, and Gabriel and Priest slid into the back seat. "Let's get rolling. I've got more important things to do," Gabriel said in his typical, narcissistic fashion.

"You have no heart," I shot at him over my shoulder.

He placed his hand on his chest. "I most certainly do," he responded, "and it would very much like to get on with chasing its desires instead of those of an insignificant human."

He didn't deserve the effort required to verbalize a response.

Connor glanced in the rearview mirror, his eyes locked on Gabriel. "One more remark like that, and I'll throw your ass out of the Jeep."

"Fine," Gabriel replied in a flat tone. "I'll behave."

"We need to work together, not against one another," Priest advised. "Also, we need to prepare for what lies ahead."

"And what do you mean by that?" I asked.

"If JJ is at the cabin, we don't know what his state of mind will be. We must be cautious."

"I'm sure there's nothing to worry about," Gabriel stated, drawing his own conclusions.

"There is a possibility that he will be there, and we need to be prepared for that," Priest affirmed.

"I need to see my brother, so I hope he is there."

"He's ill and might even be dangerous," Priest pointed out, in keeping with his intention to foretell doom.

"I won't be afraid of my brother."

"Perhaps you should be."

The urge to kick Priest out of my car right now spread through me. Instead, I simply said, "You act like JJ has barricaded himself with an arsenal of weapons."

Connor finally decided to come to my defense. "He's a boy in trouble. He's most likely terrified and doesn't know where to turn."

"JJ's unstable. He's not the same boy you grew up with, Claire," Priest said, darkening the mood even further.

"I'm his big sister. He's not going to hurt me."

"You have to be prepared for the possibility he won't recognize you, even if you stand before him. He may unwittingly attack you."

His depressing chatter reminded me of the annoying, steady ping of a dripping faucet. "Do you ever have anything positive to say? I trust my brother; end of story." I didn't leave room for a reply and turned to Connor. "Can we please get going?"

Connor backed my Jeep onto the street and said, "Priest is just trying to help, in his own way."

"Why, thank you," Priest said, seemingly pleased.

I looked at them both and rolled my eyes. *Men.* Human or vampire, it didn't matter; they were all the same.

"Take I-8," Priest suggested. "It will be the fastest way."

"Not fast enough," Gabriel grumbled. "Mount Laguna's at least an hour's drive."

"Mount Laguna seems to be the source of all the trouble," I muttered.

"Claire?" Connor questioned.

"The storage unit," I said, reminding him, and then turned to face Gabriel and Priest. "My parents have a storage unit in Mount Laguna as well. Detective Reynolds found videos and journals inside it."

"Videos and journals of what?" Priest asked.

"My..." I cringed, not wanting to speak the vile words. "My parents' kills."

"Then the detective may soon find the cabin if he hasn't already," Priest said in an urgent tone. "As well as JJ's formulas."

CHAPTER 19

Other than pockets of moonlight peeking between the brownish-gray trees, darkness surrounded us. Priest dictated directions from the back seat. "Coming up on the right, there will be a dirt road. Follow it until I say otherwise." In the next minute, he shouted, "There!"

Connor nodded, maneuvering my Jeep onto a bumpy side road. I tuned out Priest's voice and focused my thoughts on JJ. What were these formulas both Gabriel and Priest had mentioned? And how could JJ bring himself to stay in the cabin where our parents had taken so many lives? Maybe he reached a mental breaking point? Was there a reason to fear him? Finding JJ was the only way to solve the mystery.

"Are you okay?" Connor asked, squeezing my hand.

The touch of his hand sent my pulse racing. He was my constant bright light, steering me away from the darkness plaguing my family. I smiled the most I could muster. "I'm okay."

He caressed my fingers. "I'm here for you."

Gabriel groaned loudly. "Do I have to bear witness to such sappiness?"

"I find it refreshing." Priest chimed in. "In such times of sorrow, it's delightful to see two people find happiness."

Gabriel dismissed him with a wave of his hand. "For the love of God, you sound like a Hallmark card."

"How did you become so cynical?" I asked him. "Does anything at all please you?"

"Blood sends me over the moon. I live and breathe for it." A wicked grin occupied his face. "Care to offer a sample of yours?"

Connor growled at him. "Careful, Gabriel. It's a long walk home from this point."

"Silence," Priest commanded. "We're coming up on the turn to the cabin. There, Connor." He pointed at a fork in the road.

I was filled with a heavy feeling that something would go horribly wrong. I pressed my hand against my chest as a quick prayer ran through my thoughts. "Dear God, please see us through this journey safely."

Gabriel belted out snide laughter. "Aren't you all being overly dramatic? He's just a human, for Christ's sake."

Priest retorted, "Never underestimate a disturbed mind. It tends to heighten the senses, making one well aware of their surroundings."

"Remember, this is my brother you're talking about. He learned about our evil parents through the painful experience of seeing his closest friends executed. Show some respect."

Gabriel slumped in his seat and faked a yawn. "Whatever you say, Claire."

I bit the inside of my cheek and wanted to strangle him.

"Turn here and go slow," Priest said, his voice low. "Better shut off the headlights."

"We won't be able to see the road," I said, pointing out the obvious.

"We're vampires, my dear. We're quite comfortable in the dark. Lights are for humans," Gabriel declared, wearing a smug expression.

"Our eyes adjust," Connor explained. "I'll be able to see, don't worry."

As my Jeep's lights cut away, the trees vanished, as if plucked away by some giant god. Moonlight flickered in and out of the trees, bringing all the shadows to life. A passage from William's journal came into my mind. *Their razor-sharp sight, a keen sense of smell, and perception of sound exceed my human capabilities.* Now it was my turn to experience the same thing firsthand. I squinted, trying to make out shapes in the pitch-blackness. It comforted me to know they could see all I could not.

Connor looked in the rearview mirror and asked, "How far up the road, Priest?"

"Not far," he answered.

Distorted images of JJ haunted my mind. They floated about inside the haze, never allowing me a clear picture. I rubbed the heel of my palm against my aching heart. I wished I could travel back in time and undo all the negative experiences. JJ and I would have run somewhere far away from our parents. I would have given him a different life, one without lies, betrayal, and violence. Yet, I knew there was no going back, only moving forward amidst the unknowns and accusations, but it eased the ache in my heart to imagine I could.

"There it is," Priest conveyed to the rest of us. "Pull off to the side and park under that cluster of trees."

Would I be able to even enter their horrific, crime-filled cabin? Would I find JJ staring madly at his formulas in an empty room...or would I encounter something even more horrific and terrifying?

Connor guided my Jeep forward a couple of feet and then cut the engine. "What now?"

"Let's hang back for a moment to see what we can gather from the car," Priest suggested.

A glimmer of moonlight exposed the tip of the stone chimney. My gaze followed the shaft of light, which revealed the outline of the small cabin. Darkness obscured every window; not even the gleam of the porchlight greeted us, yet something yellow in color fluttered just inside the doorway. The familiarity of it tugged at my brain, and I felt certain I'd seen it before. I leaned forward, squinting to make it out. The breeze lifted it just enough to uncover large black letters spilling across the yellow banner. The tape resembled a crime scene! Sweat covered me, and a sickening cold sensation washed over me. My body tingled with a sharp, prickling alert, as if silently warning me. "Reynolds has JJ," I screamed and threw open the door. I jumped down and landed on uneven ground, falling onto the dirt. Rocks dug into my knees, but the pain didn't matter; only JJ did. Scrambling to my feet, I dashed toward the cabin.

Connor bolted in front of me, holding me back. "Claire, wait. It may not be safe."

I thrashed and struggled to break free. "Get out of my way. Let go of me. I have to know."

He tightened his grip, forcing me to stay at his side. "And you will, I promise. Just let me check it out first. We don't know who or what may be inside."

Tears gathered in my eyes, more out of frustration than anything else. After all this time, the truth, or some version of it, remained just out of reach, but would it establish JJ's guilt or innocence? I had to believe in his innocence and not give up on him. My quest would end when JJ was standing in front of me, telling me what had happened from his mouth. Then I could rest, but for now, I needed to keep fighting. I reached inside myself, summoning up the deepest remnants of strength left inside me. "Please, someone go inside. I need to know what happened, please."

"More crying. Just like a human," Gabriel grumbled.

Connor released me and propelled himself full speed at Gabriel. Clenching his hands, he yelled, "Will you shut the hell up!"

"Quiet," Priest urged.

Gabriel held up his hands in surrender and backed away. "Fine."

I focused on the tape blocking the doorway. "Connor. Just go inside. See if JJ is there. Please!"

He held up a hand. "Okay, okay, just wait here. I'll come back for you when it's clear."

I nodded, shuddering and pulling my jacket closed. The three vampires headed up the dirt path and onto the front porch before I could blink my eyes. Connor ducked under the crime tape first, followed by Priest and then Gabriel. There might be a clue hidden within those walls that could mean the difference between life and death for JJ. Fixated on the doorway, I channeled positive thoughts, anticipating Connor's return with positive news.

After he waved me ahead, I raced toward the cabin. Wind chimes welcomed me as I stepped onto the porch. Connor took my hand and gently squeezed it as he divulged, "He's not here."

My shoulders slumped forward as I exhaled a breath. "That would've been too easy."

"We're getting closer, though. Do you still want to go inside?"

"Yes, of course."

"All right," he said, wrapping an arm around me and leading me through the open door.

The cabin looked peaceful and ordinary—filled with everyday country décor. Not a single trace of anything sinister or wicked met my sight. I'd imagined bloodstains or battleaxes mounted on the wall but instead found only normalcy. Cabin-like furniture filled the room, and photographs adorned a wooden mantel.

I crept closer, taking inventory of all the pictures. My parents' smiling faces filled every frame, yet not one held any image of either me or JJ, not a single one. The cabin was theirs, my parents, the strangers. Within these walls, they had erased mine and JJ's existence. I surveyed each snapshot, hoping for some sign of recognition, something familiar that I'd remember.

As I took in the photographs, one in particular sent a sickening feeling sweeping through my stomach. A waitress snapping the celebration photo of JJ's International Science and Engineering Fair first-prize win flashed across my brain. It was two summers ago at Tortellini's Restaurant, but my parents altered it, cutting me and JJ out of the frame.

Gabriel came up behind me and offered, "Maybe they did it to protect you."

My eyes remained glued to the picture. "How would such a thing protect us?"

He stepped in front of me, blocking my view of the photo. "I'll spell it out for you. They tortured and killed vampires. What if one got away? Wanted revenge? Maybe the two of you aren't in any of the photos for a beneficial reason."

"But vampires read minds," I protested. "Cutting us out of pictures wouldn't have been foolproof."

"Maybe, maybe not. The mind of a slayer is practiced and cunning, and a complicated mind for a frightened vampire to penetrate."

Connor joined us and added, "Fear inside a vampire's head is like a lit fuse. When panic sets in, logic and reason are the first to crumble."

I studied the picture again before turning away and thinking, *maybe they* did *do it to protect us. At least it's something positive to hold on to.*

"In here," Priest shouted from down the hall.

My arms tingled with goosebumps as I heard the strain in his voice. Breath caught in my throat as I hurried down the hallway and into the room.

With a slack mouth, Priest pointed at the walls, covered with bits and pieces of torn paper. "JJ's formulas covered these walls. Now they're gone."

"What the hell is up with those formulas?" Gabriel asked sarcastically.

"It looked like a bunch of chicken-scratch to me, hexagon shapes and stick figures with numbers or letters," Priest responded.

"A DNA sequence perhaps?" Connor suggested.

My gaze settled on the two empty chairs in the center of the room, drowning out their conversation. This had been my parents' kill room. The chairs resurrected the haunting videotape, and I cowered with shame.

Connor turned me away from the chairs. "Don't look at those, Claire."

Priest threw his hands in the air. "Is anyone listening to me? The pages have vanished."

"Maybe the police took them as evidence," Gabriel offered, glancing at me. "Perhaps you should call that detective of yours?"

"Reynolds?"

"If he has JJ and the pages, then we're wasting time here."

"Gabriel's right," Connor agreed. "You should call Reynolds and see what he knows, if anything."

Drawing strength from childhood memories, I clung to the part of myself loyal to JJ as my composure deteriorated. Gabriel and Connor were right. It was time to contact Reynolds. "I'll make the call."

Connor lightly stroked my forearm. "Remember, I'm here if you need me."

I touched his face, allowing my hand to linger for a moment before turning to leave. On the front porch, the stars flickered against the backdrop of the dark sky. I released a shaky breath as I pulled out my cell phone and dialed the station. Closing my eyes, I listened to the steady ringing in my ear. When a man answered, I asked to talk to Reynolds.

After several minutes on hold, he finally picked up. "Reynolds."

My body shuddered with nervous energy as I responded, "It's Claire. You're probably not pleased with me, but first I want to know if you have JJ. I think he was at my parents' cabin, where I am now."

A loud groan came from the other end. "What is it with you and breaking into crime scenes?"

"Do you have him?"

"That area is Detective Johnson's jurisdiction. However, since it's my case, he's keeping me updated. And no, we don't have him." He paused, sighed again, and added, "Continuing down this path will get you into serious trouble, Claire. Trouble I will not be able to help you get out of."

"I'm not alone. Connor and two other vampires are here with me."

"I don't care if you're with the Pope. You can't keep interfering with an official investigation. Now, quickly leave the area to avoid detection.

"But I need answers. I can't turn my back on my family."

"I think I've made it clear that those answers will be provided by me."

Reynolds reminded me so much of my father—the father I thought I had known. Reynolds displayed the same quiet strength and unwavering patience my father did. Both made everyone feel safe even in challenging times, but at that very moment, I felt lost. "I don't know what to do anymore."

"You can trust me."

"But you don't keep me in the loop. You don't share information. Everything I've learned, I found out on my own."

"Remember, it's my responsibility to extract details from you, and you intentionally lead me on tangents."

"It's just a case for you. To me, it's the fate of my family...or what's left of it."

"It's more than just a case for me. I'm involved," he assured me, his voice softening. "Your well-being rests on my shoulders. I feel responsible for you."

My lip quivered when I blurted out, "I stood in the middle of the room where my parents murdered those vampires. I can't get the picture out of my head. I'm just trying to keep it together, so I called you for help. Please help me!"

"And I'm here to help. Let's share everything we know. Deal?"

I didn't hesitate. "Deal. Do you have new evidence concerning JJ?"

"Yes. Documents from the cabin."

"What kind of documents?"

"First, you give me something. Tit for tat."

"A vampire they call Priest knows about what happened between JJ and my parents. He has information about their murders."

He rattled off his next question. "What did this vampire say?"

"JJ came to him several times before and the night after my parents were killed…but first I want to hear more about these documents."

"I can't discuss it with you."

My frustration grew, and I raised my voice. "You have to be kidding me! What happened to tit for tat?"

"Calm down. The evidence bags from the cabin arrived yesterday. We're still going through them."

"And JJ?"

It took him a long moment to answer. "Detective Johnson did find JJ at the cabin, but they lost him. He's still out there somewhere in the mountains."

I lowered myself onto the porch steps. "Thank God he's alive. When did he run? What are you doing to find him?"

"Two days ago. De—"

I cut him off. "Two days! What about food and water?"

"As I started to say, Detective Johnson is searching around the clock. JJ disappeared in a matter of minutes. He must know the area and all the places to hide."

"That doesn't make me feel any better."

"They'll find him."

"And when they do?"

"They'll bring him back here to my jurisdiction."

A new bout of uneasiness settled in my bones. Once Reynolds had JJ in custody, what would happen next? Would Reynolds arrest him and place him in lockup? "I'm coming to see you."

"There's no need. I'll call you when I have news."

"I want to see the evidence. I want to help."

"Claire, no."

I hung up on him and ran back into the cabin, adrenaline pumping into my veins. "I'm leaving," I blurted out. "I'm going to the police station."

Connor grabbed my arm, holding me back. "One step at a time. What did he say?"

Gabriel stood with his arms folded, his eyes on me.

Priest asked anxiously, "Does he have JJ?"

My eyes moistened as I shook my head. "No. JJ...he...he ran and disappeared into the mountains somewhere. They're searching for him."

Connor regarded me with an unsettled look. "How long has he been out there?"

"Two days, but I have to believe he's okay."

Priest nodded his agreement.

"What does Reynolds have on him?" Gabriel asked.

"Evidence collected from the cabin—the formulas. I don't know, he wouldn't say. That's why I'm going to the station." I turned to Priest. "JJ trusts you. Can you please stay here in case he comes back?"

"Of course."

"I'll stay too," Gabriel offered up.

"If he comes back..."

"We'll call you," Gabriel finished for me.

"Claire, it's a long drive. We should get going," Connor said, placing his hand on my back and urging me forward.

"Go. We've got this," Priest assured me.

"Wait." I left Connor's side and neared Priest, taking his hands in mine. "If JJ comes back, promise me you'll protect him and keep him safe."

"I promise," he said earnestly.

Gabriel let out a huff. "After everything Priest put you through, you're placing your faith in him?"

"I am."

"And what about me?" Gabriel asked with a wink.

I stared him down. "I hope you'll do the right thing."

A faint smile touched his lips. "I just might."

"If we have any news, we'll reach out, and you do the same," Priest said, walking us to the door.

All the ill-fated possibilities clouded my mind. Would the evidence Reynolds had gathered implicate JJ in the murders? Would it explain why he'd disappeared and never reached out to me? I could only hope JJ had escaped the family curse and, unlike our parents, was innocent of murder.

CHAPTER 20

Connor and I sat inside the empty, dead-quiet precinct; one lone cop worked the front desk. The entire police force appeared to be pounding the streets and tracking down criminals. As the clock neared eleven o'clock, I cast a quick glance at it and let out an exaggerated sigh. Forty-five minutes ago, we had asked for Reynolds. What the hell was taking so long? Was he playing some sort of mind game with me? Did he think I would give up and leave? I would not leave the station until I saw the evidence he claimed to have. I planned to challenge every last bit of the evidence. I couldn't bring myself to believe that JJ, a seventeen-year-old boy who loved science, skateboarding, comic books, and Xbox, would kill our parents. Yes, they had turned out to be monsters, ones who had committed unforgivable, gruesome crimes, but nonetheless, they had been our parents—loving parents even—and JJ just didn't have it in him to be a killer.

I glanced at the clock once more. Ten minutes had passed. I shifted in the lobby chair, forcing my gaze to follow the neutral-colored grout connecting the polished tiles.

Connor lightly touched my forearm, turning my attention toward him. "Relax. Stressing isn't going to make Reynolds appear any faster."

"Can you pick up on anything?"

"Bits and pieces of conversation, but it's muffled. I can't make it out."

I drummed my fingers on the chair arm and muttered, "Why is he making us wait like this?"

Connor, acting as my voice of reason, said, "He's probably got a heavy caseload. Give him a little more time. He'll get to us."

"I think he's avoiding me."

"You don't know that."

I glared fiercely at the clock once more. "Then why hasn't he come out for us?"

"I don't have an answer for that."

A relentless sense of doubt hammered away at my head, causing me to rub my temples. My headaches seemed to be never-ending these days. "I'm trying to stay calm, but as time passes, I feel more restless."

"Whatever the outcome, good or bad, we'll get through it together."

Connor certainly had a way of seeing the positive side of things. "You're right. We will."

He gave my hand a squeeze. "I love being your support system."

"I appreciate it, I do, but right now, I want Reynolds to get his ass out here. Sorry. I just need answers."

He brought my hand to his lips and kissed it. "I'm sure it won't be much longer. He can't keep us waiting forever."

I stood up and glanced at the front desk. "I'm going to ask what's taking so long."

The creak of a door hit my right ear, and I jerked my head in its direction. Reynolds stood between the double doors, holding them wide open. His tie hung loose, and his shirt sleeves were rolled up to his elbows. A scowl had written itself into his face as his eyes burned into mine. Many times over the years, I'd witnessed that same look on my father's face. "Claire, what part of 'no' didn't you understand?"

"Even if you said no a hundred times, I would still be standing here. He's my brother."

His brows softened a bit. "You deserve answers, and I want to give them to you, but I don't have all the facts yet."

He had to know how much being at the center of the investigation meant to me. "Don't do this to me, Reynolds. Don't shut me out."

He took a deep breath and then released it. "I'm not shutting you out."

"Then let me see what evidence you have."

He shoved his hands into his pockets. "I don't even know what I'm looking at. How are you going to make any sense of it?"

"Because I know JJ. Maybe I can make a connection you aren't able to."

Reynolds sighed and ran his hand through his hair. "What I've got is baffling and doesn't suggest any relation to a teenage boy."

"Stop talking in riddles. What do you mean?"

He stared at me, but didn't elaborate.

My hands began to tremble as I begged, "Tell me."

He pressed his lips together in a hard line before he spoke again. "It resembles more the work of a madman."

I blinked and then just stared, my brain trying to make sense of his words.

"What the hell does that mean?" Connor asked, rising to his feet.

"It implies that I have insufficient evidence."

I shook off the daze and pressed him. "You can't just leave me in the dark. You need to tell me something, anything."

Sympathy shone in his eyes as he said, "As soon as I figure it out, you'll be the first one I call."

The doors of the precinct flew open and slammed against the wall, shutting down my protest. Shoes squeaked as they skidded across the polished tile. In his struggle to fight off four officers, a handcuffed man kicked them in the ribs. Dirt covered his tattered clothes and skin. With an inhuman growl, he screamed, "Give it back!"

The matted blonde curls covering his face parted to reveal two piercing blue eyes. For one brief, gut-wrenching second, time stood still. A rush of adrenaline coursed through my body, and I darted forward, shrieking, "JJ!"

Reynolds grabbed my arm and pulled me back. "Hang on." He turned toward the police officers and said, "Let him go."

One of the four wrestling with JJ furrowed his brow at Reynolds. "Not a wise move, Detective. We let go; he bolts."

Reynolds strengthened his voice and ordered, "I said let him go."

They released him and inched backward, but three of them kept their guns raised. The fourth carried an evidence bag. A flash of silver inside the plastic caught my eye. I squinted, trying to make out the object. The edge of the antique frame sparked recognition—I knew it well. It was my picture, the one missing from my parents' dresser.

"Holster your guns," Reynolds commanded, sweeping a hand through the air. "And give me the evidence bag."

JJ stood trembling, his eyes wide and fixed on me. His legs buckled, pitching him to his knees. Tears glistened in his eyes, his lower lip quivering. In a shrill pitch, he cried out my name. "Claaaire!"

Seeing him broken and bawling on the floor tore at my heart. I fell beside him, pulling him into a loving embrace. A pitiful howl came from deep inside him. "I can't hug you. My hands are cuffed."

"I gotcha," Reynolds murmured, bending to uncuff him.

JJ clung to me tightly, his chest heaving with sobs.

Having lost our parents, I was now JJ's guardian. I had to protect him no matter what. "I'm here now. Everything will be okay," I whispered softly.

His wails tapered off, and for a moment he fell limp in my arms. A violent shudder gripped his torso, and he pulled away. A hot glaze clouded his eyes as they darted about. He gripped my arm and jabbered, "It's not safe. It's not safe. The people may hear us."

Looking around, I asked, "Do you mean the police?"

He fixated on the left corner of the room and pointed. "There."

My eyes followed the line of his finger to the room in the corner. No one was there. I glanced back at Connor and Reynolds and then at JJ. "There's no one there, JJ."

He tilted his head and squinted. "They're tiny, but they're there." His voice dropped to a whisper. "I can feel them. They get inside your head and don't come out. I have to give them what they want."

A sudden chill crept over me as I stared at the stranger who sat before me. The crazed look in his eyes melted away, and his tears returned, trickling down his cheeks. I reached for his hand and pleaded, "JJ, tell me what happened."

He shook his head and cried, "Nate and Parker are dead. I'll never see them again." His brows pulled together, and he glared at me, pushing my hands away. "You want what the people want. I can't trust you. I'm not saying another word."

I pointed at the evidence bag in the officer's hand, which contained my picture. "You *can* trust me. It's me, Claire, your sister."

He stared intently at my photo, studying it, tilting his head right, then left. A rosy glow flushed his cheeks, a smile claiming his lips. His eyes traveled back to me and wandered over my face. "Hey, Claire."

My voice cracked as I responded, "Hey, JJ."

He sighed and hung his head. "I have to tell you something."

"You can tell me anything. You know that."

"Mom and Dad..." He paused, his shoulders tensing up. "They're monsters. They fooled you and me, but they couldn't fool the people. The people always knew."

As his big sister, I should have shielded him from our parents, but I didn't know about them myself. They fooled everyone. Picking up the pieces and trying to put him back together suddenly became my new role, and I would not let him down as our parents had. "JJ, who are the people you're talking about?"

His piercing blue eyes turned cold and flat again. He smacked the side of his head with his palm and yelled, "I don't know their names. They don't tell me their names. They just tell me what to do." He jumped to his feet and shook his fists at me. "Stop asking me!"

Three of the four police officers drew their guns again, aiming the cold steel at JJ. Reynolds stepped between them, shielding my brother. "Stand down. He's not armed."

Their stance remained hostile, guns raised in the air.

"Report in. I've got this," Reynolds assured them.

The police officer holding my picture stated firmly, "You heard him. Stand down and report in."

"I'll take the evidence bag," Reynolds said, holding out his hand.

He handed it to Reynolds, keeping a close watch on JJ. "He's wound pretty tight. On second thought, maybe one of us should stick around."

Reynolds shook his head. "That won't be necessary."

Acknowledging Reynolds' request, they retreated, disappearing through the doors and into the heart of the station.

Reynolds ripped open the evidence bag and handed the picture to JJ. "Here you go."

JJ grabbed it and tucked it under his arm, pressing it into his side like a part of his body. "Thank you."

Reynolds took my arm and pulled me aside. Keeping his voice low, he said, "This is well beyond police business. I need to bring in psych. Go home and get some rest. I'll give you a call once we've had a breakthrough."

My entire body stiffened. If he thought I would abandon JJ now, he was insane. I shook my head firmly and said, "He's a minor. I'm his only living family member, which makes me his legal guardian. You can't question him without me present."

"If I were arresting him, yes, but at this point, all I want to do is talk. I don't need anyone present for that besides the two of us."

I folded my arms and planted my feet. "He's my baby brother. I'm not going anywhere."

JJ neared me, still clinging to my picture. "You're not leaving, right?"

"Right. I'm staying here with you," I said, smiling at him.

Reynolds' mouth slanted downward and his shoulders caved. He heaved a sigh. "Suit yourself, but it may be a long night."

I nodded in acknowledgement. "I can handle it."

Reynolds pointed a finger at me. "Don't make me regret this, Claire."

I gestured with my palms and answered, "I'm not going to do anything. I'll be waiting patiently right here for as long as it takes."

Reynolds nodded toward JJ. "I have to get a room ready and bring in psych. He needs to come with me."

I smoothed JJ's curls. "I understand."

Reynolds put his hand on JJ's shoulder and kept his voice low. "I need some answers, JJ. Can you please help me?"

JJ kept his arms tight to his body and glanced at him but didn't speak.

"How about a soda?" Reynolds asked.

JJ perked up. "Do you have any Coke?"

Reynolds smiled. "Tons of Coke. Follow me." Reynolds kept his hand on JJ's shoulder as he led him through the double doors. I shivered and hugged myself, but it brought no warmth to overcome the chill.

"Try to relax," Connor said, putting his arm around me and leading me back to the lobby chairs.

I laced my fingers tightly and swallowed hard as once again I sat in one of the chairs. "Gabriel and Priest were right. JJ is sick. He's lost his way. I don't know how to get him back."

"If it makes you feel any better, while you and Reynolds were talking, I called in some reinforcements. Priest is on his way. He thinks he can be of some help."

I heaved a sigh. "Thank you. However, JJ doesn't require a priest. He needs a shrink."

"He's been through a lot. You both have. It will take time to heal."

My family's dark skeletons had paraded out into the open. The challenge would be keeping JJ from falling deeper into the insanity plaguing his mind. Witnessing the murder of his best friends at our parents' hands had sent him toppling over the edge. What horrifying images of that dreadful night, locked away inside his own deranged mind, held him captive? Could time heal him, or were his wounds so deep he would never be able to crawl out of the darkness and be trapped there forever? I had to reach him and turn the light back on, but I didn't have a clue where to begin or how to accomplish such a miracle. Maybe a mind as powerful as a vampire's could break through; however, Priest had tried and failed. As a human and his sister, I could offer him love, and love could be a compelling and persuasive tool. I settled back in the chair and rested my head on Connor's shoulder. Reynolds had been right. It was going to be a very long night.

CHAPTER 21

The precinct's ticking clock captivated me for the second time that night. Its hands crawled over the numbers, testing my patience. Letting my brother be questioned without me, somewhere on the other side of that door, was harder than I'd imagined. I was afraid that I might betray my commitment to Reynolds by searching every room in the building for JJ. As if he had read my thoughts, or perhaps through divine intervention, Reynolds pushed the doors open and gestured for us to proceed. "We're ready for you," he said, escorting me and Connor down a lengthy hallway and stopping in front of a door marked *Interrogation Five.* "We're in here."

I entered and made straight for JJ, ignoring the woman seated at the table. He jutted away from me, pacing the room with my picture still tucked safely under his arm. JJ glared at the floor, mumbling and swinging his head from left to right. Connor approached him next. Again, JJ employed avoidance, moving in the opposite direction.

I turned to Reynolds and demanded, "What's going on here? Why is JJ so upset? What questions did you ask him?"

Reynolds closed the door and gestured to the woman. "Claire, Connor, this is Dr. Phelps."

She glanced in our direction and gave us a brief nod. Her dark hair, neatly tucked away into a bun, framed her gentle face. An open notebook lay before her, the page filled with notes of some sort. She wiggled her pen between French-manicured fingernails while her almond-colored eyes focused on JJ. "I have only posed questions to aid me in my evaluation of him," she said calmly.

I approached the table and, in a protective manner, asked, "What is it you want to know about him?"

"I brought her in to assess his state of mind," Reynolds explained. "This is her specialty."

She faced me, clicking her pen. "My questions were regarding what's troubling him."

"Didn't he say?" I asked.

"He did not," she answered.

Connor continued to gain ground on JJ, inching closer. JJ faced the wall, the volume of his mumbling growing louder.

Connor meant well but was only making matters worse. "Connor, stop. Give him some space."

"I tried to read him and get inside his head." Connor frowned. "I couldn't make a connection."

Reynolds raised his brows. "Is he resisting?"

Connor shrugged. "Hard to tell."

JJ spun around and shouted, "Leave me alone!"

I reached out my hand and approached him slowly, as if drawing near a cornered animal. "JJ, it's okay. I'm here."

He tightened his grip on the frame, curled his lip, and backed away. "Stay away from me."

Dr. Phelps scribbled in her notebook and asked, "JJ, don't you recognize her?"

He quickly nodded his head. "Yeah, but I would rather not talk to Claire...or any of you. Leave me alone."

I made Connor back off, but I couldn't do the same. "JJ, please, talk to me. Tell me what happened. I've been through hell just trying to find you."

His head jerked in my direction. Spittle flew from his mouth as he yelled, "It's always about you, isn't it, Claire? What about what I've been through?"

I flinched. What was he talking about? Self-importance had never touched our relationship before. We'd always looked out for one another, like twins, sharing everything, sometimes even our thoughts. "When have I ever made anything about me?"

He stared at the floor and mumbled, "You just don't get it."

Dr. Phelps asked, "What doesn't she get, JJ?"

His gaze moved upward and focused on the ceiling. Eventually, he faced Dr. Phelps. "That I don't exist."

The desire to comfort him ached in my arms, and I stepped toward him.

Dr. Phelps rose from the table and held up her hand, blocking me. She drew near JJ and asked in her gentle, soothing voice, "Why do you believe you don't exist?"

He slumped against the wall, rolled his head backward, and closed his eyes. "It doesn't matter."

Dr. Phelps rested her hand on his shoulder. "It does matter, JJ." He opened his eyes and stared at her. "Why do you feel this way?" she pressed.

His young face withered by gloom as he said, "She's the favorite."

Dr. Phelps glanced at me. "You mean to say your parents favored Claire?"

I shook my head no. Our parents had never played favorites.

JJ let out a frustrated groan. "How many times can one person stand to hear, 'Claire this and Claire that'?"

"Parents see different things in each of their children. What did they see in you?" Dr. Phelps asked.

He ignored her, peering to his right, as if someone was next to him. Leaning in, he whispered, "I can't talk to you now."

"Who are you talking to, JJ?" Dr. Phelps asked.

He didn't respond.

Connor moved in again, his unwavering gaze fixed on JJ. The hypnotic glow in his eyes grew bright. This time, Reynolds pulled Connor back. "Stop pushing, Connor. Let Dr. Phelps handle this."

Connor held up his hands in surrender and backed off.

"Is someone here with you, JJ?" Dr. Phelps probed further.

JJ shied away. "I don't want to talk about it."

"I understand. You can tell me when you're ready. Would you be able to answer my question about what you believe your parents saw in you?"

"Disappointment," he answered, his eyes still on the floor.

JJ's suffering consumed me, ripping open my heart and stealing my breath. My mind raced backward, conjuring up childhood memories, but not a single one validated his beliefs. Where were these ideas coming from? Was the sickness warping his brain? Again, I approached him, wanting to ease his pain.

Dr. Phelps stepped in front of me once more. "It's too soon, Claire. He's not ready to confront his feelings about you."

"I agree," Reynolds concurred.

"Stop trying to keep me from my brother."

Connor came to my defense. "Maybe Claire is precisely what he needs. She might be able to reach him and help him remember."

JJ scowled fiercely and shoved my picture in my direction, shaking it at me. "I know the image is what you're after. You want to steal it from me and give it to The Society. You're on their side!" He tucked it back under his arm and vigorously shook his head. "You'll never get your hands on it, and neither will they."

"Enough," I shouted and scooted around Dr. Phelps and made a beeline for JJ. I latched onto his arm and tried to reason with him. "I'm not concerned about the damned picture. Keep it. All I care about is you." A glimmer of affection flashed in his blue eyes before vanishing.

Dr. Phelps studied JJ as he cradled my picture in his arms. She stood directly in front of him, forcing him to look at her. "JJ, may I take a look at the picture?"

"Be careful, Dr. Phelps," Reynolds warned, inching closer to my brother.

"There's no cause for concern," she stated in her calm manner.

JJ shook his head again. "I can't let anyone touch it. I have to keep it safe."

Dr. Phelps' eyes narrowed. "Are you referring to the picture or to Claire?"

JJ cracked a smile. "Claire doesn't need protection."

"Then the picture does? Or perhaps the frame?" Dr. Phelps speculated.

His smile faded abruptly. He began pacing again, turning sharply as he reached each wall. "You ask too many questions. Leave me alone."

Dr. Phelps walked alongside him as she asked, "Why is her picture so important?"

His eyes focused on me when he said, "The picture's important, not her."

My chin trembled, and I swallowed hard, trying to banish the advancing tears. Where was this hate coming from? Did he blame me for going away to college and leaving him alone with our monstrous parents? Did he hold me responsible for everything? How could I possibly fix this?

Connor whispered in my ear, "Don't let it get to you."

JJ screamed at the doctor, "Leave me alone!"

She stood still and let him pass.

He faced me with soft, tear-filled eyes. His lips quivered as he said, "You're everything to me, Claire. I trust you, but the people don't. I have to listen to them."

I balled my hands into fists but kept my voice level. "Who are they? Tell me, JJ."

"Claire, stop," Dr. Phelps said, wedging herself between JJ and me.

I ignored her and continued to press him. "There's no one around you. No one."

His eyes glazed over, and he began rambling. "You're just trying to trick me. You're all after me, working for The Society. The people told me no one could be trusted. They were right." A growl crawled up through JJ's throat as he charged me. "Even you!"

I stood motionless, my heartbeat swelling inside my chest. He was insane. Connor jumped in front of me, shielding my body with his and knocking JJ to the ground. JJ tore at his hair and howled.

"This is exactly what I was afraid would happen. Come on, both of you, out now." Reynolds hauled Connor and me by our arms toward the door. I glanced over my shoulder in time to see JJ sink to the floor, whimpering.

Dr. Phelps knelt beside him and rested her hand on his shoulder. "It's all right. Just try to relax." She helped him up and guided him into a chair. He slumped forward and burst into sobs.

JJ was no longer present. JJ was replaced by an unfamiliar person who was sitting in the chair and crying.

A sharp knock on the door interrupted us. A female detective in a gray suit entered the room and announced, "There's a vampire here who calls himself Priest. Says he's here for the boy."

Reynolds immediately turned to Connor, his eyes narrowing.

"I contacted him," Connor admitted. "He has a connection with JJ. I thought he might be able to help."

Reynolds addressed the detective. "Tell him I'll be out in five." He turned to Connor and asked, "What's their exact connection?"

Dr. Phelps raised a brow. "There are too many people involved in this matter as it is."

"Hang on, Dr. Phelps," Reynolds interjected.

Apparently displeased with Reynolds, I watched her jaw clench.

"After the deaths of Nate and Parker, JJ went to Priest for help," Connor replied.

"JJ seems to trust him," I pointed out.

"Priest might be able to reach JJ," Connor added.

Reynolds looked at Dr. Phelps. "What do you think?"

She shook her head. "I want to interview JJ further and perform some psychological tests before anyone else comes into this room."

JJ mumbled to himself as he rocked back and forth in the chair, clinging desperately to the picture frame.

I felt hopeless. He'd refused me. What could I do for him now? I looked at her and said, "I just want my brother back."

JJ's head popped up, and his eyes fixed on me, the rage gone. "Claire," he said, his goofy, boyish smile consuming his face, "I don't need to see Priest. I'll talk to Dr. Phelps." He glanced at her. "She seems cool."

I wanted to know one thing before I left him. "JJ, I'm going to ask you a question, and I need you to tell me the truth."

Dr. Phelps objected. "He's not ready, Claire."

"I'm not asking you."

"What question?" JJ asked.

I took a deep breath. "Do you know who killed Mom and Dad?"

An incredulous stare consumed his expression, and he cried out, "No, of course not!"

Could I trust JJ? Was he telling the truth? Did he even know what the truth was?

Dr. Phelps came to me and took my hands in hers, giving them a reassuring squeeze. "I'll take care of him. Don't worry."

"I'll be right outside, JJ. I'm not leaving you."

"I'm okay, Claire."

As Connor led me out of the room, I kept my gaze locked on my brother. He waved goodbye as the door closed behind us.

"I have to believe him," I said, more to myself than to anyone else.

Connor stroked my back and nodded. "I know you do."

Reynolds gave me a weak smile. "We'll find out more after Dr. Phelps conducts her assessment."

Connor regarded Reynolds with an arched brow. "Shouldn't you be in there...you know, like, monitoring things?"

"We consult Dr. Phelps on a regular basis. Her reports are very thorough. Besides, there are cameras in the room. If I need to, I can always review the footage."

"Do you have any other suspects, or are you focusing solely on JJ?" I shuddered, not sure whether I wanted to know the answer to my question.

Connor nudged Reynolds in the way people do when they share a secret. "You should be straight with her."

My gaze bounced back and forth between them. "What aren't you telling me now?"

Compassion smoothed the wrinkles in Reynolds' brow. "I'm sorry, Claire. All the evidence we have points to JJ alone. There are no other suspects."

That was a blatant attempt to avoid responsibility. Reynolds needed to put more effort into his investigation and check under more rocks—every rock. "You must have found something else. I identified their bodies, remember? I will always remember the horrific scene. Did you at least investigate any other leads?"

"I know, and I'm sorry. Believe me, I wish I had other leads."

JJ was incapable of inflicting so many bite marks and marring our parents in such a way, and how would he have drained their blood? Neither seemed physically possible for him. "But you heard him and witnessed his genuine expression of disbelief. He said he didn't know."

Reynolds showed his palms. "The evidence points in a different direction, Claire. Unfortunately, it all points to JJ."

I turned to Connor, desperate for any detail to help vindicate my brother. "You tried to get inside his head. You must have picked up on something. What was he thinking? What did you see?"

Connor pursed his lips, shaking his head. "Nothing made sense. His thoughts were disorganized and fragmented." He gave me a reassuring hug before adding, "We'll get through this, all of us, together."

"I can't begin to know what you're going through," Reynolds told me. "I wish I could tell you what you want to hear, but I have to follow the evidence trail, no matter where it leads."

What did he have on JJ that was so damning? "If the evidence you have so clearly implicates JJ, I would like to see it. At least then, I'll understand why you think he could have done such a horrible thing." He gave me that; *you know, I can't* look, but before he could open his mouth to speak, I begged, "Please, for the love of God, please."

Reynolds rolled out a hesitant nod and pointed to the hallway. "The evidence room is down there. Come on, let's get this over with before I change my mind."

I clasped my hands together, resisting reaching out and hugging him. "Thank you, thank you, thank you!"

"Don't thank me yet. You probably won't like what you're going to see."

"But she'll finally have all the pieces to the puzzle," Connor said, glancing at me. "That's all she really wants."

Reynolds stated glumly, "Just be prepared."

"I'm prepared. Show me what you've got."

"Priest should come with us," Connor pointed out. "He has more insight into JJ's situation and state of mind than any of us."

Reynolds snapped his fingers. "I forgot about him. Hang tight." He left us and hurried toward the lobby. Minutes later he returned with Priest, who was babbling on about the impending sunrise.

I gripped Connor's arm in concern. "There are windows everywhere."

He flashed that charming smile of his. "I'm well aware."

"You need to find shelter."

He laughed, seemingly completely at ease. "Vampires get arrested too. The building must be sunproof. I'll be okay. Besides, I'm not going to leave you at a time like this. My place is by your side."

"I appreciate that, but I'm not going to risk your life."

Reynolds interrupted our little back-and-forth and reassured, "We're well equipped to deal with the sun. All the windows are specially coated to block out the sun. Connor and Priest are perfectly safe."

Priest bowed his head and murmured, "Thank God."

I relaxed and released Connor. He gave me a playful nudge and teased, "See, I told you."

Priest, now calm and composed, stated, "Gabriel wanted me to inform you that his thoughts are with you and JJ."

"Thank you," I said, though I found it difficult to believe such a sentiment had come from Gabriel.

Priest focused on Reynolds. "Fill me in on JJ. What evidence do you have against him?"

Gesturing toward the hallway once more, he answered, "We're heading to the evidence room now."

"In my eyes, he's innocent," I said, sounding as confident as I could under the circumstances.

Priest pulled me aside and quietly stated, "Reviewing the evidence will not alter the facts. JJ wanted revenge for Nate and Parker."

"Wanting it and acting upon it are two different things," I argued.

"But action was taken," Priest challenged. "Your parents are gone."

"But by whose hand?" I questioned. "Whatever happened to a person being innocent until proven guilty?" JJ was my brother. My loyalties lay with him, even though a part of me struggled with the slightest possibility. Regardless, I would exert every effort to defend him and, hopefully, establish his innocence.

"You need to believe him," Priest stated. "I understand." He gave me a slight smile. "I want to believe in him, too."

"We can stand around discussing this, or we can go have a look at the evidence. Which is it?" Reynolds asked, seemingly growing impatient.

"The evidence," I answered quickly.

Waving us forward, Reynolds said, "Then let's get moving."

He led us deeper down the corridor, making a sharp left into an open door. After ushering us into the large room, he approached a long rectangular table at its center. Boxes, manila folders, and plastic evidence bags cluttered its surface. A massive whiteboard, covered with photos, handwritten papers, and a timeline scrawled in bold black marker, stretched across the far wall to our right.

Priest stood inches from the whiteboard and pointed at the papers. "The hexagon shapes with stick figures are JJ's formulas."

Reynolds placed his hands on his hips. "Our lab geeks determined it's some kind of formula for DNA." His gaze wandered over the scribblings as he shook his head. "But breaking down the strand's code was a different story. It's an entirely foreign combination of sequences. They have no idea what kind of DNA it is." He glanced over at me. "They said your brother must be some sort of whiz-kid genius."

JJ's science awards came to mind. Teachers had always praised him, stating the same. He loved science and had always been conducting some sort of experiment, but whatever the hell he'd written on those papers was far beyond me. "He's brilliant, but he's just a kid."

"A kid who just happened to create his own unique DNA sequence," Reynolds pointed out. He spoke to Priest. "Did JJ give you any clue as to what those meant?"

"Unfortunately, no," Priest replied.

Connor walked the length of the board, stopping dead center. His hands folded behind his back as he studied the symbols carefully. "The DNA isn't human."

I shivered at his words. "What?"

Reynolds neared the board and crossed his arms over his chest. "Can you decipher it?"

Connor didn't respond. His eyes remained focused on me.

"Well?" Reynolds pressed.

Connor's gaze lingered on me for a moment longer before he answered the detective. "One half of the DNA is human, and the other, vampire."

Priest gasped aloud and backed away from the board. "JJ kept repeating he couldn't get the formula right. He must have been referring to this nonsense."

My conscience wrestled with my heart. I trusted Connor more than I'd ever trusted anyone, but how could I believe the words that had just come out of his mouth? Could JJ be capable of replicating such a creature, and for what purpose? I couldn't comprehend what the possible reason for this science project was.

Reynolds dropped his arms to his sides, and his mouth fell open. "That kind of DNA manipulation can't be possible."

"I agree," Connor said. "But JJ seemed to believe it could be brought to fruition."

Reynolds steered away from the whiteboard and approached the rectangular table. His eyes darted back and forth over the items contained there. "Now it's all coming together, just like the final pieces to a puzzle."

Priest and Connor arrived at the table's edge before I even lifted a foot off the floor. At a snail's pace by comparison, I crossed the room. When I reached Connor's side, he slipped his arm around my waist. The items collected on the cluttered tabletop came into focus. Several evidence bags held dental molds with extended incisors of various sizes. One anatomy book and a *Physician's Desk Reference* were stacked on top of each other in the center of the table. Two large plastic buckets with hoses snaking out of them rested at the table's corners. A tingling, sinking sensation inched through my body as my resolve to prove JJ's innocence weakened. What purpose did those bizarre items serve, and had they found them in JJ's possession? Reynolds' earlier remarks resonated deeply—I wasn't ready for this.

Reynolds placed his hands on the table and nodded toward the dental molds. "The molds were tested for DNA but came back clean, and none matched the bite marks found on your parents. We believe they destroyed the fang molds used on your parents. These molds we have here look to be prototypes for testing prior to the murders."

"Wait. You're suggesting he wore these inside his mouth?" Priest asked, his voice shrill.

"Yes," Reynolds confirmed. "We believe he designed them to custom-fit inside his mouth. We also subjected them to testing. These molds are all sharp enough to puncture flesh."

I nearly gagged when I pictured JJ sinking fake vampire teeth into our parents.

Connor spoke up, keeping the hope for JJ's innocence alive. "What about prints? Are JJ's prints on any of them?"

Reynolds shook his head. "No prints. The person wiped everything clean, even the pumps."

"Pumps?" I questioned. "You mean those contraptions?" I pointed to the buckets.

Reynolds lifted one up and turned it over, exposing a motor underneath. "Yes. They were engineered to suction out fluid. They could've easily emptied a human body completely of blood. Your parents' bodies, to be more precise."

I swallowed hard. "Spare me the details. I get the picture."

Reynolds continued his verbal cataloging of the remaining morbid items. "The anatomy book appears to have aided in the design of the pumps, and the *Physician's Desk Reference*," he patted the cover, "is a dictionary of prescription drugs. It would've instructed him on the precise sedative dosage required to prevent resistance from the victims."

"Did the autopsies discover any traces of drugs?" I asked.

"No, but several exist that can't be identified in the body after death," Reynolds advised.

"Did they find blood in the pumps?" Connor asked, holding one up to the light.

"Only bleach."

The evidence just kept piling up against JJ. I began to understand why he had become their prime suspect. Hell, even I doubted my brother, though I kept coming back to the fact that JJ had stated he didn't know who killed them. We only have each other now. I had to believe him, have faith in him, and stand up for him, especially with the mounting evidence stacked up against him. Another thing had occurred to me. These items that Reynolds had on display could have easily been used by my parents during their torture sessions. I wondered if Reynolds had thought of that scenario. "You found these things in my parents' cabin, right? Any of these items could've belonged to them. After all, they were slayers. Wouldn't that be an explanation as well?"

"That's a logical suggestion, Claire," Reynolds said, "but after thorough examination by our forensic team, that possibility seems less likely."

"Why? What reasoning did they give?" I asked.

"The items on this table appear to have been manufactured with the intent to kill humans, not vampires."

"You can't know that for sure. What about the video you showed me in my parents' cabin? I believe the video of the two vampires bleeding out and my parents enjoying their pain conveys a powerful message. Maybe draining vampires of their blood was one of the methods they used to inflict pain or even cause death."

Priest shook his head. "Slayers always stick to the basics: stakes or the sun. Those choices are far less complicated, and there is no evidence to destroy or hide."

"There's nothing basic about torturing, which is what my parents did to vampires."

Reynolds made an impromptu T with his hands. "Okay, time out. Of course, anything's possible, and yes, I'm making assumptions, but as a detective, I study evidence, piece it all together, and deliver my best guess. In this case, my best guess is that JJ killed your parents. I'm sorry, Claire."

My gaze roamed over the items once more, searching for something, anything, to corroborate JJ's innocence. I had to make sure I didn't overlook something useful to his case.

Priest also surveyed the table, and his eyes suddenly grew wide. He snapped his fingers and shouted out, "It's entirely clear to me now. I know what he was doing." He scanned the evidence wall before continuing. "No vampire would turn him. No vampire would kill for him. He was out of options and desperate. He was trying to turn himself into a vampire."

My legs wobbled beneath me as I stumbled away from the table. My vision blurred and darkness filled the room, altering into pitch-black, and then, nothing...

The sting of ammonia rushed into my brain, and my eyelids fluttered. Muffled voices surrounded me, their words gradually becoming clear. It was my name they were saying over and over again, but I couldn't respond. My mouth refused to form words. The stink of ammonia resurfaced a second and then a third time. Hands patted my cheeks, and something damp brushed across my forehead.

"Claire, can you hear me?"

I recognized Connor's voice, but his form was a blur. I fought to bring him into focus. Detail by detail, his face emerged through the fog inside my brain.

He crouched by my side, dabbing at my forehead with a wet towel. He helped me sit up, and staring into my eyes, he asked, "Are you okay?"

"I feel sick."

Connor brought a bottle of water to my lips. "Here, take a sip."

The fresh water moistened my dry throat and eased the nausea somewhat. I sat there holding my head in my hands and breathed in and out slowly. "No more talk about blood, bodies, or Frankenstein-like vampires. I've had enough."

A deep frown settled into Reynolds' forehead. "I must admit, I've become immune to all the gore. I'm sure it was hard for you to see, and I shouldn't have allowed it. I apologize for my mistake. Why don't we get you somewhere you can rest? I have a couch in my office."

"No," I insisted. "I have to see JJ."

"He's probably still with Dr. Phelps, and she'll have to consent. For now, you might as well rest."

I knew he was right, and I decided to take his advice. I needed to gather my strength before visiting with my brother.

Connor helped me to my feet and kept his arm around me for support. "I'm going with her."

"Very well. I'll show you the way." He turned to Priest and said, "Wait here. I'll be right back, and then you and I can continue discussing your theory."

"Of course. I came to help."

CHAPTER 22

Reynolds opened the door to his office, gesturing toward a black leather sofa against the center wall. "Have a seat." After throwing his keys on top of an aged oak desk, he pulled open the bottom drawer and retrieved two bottles of water. Handing them over to us, he said, "There's more in there if you need it."

I sank onto the couch, rested my head against the back cushion, and pointed at Reynolds. "Don't forget that I still want to see JJ."

"Might I remind you that you fainted," he pointed out. "I'm trying to help you."

"I won't be able to relax unless you promise to keep me in the loop."

He held up his hand like a Boy Scout. "I promise." Pointing to the thermostat on the wall, he said, "Feel free to turn up the heat if it gets too cold."

I closed my eyes and said, "I'm fine, but please, don't take too long or I'll go crazy sitting here, thinking the worst."

"Understood. I'll be back as soon as there's news. Now get some rest."

As the door closed, I sat upright, twisting a strand of hair between my fingers. "How can I rest? My mind is constantly questioning whether JJ is guilty or innocent. I don't know what to believe anymore."

Connor sat on the couch next to me. "Dr. Phelps appears to be fairly confident in her ability to uncover the truth. Give her time."

"I don't even know if I want to find out. I mean, yes, I do want to know, but then again, I don't. Does that make any sense?"

"Of course it does." He smoothed my hair and smiled at me. "Whatever the outcome, just know you have me by your side."

I reached for his hand. "I don't know what I would do without you."

He gently squeezed my hand between his palms. "That's something you don't have to worry about. Now, lie back and try to get some rest."

"But JJ's just down the hall going through God knows what. And what if he has to face murder charges? What will we do then?"

"We can engage in the hypothetical game throughout the night without gaining any insight." He fluffed a pillow and placed it underneath my head. "Come on, try to relax."

I settled against the softness, but my mind continued to race in a thousand directions. "I can't."

"Close your eyes for a couple of minutes. See what happens."

I closed my eyes. The couch's soft leather cradled me, easing the tension slightly. My thoughts drifted. The gentle hum of the air conditioner filled the room. My mind quieted, allowing sleep to overtake me.

With a start, I bolted upright, my gaze darting about the room. "What time is it?"

"Early morning, I think," Connor replied.

"How long did I sleep?"

"An hour, maybe."

"Did Reynolds come back?"

"Not yet."

"We should have heard something by now."

"Maybe, perhaps not."

I slumped against the couch and sighed. "I believe there's a dark cloud of gloom raining hopelessness and heartache over me."

Connor scooted closer to wrap his arm around me. "Aren't you being just a tad melodramatic? We don't know anything for sure yet."

"There's something wrong. Don't ask me how I know. I have a strong intuition about it. They could be coercing JJ, filling his head with several lies to force a confession."

"You don't really believe that, do you? Reynolds cares about what happens to you. There's a strong sense of fatherhood within him."

I raised my brows at him. "You read his mind?"

He winked at me. "Yes, I did. It's a habit I can't seem to break."

"So you're saying I can trust him?"

"You can," he said with conviction. "He's on a mission to make things right, and he's broken several rules for you."

Reynolds seemed like a good guy, but what about Dr. Phelps? "Did you read Dr. Phelps, too?"

"Her mind felt like a solid wall. Couldn't even sneak a peek."

"But what do you think of her in general?" I pressed.

He shrugged. "She seems okay to me."

"That's not enough." I rose to my feet. "I'm going back there. Are you coming?"

He furrowed his brows. "In the room with Dr. Phelps?"

"Yes."

He had a point. Reynolds would likely send me back to his office and instruct me to wait. I glanced at Connor. He could do what I couldn't do. With a few whispered words and a piercing look, he could easily persuade the guard to let me see JJ. In a soft, hopeful voice, I said, "Maybe you could enchant the guard so I could slip past him."

His gaze flickered upward, as if considering it, before he shook his head. "Not a good idea."

"Then you sneak by the guard."

"So I get inside the room, and then what? It's unlikely they'll let me stay."

"Can't you make them not see you?"

He offered up a bemused smile. "You do realize I'm not invisible, yes?"

I rolled my eyes at him. "Obviously, but you do possess supernatural speed."

"Shall I race around the room a few times and report back?"

"Race, enchant, whatever it takes. Just get inside the room!"

He came to me and put his hands on my shoulders, peering into my eyes. "I'm going to enchant *you* if you don't calm down."

Tears of frustration stung my eyes, and I swiped them away. "I want to calm down, but that's impossible right now."

He gently brushed tears from my cheeks and said, "Close your eyes and take a deep breath."

After several breaths, the relentless pounding of my pulse lessened. "Thanks. I'm better."

His lips neared mine, but the door opening drove us apart. Detective Reynolds and Dr. Phelps entered. His solemn, TV-cop expression was back, and hers was unreadable. Reynolds ran his hand over his mouth. "You should sit down."

A lump formed in my throat. *This can't be good.* I reached for Connor's hand. "What? Tell me."

Connor held me close, his gaze bouncing back and forth between the pair.

In her soothing voice, Dr. Phelps echoed Reynolds' words. "Claire, please sit down."

I tightened my grip on Connor's hand. "Just tell me."

"Please, Claire, sit down," Reynolds repeated, but this time, with a stern voice.

Connor eased me onto the couch and sat next to me. "Let's hear them out, okay?"

My feet bounced against the floor as I waited for whatever news was too harsh to remain standing.

Reynolds offered his desk chair to Dr. Phelps and stood behind her. "Go ahead, Dr. Phelps."

She folded her hands neatly in her lap, and her face had that *I-have-to-inform-you* expression. "I conducted a thorough interview with JJ and performed several psychological tests."

A sense of dread gripped my body, telling me that something terrible was about to happen. No matter how much I wanted to escape her words, I couldn't.

Her voice, though gentle, was deadly calm. "He has an unshakeable belief that an underground society is after him, seeking to steal the picture of you. *The People*, as he refers to them, are his protectors. He's hallucinating as well as hearing voices. And, as I'm sure you probably noticed, his personal hygiene has grown rather poor."

Connor glanced at me before fixing his gaze on Dr. Phelps. "Meaning what, exactly?" he asked.

"JJ is a paranoid schizophrenic."

What? Had I heard her right? She'd spent mere hours with JJ. I'd been with him his whole life. She couldn't just slap a label like that on him. People don't go crazy overnight. "He was okay, healthy, and sane the last time I saw him at Christmas. How does something like that just happen?

"In men, it can surface during their late teens," she explained. "And a traumatic event usually triggers sudden onset."

"Like witnessing Nate's and Parker's deaths," Reynolds interjected.

"Yes," Dr. Phelps confirmed. "Claire, I know this must be completely overwhelming, but his illness is treatable. I can help him manage his disease with medication and therapy."

I brought a shaky hand to my forehead. This was all happening too fast. I didn't know what to believe. "Can I see him?"

"Maybe in a little while. He's resting now. I've given him a medication called Clozapine. It will help to manage his symptoms."

"Thank you," I said, not knowing what else to say.

"You're welcome. I'll see you soon."

After she had exited the room, Reynolds sat in his chair and faced me with a pained expression. "There's more."

His words were ominous and weighty. The urge to clamp my hands over my ears and refuse to listen tingled through my fingertips. "More?"

"JJ may have to face criminal charges for the murder of your parents."

Thoughts flooded my mind of that earth-shattering day when I had stepped out of the cab and into this nightmare. After seeing my parents' dead bodies, I had taken it upon myself to find their killer. I volunteered at The Vampire Center, looking for leads. I pursued Marty, Stanley, Victoria, Priest, and Gabriel—and it had all been for nothing. I'd nearly ended my life several times. For a fleeting moment, I hated my brother, but loyalty, love, and compassion quickly replaced the hatred. He was sick and broken. This wasn't his fault. My gaze found Reynolds. "Did he say he did it? That he killed them?"

"No, but we found a sheet of paper with handwritten notes hidden inside the frame behind your picture. Getting our hands on it became quite an ordeal. JJ was determined to hold onto it, and with good reason.

Connor took his eyes off me for a second to ask, "What did it say?"

"It spelled out a plot of murder."

"What?" I uttered. "He wrote it down?"

Reynolds rested his hand on my knee. "I'm so sorry, Claire, but yes."

Connor blinked and took a moment to process. "You mean, like a confession?"

Reynolds weighed his hands side to side. "Yes and no. It reads more like an outline of his plans than a confession. Unfortunately, the story gets worse."

My stomach ached as nausea crept back. "How could it get any worse?"

Reynolds' expression turned somber. "He dated it, February tenth. This occurred just days after the deaths of Nate and Parker. That makes your parents' murder premeditated."

I literally felt the blood drain from my limbs as my body grew ice-cold. The vivid image of my parents' murder, followed by the bloody vampires my parents had tied to chairs, polluted my brain. Had witnessing the demise of Nate and Parker caused JJ's mind to snap? Had it driven him to exact vengeance? I couldn't possibly comprehend the rage inside him. Yes, our parents had done unspeakable things, but their actions didn't give JJ the right to act as their judge and jury. The content of the confession was utterly damning. There was no way to recover from this. I couldn't change what he wrote. "What can I do? How do I help JJ? Can I at least see what he wrote?"

'Dr. Phelps and I can assist him. We're going to present a plea of insanity to the DA. Hopefully, we can keep this out of a courtroom," Reynolds said, his tone fairly confident. "As far as his notes are concerned, they're locked up in evidence."

"Is the plea bargain going to work?" Connor asked while stroking my back.

Reynolds' face brightened. "She and I together can be very persuasive. I think we have a good shot at convincing the DA."

I let my hands fall loosely into my lap as I shuddered. "I just don't see how he could look me in the eyes and say he didn't know who killed them."

"At the time, he believed that," Reynolds pointed out. "It was through Dr. Phelps' questioning that we gathered new information."

"Who does he think killed them then?"

"In JJ's mind, a group of vampires, The Society, retaliated by killing your parents."

"So in his eyes, he's innocent," Connor surmised.

"He does remember your parents murdering Nate and Parker, and he's not sorry someone got revenge for his friends. But any memory of what he did to your parents is locked away inside his mind."

"But his outline states differently?" I clarified.

"Exactly," Reynolds answered. "He clearly states they must die at the hands of the creatures they destroyed."

A painful web of sorrow wound its way around my heart. JJ had gone through everything alone. I should have been there. Maybe I could have argued with him, stopped him, and saved him.

Connor squeezed my hand. "You're trembling. Are you sure you want to hear more?"

"Our lives have been turned upside down. I need to know everything, no matter how painful it may be."

Reynolds nodded his understanding. "Priest was right. When the vampires refused to turn him, your brother attempted to alter his DNA and turn himself. Of course, that wasn't possible, and he couldn't find a vampire willing to kill for him. Dr. Phelps believes that, at that point, JJ created The Society in his mind, allowing him to enact vengeance for his friends."

An image of JJ standing over our parents, fake fangs in his mouth, sent an icy chill scurrying down my spine. I shivered, fighting it off. "I just can't imagine him doing something so horrific. What I witnessed that day did look like the work of vampires."

Reynolds assented. "He fooled us all and staged a convincing vampire murder scene. He almost got away with it."

"Were my parents conscious during...I mean, did they know what was happening to them?"

In a soothing tone, Reynolds responded, "His outline stated they must be drugged. He used over-the-counter sleeping pills." A sad smile formed on his lips. "The ME believes they were already gone when he began to bite them. They didn't suffer."

A sense of relief washed over me. "Thank God. He's only seventeen and going through this madness alone. Please, let me see him. I need him to tell me what he believes happened and in his words."

"I'm telling you, Claire, he has no recollection of murdering them. He believes that vampires killed your parents. Pressing him for details may only harm his state of mind further."

"For God's sake, he planned our parents' murder. He carried it out himself. Some of that must remain inside his head."

Connor offered up his thoughts on the matter. "Maybe he blocked it out to protect himself. I mean, murdering your parents..."

"Not quite," Reynolds corrected. "Yes, he invented The Society, but he believes they actually exist. He could describe the murder scene blow-by-blow because he was there, but in his mind, he tried to save your parents. As he remembers it, the vampires came after him, and he ran."

"I have to see JJ," I uttered. "He needs to know I care, that I'm here for him."

"Let me talk to Dr. Phelps, and I'll see what I can do."

"Go get your approval," Connor urged. "Claire needs to see her brother."

Reynolds placed his hand on my shoulder on his way out. "I am truly sorry."

The sudden sting of anguish burned inside me. "I'm hurting. JJ must be hurting. We need each other," I pleaded with Reynolds. "I need him to know I haven't deserted him."

"Very well. Let's go find Dr. Phelps. She'll have to be present. You can't see him alone."

"Thank you," I whispered.

CHAPTER 23

eynolds led Connor and me down a stark-white corridor. He swiped his badge at a security door and escorted us into a restricted sector of lockup. After passing through a second security door, we came to a barred gate. Reynolds unlocked the door and released the bolt, pushing it open to expose a row of isolated cells. Dr. Phelps stood at the far end in front of a cell to her right. As I approached, my heart nearly exploded inside my chest, and a sheen of nervous sweat coated my palms.

Dr. Phelps put her hand on one of mine. "I'll be right there with you."

A tightening sensation spread through my throat. "What should I say to him? I don't want to upset him."

She smiled warmly. "Speak from your heart."

I reached for Connor's hand.

"It'll be okay," he assured me, his eyes soft and compassionate.

"Does he understand what's happening to him?" I asked Dr. Phelps.

"I've explained his illness to him, but it will take therapy, medication, and time for him to truly recognize the difference between reality and illusion."

I took a deep breath and faced JJ's cell. "I'm ready."

Reynolds unlocked the door, and I followed Dr. Phelps inside. The detective took up a spot outside the cell near the wall. JJ lay sprawled across a narrow cot, his gaze fixed on the ceiling. He mumbled to himself, seemingly unaware of our presence.

Dr. Phelps approached the bed and touched JJ's leg. "JJ, Claire is here to see you." She backed away and settled herself into the far corner of the cell.

JJ turned his head, and our eyes met. He bolted upright. "Claire, the police took my picture. I need it back. It can't fall into The Society's hands!"

I sat next to him and took his hand before lying to him. "I have the picture, JJ."

"Really?"

"Yes, and I've locked it away where no one can get to it, especially The Society."

He pressed his lips together and rocked back and forth. "I need it back."

"But we need to keep it safe, remember?"

His head bobbed up and down in agreement. "You're right." His eyes darted about with a crazed gleam. "Don't tell anyone where it is."

I crossed a finger over my heart. "I promise."

He focused briefly on the ceiling, and then his eyes burned into mine. "You need to be careful. The Society will stop at nothing to get it."

I squeezed his hand. "I'll be careful, but that's not why I'm here. I want to talk to you."

"About what?"

"Mom and Dad."

Dr. Phelps stepped away from the wall and shook her head. "Claire, keep the conversation light."

JJ curled his lips into a sneer as he glanced at Dr. Phelps. "She has to know. I want her to know."

"You're sure, JJ?" she questioned.

His voice grew solemn. "I'm sure."

"Very well. I'm here if you need me." She faded back into the corner.

"Vampires killed Mom and Dad." He shuddered violently and hugged himself. "Wanted revenge. Wanted to settle the score. The vampires held me against my will. Made me watch. Would have killed me too if I hadn't escaped."

His madness penetrated my soul. I ached all over, as if I'd been beaten to the edge of life itself. Answers no longer mattered; only putting an end to JJ's suffering did. "Mom and Dad are gone. They can't hurt anyone anymore."

He let his shoulders slump forward. "I was a disappointment to them," he said for the second time.

I slowly shook my head in disbelief. "Why would you think that?"

"I brought vampires into their home."

An overwhelming sense of responsibility for my baby brother flooded my soul. I *would* make him forget the sins of our parents. "You could never be a disappointment to me, JJ. You're my best friend."

A smile came to his lips. "You're my best friend too."

My chest heaved, and the sobs broke free. I reached for him and held him close. "I love you, JJ."

He wrapped his arms around me, holding on tight. "I love you too, sis."

Dr. Phelps stepped forward and touched my shoulder. "That's enough for now, Claire. JJ needs to rest."

I didn't let go. I couldn't let go.

"Keep the picture safe, Claire," he whispered as he released me.

"I will, I promise."

He yawned and lay back down, stretching his arms overhead. "I am pretty tired." He looked up at me and blinked sleepily. "I'll be okay, Claire. Don't worry."

I stood there nodding, wondering whether I believed him or not. He had no idea he'd killed our parents. In his mind, he believed that vampires had taken our parents' lives, a conclusion he could accept and so could I.

CHAPTER 24

Outside JJ's cell, Dr. Phelps and Detective Reynolds exchanged words until her cell rang. Turning away, she answered and hurried off down the hallway. Reynolds escorted me and Connor back to the lobby. Despite the insanity haunting JJ's mind, I grappled with my own demons and the lies I'd told Reynolds. Marty and Stanley would be alive today if I'd chosen a different path instead of meddling in their affairs. My obsession with the map had led to more vampire deaths. And what of Victoria? I'd driven her from her lair. I wanted—no, I *needed* to come clean. "The cuffs were mine."

Connor's eyes popped wide open, and he grabbed my arm. "Claire, don't."

Reynolds jutted a rigid finger toward his office. "You two, in my office, now!"

Like naughty children, we hurried after Reynolds as he stormed inside, slamming the door shut behind us. "What the hell is going on, Claire? Care to explain that little outburst?"

Connor stepped in front of me. "I can explain."

Reynolds placed his hands on his hips. "There's no doubt in my mind you're knee-deep in this too, but I want to hear it from Claire." He turned to me with sharp eyes.

Connor didn't back down. "I'm not going to just sit back and watch you rake her over the coals, especially after all she's just been through."

Reynolds took a step toward Connor. "One more word, and I'll separate the two of you. Is that what you want?"

The vein in the center of Connor's forehead throbbed dangerously. "Of course not."

"Then sit down and shut up." Reynolds glared at Connor a moment or two longer to drive his point home and then focused on me. The volume of his voice lowered slightly. "By 'cuffs', you're referring to the ones found in the park near the murdered vampire?"

My throat immediately became dry, strangling my voice, but he needed an answer. "Yes," I choked out in a hoarse whisper.

Connor kept his gaze fixed on me while biting down on his lip.

Reynolds spoke with a direct and concise tone. "I need you to tell me exactly what happened."

"I purchased them," I said, somehow finding my voice, "but not with the intention of killing anyone." I sat next to Connor and reached for his hand. His fingers surrounded mine.

Reynolds leaned against his desk and rubbed his forehead. "But you purchased them with the intent of restraining a vampire?"

"Marty died by his own hands," I blurted out. "I tried to save him, but he was so drunk."

Connor interrupted. "Please, can I—"

"No." Reynolds cut him off with a rigid wave of his hand. "Believe me, you'll get your turn." Connor fell back against the couch and groaned. Reynolds ignored him and focused on me. "Marty, is it the same vampire from the station that night? The one you wanted me to question?"

"Yes. He just showed up at The Center one night. He told me he had information about my parents' murder."

"And you believed him?" Reynolds replied, sounding surprised.

Exasperated, I threw my hands in the air. "I was desperate, Reynolds. I needed answers."

He shoved his hands into his pockets and sighed. "I provided all the answers you needed. You were just too impatient to wait for them."

Disappointed in myself, I clenched my hands and raised my voice. "Don't you think I know that?"

"You say you didn't kill Marty, so how did he die?"

The saying, *the truth shall set you free,* came to mind. It was ironic; I didn't feel free at all, but rather trapped. "I did restrain him but released him when he begged me to. Marty grabbed the restraints and cuffed us together, got drunk off three bottles of tequila, and passed out."

His thick brows came together. "I assume something went terribly wrong."

I rattled off the rest in one breath. "The sun came up. We tried to escape it, but he was still drunk. He couldn't stand, let alone run. He just kept falling. Maybe the alcohol combined with the silver cuffs weakened him. I don't know. I tried to save him, but the sun was too strong. He died right in front of me, and I couldn't stop it."

Connor jumped to his feet and shouted, "To hell with this. Lay off, Reynolds. Can't you see you're upsetting her? It's breaking my heart. I love her!"

Reynolds hung his head and stared at the floor. After a moment, he gestured to the couch. "Please, sit down. I understand you have feelings for Claire, but I can't have you interfering."

Connor scooted next to me, wrapping both arms around my shoulders and holding on tight. "I can't just sit here and say nothing. She's obviously hurting."

"I get that," Reynolds said, "but I need her to speak truthfully with no enchanting or coaching from you." He wagged his finger at Connor. "And you're not off the hook. I've got questions coming your way next."

"As you wish."

Reynolds narrowed his gaze at Connor before turning his attention back to me. "*Did* Marty know anything about your parents?"

"He only told me he did so I would have a drink with him."

Reynolds frowned. "So what brought on the need for you to cuff him and him you?"

I didn't have a reasonable explanation. "He was stalling, and I was impatient. I wanted to scare him, make him tell me what he knew. The cuffs seemed like a way for me to get to the truth."

"You threatened him?"

My eyes retreated, focusing on the floor. "Yes, I threatened him." I looked up into his eyes again. "But like I said, I also *uncuffed* him."

Reynolds appeared puzzled. "So what went wrong? How did Marty end up dead?"

That dreadful morning replayed inside my head, frame by frame. I clutched my arms against my chest and, in a quiet voice, said, "He got angry, told me two can play this game, and cuffed us together. I tried to reason with him, but he got inside my head. There was so much pain. I could only sit there, unable to move." I squeezed my tear-filled eyes shut.

"The sun came out of nowhere, and I woke him. He uncuffed us, but his legs were so wobbly. He couldn't walk."

"She tried to save him," Connor offered up in his most sincere tone.

As I continued, my voice kept growing softer and softer. "I pulled him to his feet and made him run, but he kept falling." I opened my eyes and let the tears stream down my face. "There wasn't enough time. I threw myself over him in an attempt to shield him, but it was pointless. The sun engulfed him completely. In seconds, he'd turned to ash."

Reynolds mercilessly fired off another question. "The cuffs were clean, no prints. How is that possible?" Realization sparked in his eyes as he faced Connor. "I suppose that's where you came in."

"Yes," Connor confessed. "And wiped them clean."

"I asked him for help," I said in Connor's defense. "I was scared. I couldn't prove it was an accident."

Reynolds' eyes brimmed with disapproval. "You could have trusted me. Instead, the two of you dug yourselves into a deep hole."

"I'm responsible for wiping them clean," Connor professed. "Not Claire."

"You're both responsible," Reynolds barked.

He spoke the truth. We were both responsible. Whatever bitter medicine he delivered, we deserved.

"What about the vampire I shot at your condo? Why did he come after you?"

"His name was Stanley. I met him at The Center too. He also told me he had information about my parents. I agreed to meet him so he could tell me."

Reynolds raised his brows. "Hadn't you learned your lesson from Marty?"

"I deserve that."

"I was supposed to go with her but got delayed." Connor let out a nervous laugh. "Taking care of the cuffs and all."

Reynolds jerked his head back and crossed his arms. "Do you think this is funny?"

"No," Connor said, ironing out his expression.

Now that the truth had finally surfaced, I felt lighter somehow, but I still had more to tell. "Stanley said he knew Nate and Parker. The girls from The Center told me he'd killed a volunteer, so I reasoned he could have been my parents' killer. Turns out, what he wanted was a taste of my blood."

"When I arrived at the graveyard, I found Claire pinned down and Stanley trying to feed on her," Connor explained. "I threw him into a tombstone, and we ran."

"So he'd come to finish what he'd started when I shot him," Reynolds concluded.

"Yes," I concurred.

"The vampire map and the field trip to the crypt—another attempt to gain information about your parents?"

I shifted in my seat. "I know it all sounds ridiculous, but my obsession with finding the killer and JJ clouded my judgment."

"I'll say." Reynolds leaned back, eyeing us both and rubbing his chin. "What am I going to do with the two of you?" A knock at the door interrupted his contemplation. "Come in," he called out.

Dr. Phelps popped her head in. "I just wanted to give you an update." I've been on the phone with the DA. He agreed to release JJ into my custody, so I'm filling out the paperwork to transfer him to the hospital."

I ran to hug her. "Thank you." I looked at Reynolds. "Thank you both so much."

She gently returned the hug before pulling away. "JJ's got a long road ahead of him. He's going to need a lot of support."

"I'll be there every step of the way."

"Excellent. I've got a mountain of paperwork to complete, but I just wanted to give you some good news. I'll be in touch soon." She spoke to Reynolds next. "Can you stop by my office in, oh, say, an hour? I'll need your signature."

"Will do."

Once again, we were alone with Reynolds. His thick brows came together, just like my father's used to. He reached for my hand and squeezed it. "I'm going to go easy on you. You lost your parents, and your brother has lost his way. You've been living through hell, and I say you've paid your dues. Can I assume your days of playing cop are over?"

I pressed my hand over my heart. "Absolutely."

He gave me a curt nod and turned to Connor. "As for you, I've been looking for a vampire grunt to lessen my workload and help me solve my backlog of cases." He grinned wickedly. "And that vampire is you."

Connor smirked and rubbed his hands together. "Sounds like a blast. I'm in."

He shooed us away. "Go, get out of here."

I hugged Reynolds and kissed his cheek. "Thank you, thank you, thank you. I'll never forget what you've done for me...for us, never."

Reynolds patted my back, turning a slight shade of red. "Well now, you're welcome." He pointed a finger at Connor. "I'll see you tomorrow. Say around seven? Gives you enough time to finish up at The Vampire Center."

"I'll be here."

"Now beat it."

Connor held out his arm, and I hooked mine underneath. We nearly bolted out the precinct doors, fearful Reynolds might change his mind. I couldn't breathe until we stood outside on the front steps of the station. I fixated on Connor's jade-colored eyes and asked, "What now?"

He slid closer to me and scuffed the sidewalk with his combat boot. "Well, there is that unresolved matter of forever."

I managed a real smile. "Yes, there is that."

"I know you're not ready for forever yet. I thought maybe we could start with something simpler...like living together?"

I gave him a sidelong glance. "Simple would be something like a first date."

"With everything we've been through, we're way past a first date." He took my hands into his. "I don't want to go home alone to my dreary apartment in the Vampire District anymore. I want to get to know JJ. I want all of us to be a family. I want your face to be the last thing I see before I go to bed and the first thing I see when I wake."

My pulse raced beneath my skin. He was serious—I could see it in his eyes. Who was I kidding? I wanted all of that too. I wanted every waking minute to be at his side, this beautiful, kind creature who loved me as much as I did him. I circled my arms around his neck and let out a squeal of joy. "Yes!"

"Yes?"

I shouted at the top of my lungs. "Yes!"

He scooped me up and twirled me around, shouting into the night, "Hell yes!" When he set me back down again, he studied every inch of my face as though he might never lay eyes on me again. I brushed the back of my hand across his cheek, hypnotized by the fireflies dancing inside his eyes. His mouth covered mine, and I surrendered to the dreamy touch of his lips. My breath became entangled in his, and our hearts pounded in tandem, as though they were one. He had captured my heart, and I loved him completely.

In my ear, he whispered, "You have three years until forever."

I pulled away and eyed him suspiciously. "Why three years?"

"I was twenty-three when I turned." He smirked and nudged the tip of my nose with his own. "If we wait more than three years, technically, you'll be older than me."

I gave him a flirtatious wink. "We can't have that, now, can we?"

He winked back. "No, we most certainly cannot."

About The Author

LAURA DALEO is a multi-genre author, specializing in dark fantasy, urban fantasy, supernatural fiction, science fiction, and young adult fiction. Immortal Kiss, her best-known vampire series, explores the Egyptian pantheon that gave rise to vampires. Currently, she is working on her ninth book, The Wolf Experiment, an urban fantasy.

A native of San Diego, California, Laura now lives in Tucson, Arizona with her two dogs, Rose and Cooper.

www.ingramcontent.com/pod-product-compliance
Lightning Source LLC
Chambersburg PA
CBHW031238120726
47905CB00002B/647